THE LURKERS

Other Titles by Kristopher Rufty

All Will Die
The Devoured and the Dead
Hell Departed: Pillowface Vs. The Lurkers
Anathema
Master of Pain
(Written with Wrath James White)
Something Violent
Seven Buried Hill
The Vampire of Plainfield
The Lurking Season
Bigfoot Beach
Desolation
Jagger
Prank Night
The Skin Show
Proud Parents
Oak Hollow
Pillowface
The Lurkers
Angel Board

Jackpot
(Written with Shane McKenzie, Adam Cesare, & David Bernstein)
Last One Alive
A Dark Autumn

Collections:
Bone Chimes
Bone Chimes 2

THE LURKERS

Kristopher Rufty

This book is a work of fiction. The names, characters, places, and incidents are products of the writer's imagination or have been used fictitiously and are not to be construed as real. Any resemblance to persons, living or dead, actual events, locale or organizations is entirely coincidental.

The Lurkers
This Paperback Edition Copyright © 2022 by Kristopher Rufty
2011 edition edited by Don D'Auria
Cover Art © 2022

All Rights Are Reserved. No part of this book may be used or reproduced in any manner whatsoever without written permission, except in the case of brief quotations embodied in critical articles and reviews.

ISBN: 198189926X
ISBN-13: 978-1981899265

For my family.

PROLOGUE

Annoyed that she couldn't get her husband Hank out of bed, Nancy Hamilton decided to find out what had made that damn racket downstairs. She kicked off what blankets she'd been able to pry away from her husband during the night and climbed out of bed. Every night was a constant battle with him to get even a minimal amount of the covers.

On her way to fetch her robe from the chair in front of her dresser, she caught a quick glimpse of her reflection in the mirror. Lit only by the feeble glow from the moonlight netting through the bedroom window, her naked skin looked as if it had been painted with milk. Her mussed red hair was out of control. She'd looked better but was happy with what she saw.

Could be a lot worse.

She turned sideways, rubbing a hand across the smooth flesh of her stomach. *A tan wouldn't hurt, though.* Trying to tan was pointless with her sensitive skin, but a darker shade would help hide the throngs of freckles on her body that she'd been insecure about since she was a kid.

Nancy snatched her robe and threw it on, not fretting to tie it. The silk rubbed her breasts, tickling them. Normally, she liked that feeling, just not tonight. Her nipples were sore and tender. She and Hank had gotten awfully frisky earlier in the evening. Hank, in rare form, had gone the extra mile, making sure she got hers too. That didn't happen very often, so she savored it. When her release finally came, it had been massive. Convulsing as if having a seizure, she'd felt the orgasm all the way to her toes.

She'd fallen asleep right after.

Not bad for a couple of forty-year-olds.

She slept soundly, probably would have all night, until being awakened by the clatter of breaking glass from downstairs. It had sounded as if it had come from the kitchen, so she'd shaken Hank, demanding he go check it out. He hadn't budged, just continued lightly snoring behind slow, heavy breaths.

He *should* be tired. He'd done a lot more tonight than normal. She was pleased with him and decided to let him sleep while she investigated it alone.

He earned that snore.

As she stepped into the hall, something else shattered from down below. She flinched at the light crash sounding like one of the coffee mugs falling off the rack. Nancy hoped it wasn't the *I love L. A.* mug she'd picked up while visiting her sister in California last summer, the only souvenir she'd managed to purchase during the entire trip. Hank, pinching pennies as always, wouldn't swing for anything else. He claimed that was how *they* got you.

How who got you?

Nancy briefly thought about cutting on the hallway light but decided against it. It would kill her night vision, plus she didn't want to announce her location. In bed, she hadn't considered the possibility they might have intruders. But as she descended the stairs, she began to wonder. It terrified her to think that someone who didn't belong may be prowling around in her kitchen.

Breaking every damn thing in the process.

Turning on the light would broadcast her approach.

And what should she do if there *was* someone down here?

Run like hell.

Take her nosey ass right back upstairs and make Hank get up. If she had to turn the mattress up and dump him onto the floor then she would. He had a gun in the closest. She wanted to slap her forehead for not taking the gun with her to start with. She didn't like handling firearms, but maybe she should go back and get it now. At least she'd have something to frighten whoever might be down there.

But what if she had to use it? She wasn't sure she even knew how.

Nancy listened to herself and couldn't believe how frightened she sounded.

It was the dark, she realized, making her think like this. Just a simple case of the jitters. No one was in the house, not an intruder, not out here.

Unless…

A pitter-patter of tiny footsteps scampered within the kitchen, making light scuffling sounds across the tile, too weak to be a man's, or even a woman's. They sounded to Nancy like a small animal, or possibly even children, which would be odd since they didn't own any pets. And Nancy had been cursed with the inability to bear children, so none of those should be in the kitchen, either.

Nancy reached the bottom of the stairs and stopped, wondering whether to continue on or go back for the gun. She decided to forge ahead. Going back upstairs now seemed pointless and might be more trouble than what it was worth. She was already down here, might as well see what she was up against.

Up against?

She shivered. If she was actually up against something, then she should definitely go back for the gun.

The scurrying repeated. From where she stood, the kitchen was just to her left, near the front door that was closed and should be locked. Nancy looked at the kitchen doorway, a blackened rectangle that seemed like an ominous entrance to another dimension. Inside looked even more vague and unfamiliar. A gray square of light from the window over the sink glimmered on the tiled floor. Tiny shadows raked across it. Something was moving in there, she could see it, hear it.

Smaller than kids.

Oh God, what if it's rats?

Her skin stiffened with a sensation like furry spider legs sprinting over her body, pimpling her skin with goose bumps. She felt a chill, yet rivulets of sweat streamed down the curve of her back, ribcage and hips. She shuddered at the sensation. Reflexively, she scratched her head and her back, but found no trace that spiders had actually invaded her body.

With the countless meadows around the house, not to mention the vast terrain of cornfields that served her hometown of Doverton, it very well *could* be rats. Field rats. *Big suckers.* Maybe they'd given up on trying to feed on the produce that just wasn't growing the way it should be and finally made their way out of the plains and down to their house. *Inside the house.* They'd never had any problems with vermin before, but it was sure to happen sooner or later.

Nancy stepped onto the hardwood floor, half-expecting to place her foot down directly on the back of one of those disgusting bastards. Thank God the floor was all she got. After the warmth from the carpeted stairs, it felt cool and slick under her feet. She wiggled her toes.

Nancy stepped softly to the kitchen doorway. If there were rats in there, she surely didn't want to see them—or them to see her. She knew they wouldn't run until she turned on the light and exposed them. Then they'd scamper across the floor, darting in different directions in a panicked fury like hairy cockroaches. The idea of seeing their small, dingy bodies and wrinkled noses with their lengthy whiskers flickering this way and that made her uneasy. She reached around the panel, quietly fumbling for the light-switch. Finally, her hand brushed against the switch, and she flipped it upward. Light exploded through the kitchen, pushing all the darkness up the walls and away.

Instantly, she felt much better. She kept her eyes squinted until they adjusted to the beaming light bouncing off the white walls of the kitchen. Although, she'd been half-blinded she was happy to not be in the dark anymore.

Then she spotted the mess.

A container of flour had been tipped over. Its opened mouth hung off the edge of the counter with the lid nowhere in sight. Flakes of flour fell like snow to a fluffy pile on the floor. Footprints were stamped in the mound, and ghostly white tracks were sprinkled across the floor, cabinets, stove, and table.

Everywhere.

Even on the goddamn walls.

She stepped closer to the muddle, inspecting the tracks carefully. Unlike any rat prints she'd ever seen before, these were petite, oval-shaped marks like babies feet in booties. And the smell—a thick lingering odor that hung in the kitchen like an atrocious, invisible fog made it miserable to breathe. It burned her nostrils and stung her eyes.

Nancy glanced at the sink, gasping when she noticed the toppled-over rack. The shattered remains of her favorite coffee mug littered the bottom of the sink. All that remained of the logo was a shard with the heart cracked down the middle. It teetered on the edge of the drain. She wanted to cry. The broken shards were all that remained of the mug she'd spent so many mornings at the table with while reading a paperback and guzzling countless cups of coffee. Who knew when she'd make it back to California for a replacement? Maybe Elizabeth could send her another one. That would be a temporary fix, but wouldn't be the same. The memories of the trip had also made the cup that much more special.

Something thumped inside the cabinet above the stove, pulling her out of the broken cup blues. It landed with a metallic thud. *A can?* Somehow, the bastards—whatever they were—had gotten inside the cabinets.

Nancy moved away from the sink, glancing at the tracks in passing. Seeing them again caused her stomach to tighten. Something about them frightened her. They weren't normal, but unusually small and out of place.

Looks like a damn baby. Not just a baby—babies. More than one. Different shapes and widths left the kitchen peppered in the white dust. The only thing they had in common were their diminutive sizes.

She regretted not going back for the gun.

Nancy attempted calling for Hank, but her cries only tickled the back of her swollen throat. Yet even that in the silence of the kitchen sounded earsplitting. She could barely release a squeal, let alone a howl for her deep sleeping husband.

She was truly alone.

Before going to the cabinets, Nancy took a detour to the fridge. Walking slow and stilted, she snatched the broom out from behind it. Now she had some kind of a weapon, at least. Not much of one, she realized, but it felt good to at least have *something*.

Hunched over, she slunk back to the stove with the wooden tip of the broom pointed ahead of her, the dried straw silently scraping the floor behind her as she moved. With her left hand, she gripped a cabinet door by its bronze handle. The metal was cold and clammy in her sweaty hand. Taking a deep breath, she mustered up a hint of courage to peek inside. As she was ready to wrench it open, she caught the hushed sound of raspy whispers inside. The intruders spoke to one another animatedly, talking so fast she couldn't decipher the syllables. The hairs on the back of her neck stood on end.

What little bit of bravery she'd managed to obtain had promptly retreated.

The cabinet door lashed from her hand.

She jumped back, shrieking so vigorously that something ripped. A scorching wetness coated the back of her throat.

Blood.

Standing inside the cabinet were four things huddled together. They looked to have been arguing over a large canister of Chicken In A Can until detecting her presence. Simultaneously, their heads turned to her. She was met with a boundary of relishing stares, and watched as triangles of white stretched across the dimness.

Smiles! They're smiling!

Then she looked at the cabinet door. Hanging upside down from the spice rack by its feet was another one of the tiny creatures. She stood face to miniature face with the inverted munchkin. It appeared human-like, but as if it had been left in a drier for way too long. Its skin was pruned and withered like a rotten apple, and it wore what looked like some kind of burlap sack as a hooded suit. Suddenly, it erupted with squeals like shrieks from an injured cub.

Nancy tried hollering in retort, but only produced a wet burble.

Laughter, high-pitched as if on helium, reverberated around her, in front of her, and behind her as the cabinets throughout the kitchen sprang open, filling the tight room with an explosion of slamming doors. The central air vents on the floor flipped upward as the minuscule things climbed out from the ducts, revealing that more and more of them had been hiding under the floor. They poured from under the sink, above the counter, and even from behind the same damn fridge she'd just taken the broom from. She stopped counting crescent-shaped heads at thirteen, but there had to have been more, so many more.

They'd been watching her all this time.

Waiting.

And none of them looked to be above two feet tall.

Nancy tried to scream again and couldn't. Whatever had been damaged inside her throat flapped loosely like a piece of lettuce. It gagged her.

The creatures slowly pressed in on her, encasing Nancy in a horde of dwarfed persons. She was the beetle with an army of hungry ants all around her, stranded with nowhere to go and no point in trying.

Where the hell are you, Hank! Why aren't you helping me!

As if to answer her, his muffled screams resonated from the bedroom, but were quickly drowned out by more screeching laughter. Then she heard nothing more than the juicy rips and slashes of her husband being devoured where she'd left him sleeping in their bed.

Nancy started to cry.

What have we done? she wanted to scream at them. *Why us? Why did you come after us!* Of all the possibilities as to what may have been in the kitchen, she'd never once considered it to be them.

We've done our part, kept to ourselves, let you take whatever the hell you wanted from the barns and sheds. We did nothing wrong!

The snarling and drooling assembly inched in. She could feel their tiny hands petting her, fondling her. Hatchets, knives, and scythes—anything small enough to hold —were clutched firmly between their teensy digits. The weapons were nearly the same size as the intruders. Others were armed with artillery they'd made themselves: sticks with rocks filed to points that had been strapped down with leather twine, stone knives and miniature replicas of the weapons the others were struggling to hold.

Their clothes, concocted from potato sacks, were crudely stitched, home-bred garments that were either bleached white or dyed an assortment of colors like camouflaged fatigues. Their heads and faces were hidden under burlap hoods that hung low, obscuring the majority of their features. All that remained were their hideous smiles, dripping drool around crooked teeth.

Then they lunged.

Nancy swung the broom and smacked a few. She fended them off momentarily, but it did nothing to help her. She only prolonged the assault and angered them even more. They tore through her robe as if it hadn't been there at all. She could feel their bare hands, their calloused flesh, as they swam over her naked skin. She could feel the cold and the pain of their tiny weapons as they punched into her abdomen and her chest.

Then she felt her thighs powerfully being parted as they brought her down to the floor, pinning her on her back. They swarmed over her like maggots on feces, spreading across her and restraining her arms and kicking legs.

Nancy writhed as their flexing hands entered her.

She heard the sloshing sounds, saw her stomach bulging and contracting. She briefly remembered losing her virginity. How it had felt like her inner walls had been torn down like an old curtain. It had hurt, but she'd faked her enjoyment quite well even though she'd bled for the following two days. She healed from that and, to her surprise, found herself wanting it again. What she felt now, with the three pairs of infant like arms elbow-deep inside of her, was insufferable. If she survived this, she'd never want sex again. Peeing would be impossible to do without waves of pain.

Something inside of her was poked. Her belly button domed, and as she studied it through her tear-sodden eyes, she realized it was actually a finger trying to jab its way through. The way it looked reminded her of a deflating balloon, or pushing a finger into putty.

She found her voice momentarily and destroyed what was left of her throat with her yells.

The peaceful night of chirping crickets and singing frogs became a tumult of screams and chortles in the madness of Nancy's devastation. But just as quickly as it had started, it all ended. The creatures of the night held their breath, listening as the intruders devoured what was left of the Hamiltons.

GARY

"Why is *she* calling so late?"

Gary Butler was certain that Wendy's disapproval was loud enough to be heard on the other side of the phone call. He whipped his head around and shushed his girlfriend before he returned his head to the pillow, his cell phone nuzzled against his ear. He checked the time on the alarm clock across from him on the nightstand. It was nearing midnight.

No wonder Wendy's pissed.

"What happened?" he said into the phone. He could practically feel the biting cold temperature coming through the earpiece. Wherever Amy was calling from had to be isolated if the insect concert he could hear behind her was any indication.

"He did it again," Amy said. Her voice was heavily distorted from the cruddy connection.

Gary knew just by those four words exactly what she meant.

Piper had gotten rough with her again, and this time possibly *too* rough. He'd hoped that one day Amy would finally find the sense she needed to leave him. Sadly, after countless wounds that had healed on the surface, but had left much deeper scars on the inside, she had not.

"It was bad, Gary, so bad." She started to cry. Her tears and moans were audible despite the bad connection.

Gary's throat tightened. He wished he could be there to console her, hold her.

Why does she keep putting herself through this?

Wendy sighed from beside him, throwing the blankets off her. She marched to the adjoining bathroom. The light clicked on, casting a glowing cube on the bed, but it vanished when she slammed the door.

Ignoring Wendy's tantrum, he focused on Amy. "Explain *bad*."

Amy took a deep breath. "We got into an argument over money, and it's usually money with him. We've always done all right with the bills and stuff, never been late on any of them. But last week he went out and got a new motorcycle. I was pissed at him for giving us *another* bill to pay, especially after we'd just finished with the payments on that boat he'd wanted. So, out of spite, I went shopping for myself."

Here it comes…

"I picked up a new camera. A nice one too. Well, it *was* a nice one. A digital SLR."

"You? You *finally* switched over to digital?" He was dumbstruck. After all this time, she'd actually welcomed the digital revolution when it no longer was considered one.

"I'd preached for years that film was better, but I finally joined them since I couldn't beat them." She laughed softly. "And it's actually a wonderful world to be a part of." A sound that stopped her words short was either more laughter or more sobs, but he couldn't tell which.

Her laughter always made him smile. Even now, it was hard for him to hide his admiration for it. When she really let it loose, it could stop traffic. Even as thin as she was, Amy could bellow a laugh that would give Santa a run for his money.

She had a great singing voice too.

They'd visited a karaoke bar in Saint Paul a couple years ago. After way too much alcohol, they'd spent hours on stage singing tracks from Rush's definitive album, *2112*. Gary was the master air-guitarist while Amy rocked the air-drums. They were quite the duo.

They'd often talked about going back to the place, because who knew how they'd end up topping it, but time had slipped away from them. Gary had gone on to meet Wendy after Amy moved in with Piper. They were lucky if they saw each other once a month now.

"Piper never liked the idea of me being a photographer," she added.

He never liked her doing much of anything except waiting for him to come home. "But it's what you do. It's what you've *always* done. And you're damn good at it too. You've thrown away a great career as a photographer for him. You have a wonderful eye for it, and not many people can claim that."

"That's what you always say, but Piper doesn't share your opinion."

"Screw him. I can't let you forget just how amazing you are."

He stopped talking. Gary could feel his skin growing hot with a blush. How could that comment have slipped out of his mouth without his brain's prior approval? It was as if his tongue knew he'd never have the balls to say something like that on his own. He'd never gathered that type of courage to inform her of that fact before, although he'd wanted to many times. They'd been friends for years, but had never once considered their relationship more than that.

Well, he had, but she hadn't, so he'd kept his comments to himself.

It's not like you're bullshitting her, or just telling her stuff you think she wants to hear. It's the truth.

She's amazing.

Gary listened, holding his breath to make sure there was nothing to distract him from hearing her reaction. His stomach buzzed. Then he heard her take in a deep breath and could hear the smile in it. The night out there must have gotten a little brighter from her vivid smile.

He was thankful he'd dodged that bullet. The last thing he wanted was to make Amy's downer mood even more awkward.

"You don't have to tell me the specifics of what happened tonight, Amy. Not over the phone. Just tell me what I need to do to make it better."

She sighed, as if wary of telling him.

"Come on," he said as if trying to lure a cat down from a tree. "What can Big Papa do for his Sugar Bear?" He quickly pulled the phone away from his ear before she laughed. Holding it out from him, he heard the guffaw as if she were in the room with him, but it stopped as abruptly as it had begun.

"I didn't want to bother you with this, again."

"Don't ever say that. You've bothered me with this so much now, it's lost all meaning." He laughed, hoping she would too.

She didn't. "I bet I have…"

He felt as if he'd been kicked in the ribs. "I'm sorry, that was a bad attempt at humor."

"It's so funny because it's true."

"But you're not laughing."

"I am. On the inside."

"Seriously," he said, wishing he hadn't tried to make light of the situation. "You know who you can call anytime you need to, right?"

"Ghostbusters?"

"That's right. I sure as hell can't help you."

They laughed together. This time, he didn't take the phone from his ear. It was the best laugh they'd shared in quite some time. Gary hated that their first laugh together in months was being shared because of a situation like this.

The bathroom door popped open behind Gary, vibrating loudly on its hinges. He glanced over his shoulder and saw Wendy standing in the doorway, her head tilted to the same side that the smirk on her face was pointing. She folded her arms across her chest and propped one leg forward, the other bent behind her as she watched him. The light shining behind her in the bathroom made the thin, violet nightie she wore practically translucent. He wondered what she'd been doing in the bathroom all this time. For a brief moment, he thought he'd detected the electric razor, but he'd tuned it out so Amy could have *all* his concentration.

Gary examined the nightie closer. Through the sheer silk, he saw that the small patch of coiled hair she normally kept in a trimmed line below her abdomen was gone.

Bare. Shaved clean.

Gary had been begging her for weeks to trim up, but she'd balked, blowing it off as a little hair had never hurt anyone. She was right, he didn't mind a *little* hair, but she'd let that area get out of control. It had been a long time since she'd spruced herself up for him at all, and what he'd been asking wasn't something unreasonable. But now as he sat on the phone comforting a friend in need, she'd snuck off to the bathroom and taken care of the frizzy nuisance out of spite. She'd hoped to seduce him with her new *haircut*. She knew exactly what she was doing. She wanted to lure him off the phone and away from Amy using any means necessary.

That's cold.

Wendy grabbed the sides of her gown, hiked it up, and gave his eyes a bit more thigh to linger on. Knowing he'd obsessed over her legs since he first saw them, she now used them as a weapon. It was one of the few things he still enjoyed about her. She tilted her leg outward, rubbing the velvety skin of her inner thigh. She was just an inch away from the recently smoothed, caressable center.

Her plan was working.

Gary felt heat in his crotch. His penis was rising. Adjusting his plaid sleeping pants, he allowed it room to grow.

"Are you still there?" asked Amy's distorted voice. Her pitiful tone helped fight away his oncoming erection.

Tearing his gaping eyes away from Wendy, he said, "Yeah, I'm still here."

Groaning, Wendy threw her arms in the air. Defeated. "This is just fucking great!" She stormed away from the bathroom, stomping her feet with each step, and plopped her ass down on the edge of the bed with her back to him.

"Can you come get me?" asked Amy, finally caving in and admitting she needed help.

Gary remembered when he would be homesick as a kid and call his parents in the middle of the night to come get him from a sleepover. He'd put on his best miserable voice, because he knew his mother wouldn't be able to stand leaving him there if he was that unhappy. Amy sounded worse than any of his best efforts. But her circumstances were different; she wasn't homesick, not entirely. She was frightened. And she wasn't a kid putting on an act, either. She was a thirty-three-year-old woman on her last legs that desperately needed his help.

Gary knew it. Amy knew it. And behind Wendy's wall of cattiness, deep in her jealous, uncaring mind, she knew it too. This also explained why she was doing everything in her power to lure him off the phone. She'd always accused him of caring more about Amy than he'd let on, but he had never figured she was right.

"Where are you at?"

"I'm outside of Petersburg in the sticks. A little town. I think the sign said Hortonville. Nothing but farms out here, and I was lucky to find a store with a phone booth in the parking lot."

"Why didn't you just call from your cell phone?" He almost hadn't answered the call when he first saw the number on his ID screen. Thank God he'd taken the chance or Amy might still be wandering through the night.

"I smashed it," she said, choking up again.

"Smashed it? How?"

"Across his fucking face."

"What?"

"He wanted to hurt me. Actually, I think he wanted to kill me. I was trying to get away from him and it was all I could do."

"That bastard." Fire burned in Gary's stomach. He wanted to tear Piper limb from limb and beat him to death with his own appendages, but deep down he knew it would be his ass that got kicked. "How'd you get to…?" He'd already forgotten the name of the town.

"Hortonville?" she asked.

"Yeah, Hortonville."

"Hortonville?" hollered Wendy. "She's all the way out there? That's near Amish land."

"She's right," said Amy with a snort.

Gary's cheeks flushed hot. Just as he'd suspected, Amy had been able to hear all of Wendy's flare-ups. He had verbal proof now and wanted to kick Wendy off the bed because of it. Instead he said, "Amish land? Thinking of converting?"

"Maybe I should," she said, laughing.

"What the hell are you doing all the way out there? Why didn't you go to a bus station? Or call a cab? I would've paid for it."

"I couldn't."

"Why not?"

"He'd find me there before I even had a chance to escape."

Escape?

This was even more serious than he'd originally thought. It was always a scary and very delicate situation when Piper got like this. But it seemed to have gone beyond that. Normally, she could keep her head floating above that river of fear, but it seemed to Gary that she was sinking.

He'd find me.

Like hell he would.

"How far is Hortonville from Petersburg?"

"Too damn far. I've been walking for three hours. Probably would take no time by car, but I didn't have time to grab my keys. I just ran out of there as fast as I could. I imagine Stone Quarry, where you are, is *a lot* farther."

"I'm sure it is, but that's all right. You walked all that way?"

"Through the woods and fields. I didn't want to take the roads just in case he was driving up and down them looking for me, but I saw this store and had to take a chance. I was so glad the payphone wasn't dead."

Me too, he thought, *or you might have been.*

"All right, tell me the name of the store, I'll search for it online and figure out how to find you. Also, give me the number on the front of the phone in case I need to call you."

"Uh, it doesn't have one."

"Wait." He pulled the phone away from his ear and thumbed the display button back one notch. When he saw the number she was calling from was still there he sighed with relief and put the phone back up to his ear. "Never mind, I have it."

"Does this mean you'll come get me?"

"If it's not *too* far. I don't want to be trekking all over Amish Country looking for you all night."

"Hardy har-har."

"You love it."

"Yeah, yeah, don't remind me. Call me back, let me know how long it is before you'll be here."

"I will. Stay out of sight, but close enough to the phone that you'll hear it ring."

"I promise."

"Bye-bye."

He hung up the phone, and sat there for a moment, letting it all absorb—the conversation, the hurt in her voice, knowing that Piper had really gotten out of hand and realizing the true terror she was feeling. *Out in the middle of nowhere, and hiding in the woods.* All of that flickered through his brain in a few seconds. How was *he* going to make this better for her? He had no idea, but that wouldn't stop him from trying.

Rolling over to his side, he found Wendy on hers, facing him with her elbow bent and her head propped on her hand. "What's going on?"

"I'm going to pick her up."

"Alone?"

Gary sighed. "Well, I had planned on it because I assumed you wouldn't *want* to go."

"I don't, and I don't want you to go either, but I know you will. And if you think I'd allow you to drive all the way out there by yourself then you *are* fucking crazy." She laughed. Not a funny laugh, but cold.

Allow him? When had Wendy decided it was her position to allow him to do anything? *She must be livid.* She only cursed at him when she was furious. "Whatever. If you want to come, then come. I imagine it's a pretty long drive to do solo, anyway."

"Yeah, I imagine it's a couple hours at least, but I bet she's worth all the hassle."

Gary crawled out of bed with a groan. "Honestly," he said, "she *is* that important. I've known her for a long time. A *long* time. If you're coming along, that's fine. But if you do, then you had better drop that bitch attitude of yours right now, because if you don't, I'll drop you off at your house on the way out there and *forget* about picking you up when I'm done."

Where had this sudden valor to stand up to her come from? He had no clue, but he liked it and wished it had come much sooner.

From the look on Wendy's face, she was wondering the same thing. Her eyes were bulging, mouth agape, and her body rigid from the pure shock. She moved her lips, but the words weren't coming. It was as if her mouth knew she should say something back, but her brain hadn't figured out what.

"I'm going to grab a quick shower," he continued. "Be ready to go when I get out. Just tell me then if I'm taking you home, or if you're tagging along."

Wendy nodded.

He walked into the bathroom and slammed the door behind him, leaving Wendy alone on the bed. He wouldn't be surprised to find her still frozen with the same expression when he was done.

He got the water to his preferred temperature, and stepped into the shower. The water raining from the nozzle pounded down on his head and neck. It felt wonderful.

While he was in there he masturbated, but he was too stressed for Amy and too angry at Wendy to enjoy it.

PIPER

"Fucking cunt," Piper muttered.

The freshly jutting knot on his forehead pulsated with each bump of his heartbeat, shooting intense jabs of pain through his skull. Hard to believe this came from a lousy cell phone, but it had. He hated to admit it, but she'd gotten him good. The last thing he could remember was seeing a flash of pink.

Then there was only black.

She'd been making a break for the door, and trying to leave again, but no one makes the decision on when they're through with Piper Conwell—*no* one. Especially a dim-witted whore like Amy Stone with stupid ambitions for art and photography.

Pointless wants and needs.

He remembered her at the door. She'd opened it slightly. A few more inches and she could have squeezed through and run into the yard. If she'd done that, then there was really nothing he could have done except let her go. There were too many neighbors, too many eyes. How would it have looked if their decent, laid back Sheriff was chasing his girlfriend into the front lawn and beating her stupid?

Not good at all, that was how it would have looked.

He'd jerked her back inside by her hair, and pinned her against the door. Her back crashed it shut with a bang. He'd feared someone across the street may have heard it, but doubted they'd known what it was if they had. Then he'd gripped his hands around her throat and squeezed hard, but not enough to kill her. He'd only applied enough pressure to cut off the air so she'd pass out. Normally when he did this, she would tense up and freeze. Not this time. She had expected it. That's how she was able to catch him off guard. He'd allowed himself to become stale and predictable with his punishments.

With her jammed against the door, he saw the movement in the corner of his eye. A flash from a small lighted screen, then the pink body of her phone coming at him full speed. Without a chance to dodge the blow, she'd planted the phone squarely on his brow, shattering the phone on impact.

Then it was lights out for the good Sheriff of Petersburg, Wisconsin. When he awakened, he was lying in a pool of broken glass, and his skin was lacerated with nicks and scrapes. Sitting up, he looked around and realized that he'd fallen through the glass coffee table Amy had brought home last year from Marshall's. Out of all the useless bullshit she would normally buy, he'd actually liked the table. But, just like Amy, it was gone too. The bitch had used up the last of her three strikes. She'd smashed his head, his table, and walked out on him before he was willing to let her go.

She really messed up this time.
Messed me up too.

Now, Piper stood in the bathroom, looking at himself in the mirror. He'd already cleaned his cuts with an alcohol swab. His skin still burned and prickled as the alcohol killed any infection trying to set in. He tapped a finger against the welt on his head and recoiled from the blasting pain. The wound felt solid, like a small rock under his skin. Judging by the severe pain he had now, he was certain a migraine would soon follow if he didn't pop some aspirin. He could already feel the muscles in his neck starting to stiffen.

He spread out a bandage on the sink from the first-aid kit he kept in the medicine cabinet. Using both hands, he picked it up, gently settling the X-shaped dressing over his wound. Then, very carefully, he applied the sticky edges to his skin. The pain seemed to slacken.

Just like when I was a kid. Band-Aids always make it better.

He chuckled, but winced from the twinge in his head. It may have lessened the pain, but it was still there.

Piper sifted through the rusted aluminum kit and found a travel sized bottle of aspirin. Shaking it, he heard a few pills clamoring inside. He popped the cap with his thumb, dumping three tablets in the palm of his hand, and then dry gulped them. They lodged in his chest until dissolving enough to drop into his stomach.

That was that. His head should be feeling better in a few minutes.

He left the bathroom, making sure he left evidence behind that he'd doctored himself, just in case Amy came home. She would see that he was healed and she'd sit here, dreading the moment he returned. When he did, she'd be in hysterics and begging him not to punish her.

He loved it when she begged. It never stopped him from punishing her, but the begging made it a lot more fun.

But for whatever reason, Piper doubted that would happen this time, that she was gone for good. Amy wouldn't strike him like that only to come crawling back with her tail tucked under her tight little ass.

On the bed waited the suitcase he'd prepared. He'd packed enough for a few days. Four changes of clothes, some boxer shorts, his razor and shaving cream, hair gel, and all his toiletries. Sure, he'd probably over-packed, but he was prepared to be out there until he found her, or at least for four days, whichever came first. He doubted he'd be able to get any more time off from the station, but he also didn't think it'd take any longer than that to locate her.

And at the bottom of the suitcase, and concealed by the clothing, he'd also packed his .357 caliber pistol.

With that gun, he'd never missed. From the first shot he'd ever fired from it, he'd always put a bullet in what he'd pointed it at. The way he had it figured, he'd be returning home from this trip alone one way or another. Either he wouldn't find her, and give up his search, or he'd find her and, well, his .357 never missed.

He hated it really…such a waste. But Amy knew things about him that could get him in a lot of trouble, and not just the fact he enjoyed smacking her around a little. She knew things that could put him away for a long time.

Piper zipped the suitcase shut. He did a quick scan of the bedroom and was convinced he had everything he needed. Then he grabbed the bag, leaving the rest behind. He'd clean up everything when he got back.

After throwing the suitcase in the back of his '88 Bronco, Piper sat behind the steering wheel. He was tempted to take the motorcycle that had been the reason for this fight, but doubted he could get the helmet on over the ridge on his head. He leaned up, reaching his hand under the seat. His fingers brushed across a leather sheath. He smiled. His hunting knife was there like normal, waiting for him like a loyal pet. It'd been more of a companion than any bitch he'd ever found himself shacked up with, and there had been many bitches over the years. None of those relationships had ended well either.

Piper had used this knife to gut many things. The blade, seven inches in length, curved upward at the tip. It wasn't picky. The knife could hook and pull any entrails.

And right now, Amy's were the desired entrails.

Piper cranked the engine. Unsure as to where he should begin his search, he assumed the bus station was a good place to start. He popped the emergency brake and shifted into first gear.

The bus station was fifteen miles away. Amy had plenty of time to make it there. Her car was still parked in the driveway—he always made sure to take her keys in the evenings and hide them—so she'd fled on foot. He'd been out cold for almost two hours and had spent another thirty minutes fixing himself up and packing. Even if she hadn't hitched a ride there, she could have easily walked there by now.

Already has a bus ticket to Stone Quarry, probably. Gary will likely be getting a surprise visit from her.

Piper had always taken Gary for a fag until he'd met his girlfriend. Talk about attracting opposites, she hardly seemed the type of girl that would go for a pussy like Gary. She was too high-maintenance for him, and very outspoken. Gary was homely and quiet, which was the type of person Piper hated more than the ones that wouldn't shut up. If they were quiet then they were thinking, and that usually meant they thought they were smarter than him. It wasn't an exact logic, but it had suited him just fine throughout life.

Plus, Gary was a goddamn writer. Writers were *always* the silent type. Amy had told him it was because he was observing the situations around him, studying them, so that way he'd be able to write about it later. *People watching.* Piper chalked it off as Gary making bastardized assumptions of real life.

One thing he'd noticed about Gary, when he was in that tranquil zone that Amy admired so much, was his eyes, where they were aimed and the longing inside of them. Piper may just be some dumb redneck born in Amity Hill, but he was a good enough cop to detect that Gary was madly in love with Amy. Sometimes, he thought that Amy felt the same way about Gary.

It made sense. Amy was an artist. Took pictures, painted, and could actually draw really well. He'd never vocally acknowledged her talents or supported them, but they were too good to ignore completely. Piper found them to be a waste of time. No one could ever make a living doing it, so why bother? But Gary welcomed her talents with open arms. If he wasn't always there cheering her on—building her confidence—Piper could have discouraged her from such nonsense a long time ago.

He *loathed* Gary.

That was where she was heading, though. To be with a damn fag that buries his nose in books and sits at a computer all day long typing.

Yeah, that's real hard work, buddy. Type, type, type. Such a goddamn exhausting job you got there writing that horror shit. A useless talent, if you could even call it that.

If Piper found her there, he'd have no problem using that knife on Gary too. In fact, he'd been hoping for it since realizing Amy had run away. Maybe he'd gut Gary first, then move on to Amy, make her watch what he did to the love of her life. *That fag.* When he was done with the two of them, maybe he would have a little fun with Gary's snobby girlfriend too. Might as well go all out. Her personality was self-involved—which to Piper meant shit—but he couldn't deny that she was a ten on all counts as far as appearance was concerned.

Piper tried remembering what it was she did for a living. Amy had told him once, but he hadn't cared enough to listen to what she'd said. As he drove, he wished he would have paid attention to Amy's useless blabbering that one time, at least. That way he could call her work, possibly find out her shift. Pretend he was calling about an unpaid traffic ticket. That could work. The last thing he needed was for her to walk in on him taking care of business with her fag boyfriend and his bitch, soon to be ex-girlfriend.

Piper wanted to be hiding when she walked through the front door. Ambush her, rip her clothes off, and—no, use his knife to slice them off, right up the middle like a deer. Put the blade to her throat to keep her still. He could have his fun while she sobbed, seeing her own reflection in the shiny blade.

Piper grew hard thinking about it. The crotch of his pants looked like a dune of denim. Dancing in his seat, he rapidly drummed his fingers across the steering wheel.

Never know. She may turn out to be a masochist, someone that gets hot and turned on by being brutalized.

Hell, Amy sure did.

Brutal he could be, and that was just what he planned to unleash on all of them.

GARY

"Would you slow down?" hollered Wendy from the passenger seat. "You're going to get into an accident!" Her right hand gripped the door handle so hard, her knuckles were turning white.

Gary had been going thirty over the speed limit since they'd hit the back-roads and wasn't planning to slow down any time soon. "I have to get there."

Wendy rolled her eyes and looked out the window.

The moon-peppered trees zoomed past them in a smudged blur of black and white. At times, the trees would clear out to open fields, a barn here and there, some pastures, and then the scenery would return to dense wooded areas.

She huffed.

Gary glanced at Wendy. He wished she'd stayed home. She'd already been snappy and grumpy about his driving, and he knew her mood would only worsen the closer they got to the store. He didn't understand why she was scolding him for his lead foot. It had been *her* fault they took so long getting the car on the road in the first place, so he had to drive like this, she'd left him no other choice.

After his quick shower and cheated release, he'd rushed downstairs to the computer he kept hooked up to the internet (the other that he used for writing was in the bedroom without any ties to the outside world). He hopped online to search out the directions to Hortonville. It didn't take long to find them, ten minutes at the most. He raced back upstairs, called Amy back, confirmed the store was Hawking's Grocery, hung up, and then took another five minutes to pack and program the address into his GPS. He was ready to go in less than half an hour. But Wendy had delayed when she should have dashed.

If anything happens to Amy because of her...

He didn't want to even consider arriving at the store only to find Piper had gotten there first. Being alone with Amy that deep in the country, he was certain Piper's reaction would be less than pleasant.

Gary needed to focus on the road. Getting there in one piece was the first priority, everything else would be handled afterward. Worry about one thing at a time.

The GPS informed him he had thirty miles left to go and judging by the green smudges on each side of the purple track in the center of its narrow screen, they were completely surrounded by trees.

He gazed through the windshield. The yellow lines on the road, illuminated in the high beams of his Jeep, had faded with age. In Green Bay, the roads had been kept up, each line freshly painted with attached reflectors on top. This road he was on had no fresh paint and the reflectors had been plucked off long ago and never replaced. He figured that the snowplows had seen to that. It was pretty pointless trying to keep the small, plastic rectangles on the road when it snowed for months straight. The plows would come by and plop them off like warts when scraping the roads.

He would have been very grateful for their help in keeping the car on his side of the road. He guessed that really didn't matter, though. He hadn't passed another car since pulling off the main highway and getting on Route 45. Gary checked the time on the digital clock in the dash. Two forty-five. They'd been on this journey for over two hours, but it felt so much longer.

What if we get there and she's gone?

He really needed to stop thinking like that. She'd be there waiting for him with a smile on her face, and a hug ready to give. He longed to feel her pressed up against him, her arms curved around his back and her head snuggled up under his chin where he could smell the scent of her shampoo. It brought a smile to his face. He wasn't so sure why the sudden affection for Amy had come over him, but he wasn't ashamed of it.

It wasn't like he was going to shove his tongue in her mouth or anything.

That image played in his mind, nearly making him laugh. Even if he tried to kiss her, she would kick him in the balls. He knew that. Amy had no feelings for him beyond mutual friends, and he didn't have them for her either.

Probably.

"Yep," he muttered, verbally agreeing with his thoughts.

Wendy pulled her stare away from the window and pointed it at him. "What'd you say?"

"Just thinking out loud."

"Maybe you should try speaking *all* of your thoughts. At least you'd be talking then."

Gary looked at her, squinting his eyes against the dark. Her face, accentuated by the green light from the dash, appeared inhuman like some of kind of fiend from EC comics—a ghoul rising from the grave to feast upon the living.

"You haven't said a word to me this whole time," she continued, her head bopping from side to side.

Not wanting to argue, he just shrugged his shoulders. "Sorry."

Apparently giving up on him, Wendy returned her attention to her window.

Gary hated to agree with her, but she was right. He hadn't spoken to her at all since leaving his house.

He'd focused all his thoughts on Amy and had worked himself into such a frenzy he'd debated stopping somewhere to pick up a pack of cigarettes. He'd been smoke-free for over a year, but the events of the night had turned his emotions into a jumbled mess. A cigarette could take care of that, but Amy would ring his neck if he smoked.

If she's around when I get there to pick her up.

Amy had been after him for years to kick the habit. He despised it when people would offer unsolicited advice informing him how unhealthy it was to smoke, as if he hadn't read the warnings on the side of the boxes himself. He understood the risk associated with each puff he took. It just seemed impossible for him to quit. However, when Amy would say those things, or go as far as to research ways to help him quit, he detected the sincerity of her attempts. It seemed she was really worried that he may actually get sick, or even worse, die from his addiction.

The last time he received one of Amy's notorious lectures about the dangers of smoking, he made a promise to her. If he were to ever sell one of his manuscripts, he'd stop and never pick one up again. Cold turkey. Amy, being a diligent committer, whipped up a binding contract that outlined all the details of their agreement. At the bottom were two lines, one with her signature already inked in, the other spot was for his.

He signed it.

Then they sealed the deal with a spit in their palms, followed by a handshake. Mountain-style.

The joke should have been on her because he'd never actually considered someone would be willing to buy one of his books. Never thought he could actually sit still long enough to write one, either. To his surprise, it wasn't as hard of a task as he'd feared it would be. Sure, it had its moments, and some days he could have pounded his head against the wall and still not conjure up some good narrative, but he'd never given up.

Turned out to be rather therapeutic for him.

After a few false starts, he'd managed to whip up a novel about a dog driven mad, attacking and killing anyone it laid its eyes on. Calling the book *Shep*, he had put characters in the story that were inspired by Wendy and himself. A young couple that really shouldn't be together, but for whatever reason was. The dog, feeding off of their negative energy and an atmosphere corroded with hate, started showing signs of violence. The nagging girlfriend—who he'd named Michelle—had demanded the boyfriend, Barry, get rid of it. He drove it to a remote location and left poor Shep to fend for himself. Neither one of them had expected him to come back at all, let alone for revenge, but he did, and left a trail of grisly killings in his wake.

It clocked in at ninety-thousand words. Amy, of course, was the first to read it. She thought it was great, perfect from start to finish, and especially loved the ending when Shep tore Michelle apart, and, instead of going after Barry, he reverted to the fun-loving dog he used to be. Barry and Shep lived happily after.

The wicked witch was dead.

Amy convinced him to submit the manuscript to some publishers. Since he didn't have an agent—or a clue how to obtain one—the number of companies willing to read unsolicited material were scarce. He submitted it to all that he could find. A few agonizingly slow months later, he was surprised to find out the few companies that had read it *all* wanted it. He finally decided to sell it to Repose Publications. It was released eight months ago. Not a bestseller by any means, it had made quite a bit of money for Repose, and Gary.

Plus, he'd recently sold the movie rights, and had already received the advance check for his second book.

But none of that mattered to Amy, a deal was a deal. On the day—nearly a year ago—he received his first ever advance check, he handed over all his cigarettes, lighters, and ash trays to her. He watched as she chucked the trays in the trash and used a hammer to smash the cigarettes and lighters to morsels of plastic, tobacco shreds, and paper.

She'd probably use that same hammer on him if he smoked again.

"What do you plan on doing with her once you pick her up?" Wendy asked, ruining his fond reverie.

"What's that supposed to mean?"

"It means what it means. What are you going to do with her?"

She's not a pet, he thought, but said, "Bring her back to my house, I guess." He hadn't really planned it that far. All he was worried about at the moment was just fucking getting there and making sure she was safe.

"And then what?" she asked, rolling the window down an inch. She reached into her purse, dug out a pack of cigarettes, and offered him one.

He shook his head.

She always did that to him so he'd break his promise to Amy. It was a sick game Wendy liked to play.

She planted the cigarette between her thin lips. Using a match, she lighted it, then took in a deep drag, and exhaled. She sighed with exaggerated relief.

Gary pictured himself leaning over, opening her door, and shoving her out of the car. Looking in the rearview mirror, he'd see in the red glow of taillights her body rolling and twirling along the asphalt behind him, coming to a stop in a heap of broken bones and frayed clothes.

"You never answered me," she said, taking another drag. "Are you afraid to?"

"No."

"Then, do it."

"I haven't exactly figured it all out just yet."

"Oh, that's just great. We're driving all this way, but you don't have a plan?"

"No, Wendy, I don't. I think we should all get a hotel room tonight on the way back. I'm sure we could *all* use the rest. Then, in the morning we'll drive to my house and go from there. Cross that bridge when we get to it."

"So, your plan is not having a plan?"

"Exactly."

Wendy laughed. "You know, to be a writer you sure don't think things through. I thought you types did nothing *but* think of scenarios all day. You know? Building up fantasies in your heads and jotting them down so you can whip it into a story of lies?"

"If you can't say anything nice, Wendy, you shouldn't say anything at all."

"Ohhh, I get it. That's your cute little way of telling me to shut the hell up, right?" She scoffed, tilting her head, and exhaling a cloud of smoke in the car.

Gary shook his head. "No, not at all. *Saying* shut the hell up is my cute way of telling you to shut the hell up."

Wendy's mouth yawned open. Without saying another word, she whipped her head around to stare out the window some more.

Smooth move, asshole.

He was pushing his luck. The last thing he wanted was being partly responsible for pushing Wendy's jealous fury in Amy's direction and unleashing a cat-fight inside his Jeep. It was large enough and strong enough to contain that style of dirty fighting. However, that would undoubtedly put a damper on an already dreary night for them all.

Gary smiled.

Sure would be fun to see, though.

AMY

The moon looked as if it was slowly tracking its way to Wisconsin and would soon be low enough to touch. Not completely full, but it was close enough to be mistaken for it.

Amy pulled her admiring gaze away from the moon to peek at her watch. She pulled back the heavy sleeve of her coat, using the moon's gray smolder to read the time: 3:32. Quickly, she tugged the sleeve back down again. From the small amount of time her skin was exposed to the nippy air, it had become pebbled with goose bumps.

It felt as cold as Christmas outside.

She'd been lucky enough to grab her coat on the way out and better yet, she'd found her debit card and license in her pocket. Thank God it had slipped her mind to put them back in her purse.

The sweet aroma of fall was in the air, but dimly mixed in with it was a stale, underlying odor of manure. It shielded Wisconsin like a dome. Thanks to the myriad cow pastures and pig farms, the smell was everywhere, though she hardly noticed it anymore.

But from where she was hiding, it was hard not to smell shit.

The only place she'd found to hide and stay within hearing distance of the phone was behind an old outhouse. Made of wood, seemingly centuries ago, the structure had warped to one side, and was slowly decaying. At first, she'd attempted to hide inside of the crooked privy, but after one whiff in there, she realized that wasn't happening. Although it looked older than the land it was built on, it appeared people were still regularly using it. Being behind it was bad enough, and she could still smell the retched odors of old feces, but at least it was somewhat muted by the rotting boards.

She just needed to be careful not to step in the drain that led to a nearby creek or she'd be up to her ankles in body waste.

Anxious for Gary to come, she was ready to get out of the cold and into his familiar arms. He gave the best hugs she'd ever had.

Then she heard the stranger's question.

"Are you out here all alone?"

Amy froze at the sudden timbre of a man's voice. It boomed in the still air. She pressed her body against the outhouse wall. Afraid of risking a peep around the corner, she tried looking through the gaps between the moldering boards. There was just enough space between them that if she angled her head just right, she could see through.

"Is someone after you? Is that why you're back there?" A man, all right, but neither Piper nor Gary. *Who the hell is it?* The moonlight clashed with the dim floodlight on top of the power pole by the store, casting a deep river of blackness all around its foundation. The man stood in that blackness. *Perfect spot if you don't want to be seen.* All she could make out of him was a vague shape. He was thin. The top of his head seemed flat and level like a new eraser. Either he was Frankenstein, or his hair was cut *very* short.

Across the parking lot behind him, she could see the pale shape of a car that had somehow parked by the road without her hearing it. It was too dark to tell what kind it was, but it was of a smaller style. All that mattered was that it was there. She couldn't give a good goddamn as to what make and model it was.

How had it arrived without her noticing? She was thankful it hadn't been Gary. He might not have thought to check behind the outhouse, unless he had to take a squat. Or, he may have thought he had the wrong store and kept on driving. He could've easily left without her ever knowing he'd come, and he'd have been unaware she was here.

What if he already came by and I missed him?

Not likely. Gary would have searched the grounds, looking in every dark corner and under every rock until he'd found her. He was unwavering, a total sweetheart and the best person she'd ever known. Why she kept wasting her time with pieces of shit like Piper Conwell while Gary had been right in front of her this whole time was something that none of her female friends—when she still had them—could quite figure out.

Including her.

"Hello?" tried the voice, again. Now it sounded concerned.

Amy figured out the voice wasn't threatening, but genuinely alarmed. Turning around, she pressed her back to the weakened boards. The building shifted away from her. Cautious and alert, she eased herself up, keeping her arms outstretched beside her as if teetering on a cliff's edge.

"Steve? What's going on, man? I thought you were just gonna hop out and take a piss. D'you get lost?"

"Shut up, Jake," said the voice she was familiar with, who had been singled out as Steve. "Come here."

"What's up?" asked the second voice—Jake—who now shared the same alarm Steve did.

Two guys? Perfect. What if they're traveling rapists? Boy, they've really hit the jackpot tonight.

Amy twisted her body around, pressing her chest against the wood. Her breasts squished against it. Looking through the narrow slit, she saw in the gray light two guys at the edge of the parking lot where the gravel met the grass. The outhouse was just a few feet away. They didn't lower their voices as they spoke.

"Someone's hiding back there," said Steve.

"You're kidding."

"Do I look like I'm kidding?"

There was a short pause, then, "No, you don't."

"Looks like a woman."

"Should we get the girls? Maybe they could talk to her, find out what's up. I seriously doubt she'd trust two guys that just stumbled upon her in the dead of night."

Jake sounded like a bright guy.

"Yeah, might not be a bad idea."

They'd mentioned girls. Two guys with dates, and that meant they had to be travelers who just happened to be in the neighborhood.

"It's okay," said Amy, finally.

Both men gasped when they heard her voice. It cut through the tranquility like a razor-edged knife.

Jake said, "You scared us."

"Likewise," she said back.

"Are you hurt?" he asked.

"No, I'm fine, really."

"Are you sure?"

"Yes, I'm waiting for someone."

"Back there?"

Amy laughed. "Nowhere better, right?"

"Yes," said Steve. "I imagine there are plenty of better places."

"And they probably don't smell as bad," Jake added.

"You're both probably right, but this is the best I had to work with, so sue me."

"Why don't you come on out?" asked Steve.

Amy debated it, wondering how safe it was—could go either way, she realized. *It probably is safe.* But she couldn't bring herself to trust these guys completely. She took in a deep breath. The repellant odor from inside the outhouse was making her head hurt.

"All right, I'm coming out." She stepped away from the outhouse. Without its support, her body felt like it was floating. The warped boards had become a disposition of comfort to her, a safe zone between her and the two men. Now, she was stepping out into the open without the decrepit box.

Amy rounded the rear corner. The grass was much higher here. Wet with dew, it rubbed across her shins, dampening her jeans. Striding along the side wall, she was just a few steps away from the door, and almost in plain sight. She stepped around the front. The two men stood waiting, their arms nearly touching. To her surprise, they weren't actually men. *Boys.* Much younger than she'd assumed, their deep voices had thrown her off. She had presumed they were in their late twenties easily, but looking at them now she guessed they were barely twenty-one.

If that.

Both dressed in black, the first one with the straight shaped head actually did have hair, but it was cut so close to his scalp it seemed unfair to count it. The other one had longer hair that dangled in his eyes. He wore a Slayer T-shirt.

Metal-heads.

Amy was willing to bet that both of these guys were probably nice, timid and quite shy in a normal situation. But this was hardly normal. Head-bangers, in Amy's experience, often had a bad rap because of their dress code, and the inability to turn the volume on their radios down below eleven. She'd come to learn that people like these two kids were some of the nicest she'd ever met.

Amy walked closer. Judging the stunned looks on their faces, they weren't expecting a woman to step out from behind the outhouse. She had no idea what they'd thought they would see, maybe a vagrant, but she certainly wasn't that. "Are you guys all right?"

Steve, she assumed, removed a pair of glasses from his face. He rubbed the lenses with his shirt and put them back on. "Yeah, I was uh—you look—uh…"

"Different than what we thought you would." The longer haired one—presumably Jake—added.

"What did you think I'd look like?"

They glanced at each other, clearly daring the other to speak first. Neither of them accepted the challenge.

"Who's who?" she asked. "I heard the names Steve and Jake, so which one's which?"

The longer haired one spoke first, "I'm Jake. This is Steve." He flicked his thumb in his buddy's direction.

Steve, short hair, wears glasses. Jake, longer hair, does not.

"Well, Steve and Jake, I'm Amy Stone. Nice to meet you both."

"The pleasure is all ours, I imagine." Jake said, smiling.

Steve forced a smile, but its execution came off as too nervous and awkward to be pleasant.

"Oh please," she said. "I bet you say that to all the girls you find hiding behind outhouses."

They laughed.

"Yeah," agreed Steve. "We're suckers for those outhouse girls."

"Oh, yeah?" Amy laughed. "You guys are too much."

"Soooo," said Jake. "If you don't mind me asking, why *were* you hiding back there?"

"Tell you what," she said. "Why don't we let your buddy Steve there run on and take that leak he needs to, and when he's done, I'll fill you in on all the wonderful details."

"Huh?" asked Steve, dumbly.

"Didn't you have to pee?"

Steve jerked rigid. "Oh, right!" Laughing, he said, "I almost forgot. Thanks."

Where Amy stood, she blocked his path to the outhouse. As he passed her, he sidestepped to avoid touching her as if she was infected with a disease that spread by contact. She wanted to laugh at his reserve but didn't. That would surely make the condition even more uncomfortable for him, and he already seemed terribly stressed with the way things were going thus far.

Poor guy.

He entered the privy and shut the door.

Jake turned to Amy and smiled. "So?"

"So," she said back.

"You must *really* be in some deep shit to be hiding behind a shitter."

"Jake, you have quite an eye for detail."

He bounced his eyebrows and smiled.

MARY

From the front passenger seat, Mary watched through the sun visor mirror as Shannon lighted her cigarette with the flaming tip of a match, fanned it out, and tossed the charred stick away. She was leaning against the backseat, legs stretched through the open rear-passenger window. The chilled air flowed through the car, flicking at her legs and under her skirt, but Mary assumed she must like it.

Shannon's short, black skirt had slunk down her thighs, barely encasing her rump. Mary could see the silken curve of her buttocks. She was either wearing skimpy panties or none at all. Her knee-length boots were heavily laced and adorned with silver. Normally, she'd wear fishnet stockings with an outfit like that, but not this time. Her legs were bare, smooth and creamy.

Was her seductive pose intentional?

Stop gawking at her! She'll think you're fwapping up here!

Seeing Shannon so confident made Mary wish even more than usual that she was bold enough to show her own body, to be just as secure, though she wouldn't deliberately flaunt it as Shannon often did. Actually, Mary was quite happy with her figure. There were instances where she wanted to parade around showing the world that she wasn't just the quiet girl, and to prove that she had a body just as sweet as Shannon's.

Take tonight as an example. It had taken a lot more courage than she'd thought she had to wear the extremely low-cut tank top Shannon had forced her to buy earlier in the day. The reedy material hugged her body, pushing her large breasts even higher than they already were. Their rounding slopes were visible on both sides. Her nipples jutted like nail-points under the shirt. She'd tried wearing a bra, but Shannon pointed out how ridiculous it looked, and she had been right, so she'd gone without. Mary was proud of her cleavage. They had always seemed unnaturally heavy for her small frame. But as content as she was with having them, she felt uncomfortable exhibiting them.

When they'd arrived at the concert, she didn't want to shed her leather jacket. But after some beers and loosening up, she became eager to lose it. The guys at the club were checking her out, gawking at her. Two offered to buy her drinks. *That never happens!* As much as she didn't want to acknowledge these feelings, she couldn't ignore them. She'd loved it.

Steve had also gawked at her all night. When his hands began roaming her body, exploring her under the tank top's straps, cupping her breasts, massaging them, lightly pinching the nipples, she'd enjoyed that as well. He couldn't keep his hands off of her. But as the night progressed, it became less about Steve *wanting* her, and more of him showing the other guys in the club that he *had* her. Shadowing her, never leaving her side, he'd even escorted her every trip to the bathroom. Some girls might find that sort of thing flattering, but she didn't. She also didn't like how insecure he'd suddenly become just because she wore a revealing tank top.

"See something you like?" asked Shannon.

Mary's frame of mind returned to the car and found her eyes were still engrossed with Shannon's reflection. She quickly looked away. She felt as if she'd just been caught peeping through a window.

Might as well have been!

"What?" asked Mary, trying to sound confused.

Shannon laughed. "I saw your eyes in the mirror. You couldn't stop staring at my legs."

"I was not." Her response came out *too* snappy to be true.

She laughed again. "I'm not upset. I liked it."

Oh, boy. Please don't start.

"What do you expect? It's hard to miss them when you have them hanging out like that."

"You can touch them if you want." She rubbed the slant of her thigh with a pinky.

"Thanks, but we've tried that before, remember?"

Shannon closed her eyes, tilting her head upward as she reminisced. "How could I forget that special night?" She lowered her head, pointed an aggravated look at Mary. "And you wussed out!"

"You took it too far!"

"Took what too far? We were naked, kissing, feeling each other up. It was going that way naturally!"

"You started *licking* me...down *there*."

Shannon choked on the smoke in her lungs, and coughed. "Who cares?"

"I didn't want it to go *that* far."

Fanning away the regurgitated smoke, Shannon said, "We had already taken it too far and that just would have been a lovely way to finish."

"Sure." She rolled her eyes. Tired of talking to her in the rearview mirror, she turned around in the seat. "Did you ever tell Jake about that?"

"No, of course not. I doubt he would have minded, but I didn't want to risk it because we've had enough problems as it is. If he would've found out that I'd done anything with you, he might have looked at it as cheating."

"Wasn't it?"

"I don't think so. My feelings for you are so strong it felt right to me."

Mary could have gone without hearing that. Not only did it bring back memories of *that* night six months ago, but it made her recall something even more recent. Last month, after a fight with Steve, Shannon had blown off a date with Jake to try and cheer her up. Too many strawberry martinis later, Shannon confessed her unyielding love for Mary. Told her how she'd been in love with her since high school. Mary couldn't get her to shut up about it. Shannon had worked herself up into tears, sobbing against Mary's chest before finally passing out.

When Shannon awoke the next morning with a hangover, she'd asked Mary what they had talked about the previous night. Mary made something up, not telling her the truth. She'd wondered if Shannon had actually forgotten about it, or was just pretending that she had in hopes it would go away.

Mary lowered her gaze from Shannon's smile in the backseat.

Shannon quickly added, "And plus, your legs are a lot nicer than mine."

Mary scoffed, "Yeah, right. You're just saying that. Yours are long and shapely, mine are short and pudgy." That wasn't true. Actually, Mary's legs were curvy and had some meat on them without being fat. Many girls had told her how perfect her legs were more than once.

"Bitch, I'm jealous of your legs!"

"You're just saying that to try and butter me up."

"Yes, but I'm using truth margarine. It's lighter and feels better."

Mary laughed.

Shannon flicked her cigarette—which had been burning the filter—into the parking lot. She pulled her legs through the window and began to scoot down the seat to make an exit.

"What are you doing?"

Her skin made squeaking sounds against the fake leather as she shimmied her ass to the edge of the seat. "I'm going to prove it to you."

"Prove it? How?"

"Just shut up and wait."

Shannon climbed out of the car, adjusting her skirt and coat when she stood. She stepped around the opened door. Mary repeated, "What are you doing?" But her voice bounced back at her behind the closed glass.

Shannon opened Mary's door and squatted in front of her. Her skirt hung between her spread legs like a loincloth, but not before she saw that Shannon was indeed *not* wearing panties.

Figures.

She grabbed Mary and twirled her around to face her. Her legs parted and Shannon knelt between them. She suddenly felt awkward, as if some horny stranger was invading her personal space, getting closer than she was willing to allow.

That was just about right.

She didn't know this Shannon. After a few drinks it was like the *real* Shannon started to shine through. The lustful lesbian, who wanted nothing more than to pop her best friend's cherry.

Shannon's fingers found the button of Mary's pants.

"Whoa," said Mary. "What are you doing?"

"Relax. It's all part of me proving my point."

"Well, I wish you'd prove it without grabbing me like that."

Shannon laughed. "You're so funny. You listen to all those death metal bands, watch weird Italian Cannibal movies, and read the most disturbing books by authors I've never heard of."

"There are other horror authors besides King and Koontz."

"Oh, whatever… No one knows who King and Koontz are, either."

"What are you talking about? *We* do."

"Shut up about Koong and Kintz and stop getting all fidgety when I grab your pants."

"It's different."

"Getting too real for you?"

Real enough for me not to like it.

While they were talking, Shannon had managed to not only unbutton Mary's pants, but to scuttle the zipper down. Now, she was struggling with slipping them over her hips.

"Wait," said Mary.

"Too late," said Shannon. The right corner of her mouth curved up. "I'm not gonna lick you again."

"Let's hope not."

Shannon's movements stopped as she absorbed that comment. Mary regretted having said it. It had obviously pinged her the wrong way. She eventually continued on, tugging at the pants as if trying to undress an uncooperative infant. But now it didn't seem as fun to her. She'd managed them down to the rump that Mary was keeping pressed firmly against the seat. Looking defeated, Shannon sighed and let go.

"Just forget it."

Now Mary felt guilty. Shannon was trying to have some fun with her and all she could do was be a bitch about it.

But she's undressing me!

Mary was wearing jeans. Shannon couldn't see through denim. Of course she was trying to undress her. She claimed that Mary's legs were nicer than her own, so she was just trying to show her it was true.

Stop being so weird. You're making it even harder for Shannon.

Raising her bottom, she said, "Wait," and granted her the access she needed to finish.

Shannon's grin returned. She latched onto the waist band, gliding the pants down below Mary's knees. They hung there. A cold breeze drifted over her skin. Shannon slid her hands under each of Mary's thighs and lifted her legs high enough that she could waddle under them. Then she draped them over her, Mary's knees bending over Shannon's shoulders.

Looks like I'm about to give birth and Shannon plans to catch it as I pop it out.

Mary observed something in Shannon's eyes. A look. The same she was getting from the men at the club tonight. Earlier, it had made her feel good, captivating. With Shannon gawking at her like a starving carnivore over a butcher's choice-cut of meat, she felt like prey to the hunter.

"Look at them," said Shannon. "See what I mean?"

Mary glanced down at herself and then studied them up to her knees where they vanished over Shannon's back. They really did look good. But then, her eyes reversed their course back to her panties, remembering that she had worn a pair so thin they were translucent. *Of all nights to wear these.* Laced in the front, a thin string up the back, she'd worn them for Steve since they were his favorite. *Thank God it's dark outside.* Wouldn't help her much with hiding the panties, but it'd keep Shannon from noticing Mary's skin going scarlet.

She might think I enjoy her fondling me.

Probably thinks I wore these damn things for her.

"I see them," said Mary. "They're just legs."

"No, look at your thighs, babe." Shannon slid a hand up the side of one. "So smooth, comfortable, and darker than mine too. See?" She sat on her ass and turned to the side as she hiked her skirt up high over her hip, and let it slide back. Then she extended her leg straight up. Mary never realized Shannon was that flexible. It was actually pretty impressive, plus she was absolutely right. Her own thighs were much darker. And she also had the visual proof that Shannon wasn't a fan of having hair between her legs. It was all gone.

Mary cleared her throat and said, "Yeah, I see that." Her voice came out husky. She tried to sit up and grab her jeans, but Shannon eased her back, stopping her.

Crouching again, Shannon was much closer this time. Mary could smell the musty aromas of the club caught in Shannon's hair, smoky, with a hint of strawberries from her shampoo. It kind of smelled nice, a bit intoxicating. She could overlook the club stench and focus on the pleasant tangs.

"Look at the shape. The way they curve right at the middle and inward, tight and lean. They're perfect." She glided her index finger higher up, sliding to her inner thigh. Her knuckle lightly brushed over the tender lips behind the laced panties. Mary gasped. Shannon smiled. "Did you like that?"

"Um…" She paused, trying to think of a delicate way of answering.

Did I? Of course she hadn't liked it at all. *But why am I trembling?*

"You did, didn't you?"

Before Mary could reply, Shannon had hooked her finger inside the panties. She felt the coldness of Shannon's skin rubbing her in a place that had been reserved for Steve. After the way he acted at the club, she doubted it would have been offered to him tonight.

Then she felt Shannon's finger going inside her with a squishing sound. She wriggled like a worm on a hook as the finger rubbed against her moist interior. *I'm wet?* She was even more surprised by the moan that escaped her lips. She cut it short as she pressed her legs together, pinning Shannon's cupped hand against her groin, the finger still inside of her. Shannon flexed her wrist up and down, penetrating her rhythmically. Nearly screaming, she managed to push Shannon's hand away. It exited her with a *slurp*.

"Chill out, will you?" Mary's trembling voice was loud, yet broken and parched.

Shannon's coy routine transformed to one of hurt and confusion with a hint of shock thrown in. She lowered her head, obviously trying to fathom the conflicting emotions Mary had displayed. "S-sorry," she muttered.

Mary sat up, pulling her buttocks farther back on the seat. She felt a warm line of wetness trickling down her thighs. It was dipping onto the seat. *God, I hope it doesn't stain. How will I explain that?* She sniffed. The broad scent of sex was in the car, and she hoped the cold air would disperse it before Steve and Jake got back.

Shannon stood up, brushing her hands on the front of her skirt. "I was j-just joking around." Her bottom lip quivered. "I took it too far." Her eyes were swollen and damp. She turned to the backseat, found her purse in the floorboard and dug through it. She stepped back, brandishing her cigarettes, then walked around to the rear of the car.

Mary felt awful, as if she'd been the one that had done something horrible. Had she? *No, just denied someone, someone who's like a sister to me, access inside of me. No harm in that, right?* She'd often worried about Shannon's fixated behavior but had never truly thought it was a problem. She'd always chalked it off as her own fear, passing off Shannon's supposed affection for her to college confusion. *That's what happens in college, girls get lonely, confused, so they experiment. This sort of thing happens all the time.* But she was convinced Shannon's feelings were much stronger than that. Maybe she really was in love with her. If so, that would surely put another strain on their already crumbling friendship.

She rubbed me. Her finger was inside me!

Mary could still feel Shannon's touch like a ghost finger prodding around inside of her. She slowly pulled up her pants and buttoned them, then climbed out of the car and stretched. It felt better standing up. Her constricted muscles loosened, the cramp in her neck softened, but her legs tingled from hips to ankles. The enjoyment was short-lived. It was freezing outside, causing her muscles to restrict back as if burrowing against her bones. Even in her heavy coat, she was still trembling. Mary clenched her teeth to keep them from chattering.

Where the hell are the boys?

Steve had left a long time ago to take a piss with Jake going shortly after to check on him. Neither one of them returned. *Maybe Jake was molesting him too. A weird swinger game they've got going on.* She realized where he'd stick his finger and grimaced. There was only one place he *could* put it. *Gross.* Mary shook her head to jerk that image loose. She was ashamed for how ridiculous she was acting.

With reason, she thought.

Maybe so, but she couldn't stop the guilt. Shannon cared for her more than any friend should. In some way, she was honored by it. But it was something they'd have to deal with soon. Just not tonight. Tonight had been planned for fun.

"Hey," said Shannon. Mary turned around. Shannon was leaning with her hip against the back of the car, smoking. "Come here."

Before going, she snatched her own cigarettes from the dashboard. As she removed one from the pack, she walked along side of the car to join Shannon. She hardly had time to search her pocket for a lighter before Shannon had already flamed it for her. "Thanks."

"No problem."

On a desperately needed cigarette, there was nothing greater than that first puff, the way it hit the back of your throat and drifted into your lungs. *Best feeling in the world.*

"I wanted to apologize for that back there."

Mary threw up her hand. "No, don't. I was acting weird. All's fine."

"The hell you were. I was the one fingering your cootch. That was *so* stupid of me, I'm sorry."

Mary realized Shannon was forcing this conversation to happen tonight. "Shannon, it's okay, we don't have to get into this now."

"Yes, we do. I just don't want any of what I did tonight, or have done in the past, to ruin what we have."

Too late. It'd been hard enough for her to forget about what all had happened the last several months, but after what she did tonight, Mary knew it would be impossible for their friendship to be the same.

Shannon continued, "I really care about you, a lot. And if I couldn't have you in my life at least as a friend, a *dear* friend, I would die."

Being Mary's turn to speak, she didn't know where to start. She had a lot she *needed* to say but didn't *want* to say. They should be having this chat alone, at their apartment, but Shannon had never claimed to be a patient person. She'd thrown this on her all at her once. All Mary wanted to do was lock herself in the car until the guys got back. She pushed all those worries aside and worked up the best false smile she'd ever accomplished. "You wouldn't die, but your laundry would never get done."

Mary didn't think Shannon was going to find the humor in what she'd said. But Shannon's frown broke into an upward curve and her lips parted, allowing her wide smile to show. "Yeah, that's true."

Mary couldn't believe it had worked. She needed to keep Shannon's mind focused on something else before it returned to that place. "I think our boys have gotten lost."

The look on Shannon's face contorted into a confused smirk. Mary wondered if Shannon had once thought about them since they'd left. "Yeah, you're right. I wonder what happened."

"I don't know. Steve takes a long time to piss, but this is odd even for him."

Shannon laughed. "Maybe they're confused how it works."

They were distracted by movement to their right. The boyfriends emerged from the rear of the store.

They had found a friend.

A gorgeous one.

Shannon flicked her cigarette. It crashed on the gravel into a bang of orange, glowing ash. "What the hell is this?" she called out. "You take off to find Steve and find him plus one!"

Jake leaned over to the girl—woman—and whispered something. She nodded, understanding what he'd explained to her.

"We need to talk," said Jake.

"Why? What's going on?" Mary asked. His brow was creased, narrowing his eyes to slits. His mouth bore a straight line from his lips pressing tight and narrow. Something was wrong.

Very wrong.

WARDER—THE LEADER

It hadn't always been so challenging to survive. The last winter had been the harshest he could remember. Hammering cold temperatures and a two-month long snow storm that seemed to never stop took the lives of many, leaving even more sick and dying.

He stepped out of his shanty. It was a cone-shaped structure built from limbs, stalks, and dried mud. He stretched while gazing upon what was left of his parish.

Empty hovels of nothing.

The moon hung solidly behind the trees, casting its last net of gray across the decaying assemblies as morning prepared to invade.

How many are left?

After the last headcount, there hadn't been a lot who were still healthy.

It was autumn and the nights were already bitter cold. He feared what the winter would bring with its bleak days and arctic nights. They'd gathered what they could find to harvest for the winter. With the amount of snow that would come, they needed to have plenty of provisions. Luckily, the Watcher had supplied them with medicines for the cold months, but they would either be too little, or not what they needed. And what he gave in that capacity, he lacked in food.

Times were hard for them all.

But that didn't make it forgivable.

The way they had to take refuge during the wintry months, hiding like squirrels in the trees or gophers in the ground, just to survive was intolerable. Then, during the summer months, they'd migrate to the cornfields where they could live in some kind of serenity. It was hard, never-ending. He wished they would have established their colony in an area with the seclusion of caves, or mountains. Somewhere with a place of shelter where they could be warm as the snow fell, or to be farther south, where the snow barely dropped at all.

He thought back to their assault on the Hamilton farm as a smile festooned his face. The times called for drastic acts, which had forced them to break their treaty with the town of Doverton. He didn't feel the slightest dishonor in having done so, either. The town had turned their backs on them long ago, reducing them to nothing more than scary stories to be told around a campfire, or when they spoke of them sincerely it was in hushed tones. It was only a matter of time before they retaliated.

He walked along the loose dirt of his village that had once been ravishing greenery. When they'd first settled here all those years ago, he was told by the elders the soil had been rich. Their crops had grown by the thousands, so much so that they began trading with the Amish. Food was never scarce. But now the land lay flat and dying. The prosperous earth had dried to powder, and they were lucky to get even a month's worth of food from the crops. This summer had been even less.

They were slowly starving, prolonging what was surely coming, and as he passed by the realms of dried-brown corn stalks, he thought back to how much safer it used to be living here. When his father and several others had formed the village, they'd planned to live peacefully in the seclusion of the farmlands without fear of discovery, but of course, it did not last.

Land was snatched up in the decades following, devoured and turned into housing communities, strips of stores, gas stations and hotels. It wouldn't be long before they came looking this way. There was plenty of land here left to be claimed. Wisconsin was one of the remaining places on this side of the world with such a vast countryside. The Watcher couldn't protect them forever. He was old and sick himself. He would surely die soon, possibly even this winter. When that happened they would have to be finished with Doverton, but because of their dwindling numbers, he feared they would be nowhere close.

It sickened him.

A drastic new plan had been forced into action. At summer's end, he'd sent out a section of his finest warriors to the Hamilton farm on the other side of the cornfield. With all the nearby cattle farms closing down, there was no livestock left to steal. His men broke into the house with only plans of stealing meat from their freezers and canned goods from their pantries. From the retelling, they were ambushed by the Hamilton woman. They struck back, and she was killed along with her husband.

That plan had soured, but a fresh one was launched.

Human meat.

And in the weeks since, they'd returned to Doverton, striking more families, farmers, and whoever else they could find. Unfortunately, most of Doverton's populace were already relocating to better cities with more chance of employment and money, leaving behind houses with signs staked in the front yards. He'd seen people in suits come take pictures of them with fancy cameras. Warder had been tempted to move his people into those houses, but it was even riskier to do that than it was to remain in the woods and fields. They would see what the winter brought and if no one had settled into them by then, they could take refuge inside until spring returned.

And because Doverton had already been dying, Warder and his people were taking advantage of those unfortunate enough to be left behind. But they needed more if they were going to survive. Since they weren't like the grown ones, in his eyes and the eyes of God, what they were doing wasn't cannibalism.

Back in the old days, the town of Doverton was a willing bunch of Amish folk who gave them tools, seeds, food and help in structuring their village. But the drones that occupied the town now treated them as a mockery, a yarn that no one feared anymore. Even those gracious Amish folks had been pushed out into the fields, taking refuge in seclusion, and building houses to harbor themselves away from the ever-changing new world. He guessed that even though the Amish weren't angry people, they despised Doverton just as much as his own people.

His ancestors had been skillful hunters bred for the tracking and killing of meat. They would be that, again.

Doverton was just the beginning.

The way of the savage would return.

GARY

Wendy had fallen asleep, granting Gary some temporary peace and quiet. So he decided to pass the time by replaying some of the happier moments he'd shared with Amy before they'd both become trapped, him with Wendy and her with Piper. What he realized in the hush of the car-ride was the similarity of their situations. What Wendy lacked in using her hands to punish him, she more than made up for with her words; where Piper swung a fist, Wendy punched with an insult. The marks she left weren't purple and blue on his skin, but were just as damaging to his confidence. If she kept at it long enough, his confidence would become whittled down to a nub.

Up ahead, Gary spotted the store on the left. The sun was rising, illuminating the sky in red and blue like blood in a swimming pool. Soon, it would yellow, and the cold temperatures would dissipate, then the day would begin to warm.

The GPS alerted him the store was less than a mile away, and on the left. Wendy's head began to nod. Thanks to the GPS's loud mouth, she was waking up. She stirred, straightened and stretched. With a yawn, she asked, "Are we there?"

"Yeah, it's right up there." He wished she had just stayed asleep. He wanted that special first hug to be unruffled, lasting longer than a quick three pats on the back. But with Wendy awake, it'd have to be one of those awkward one-armed hugs that he despised.

"You don't sound excited."

"I'm just worried." He hadn't spoken to Amy in hours, and the scenarios he'd been conducting in his head of what could have happened to her had been overwhelming. He hated having an ever-growing imagination at times like these. It was the best and worst thing about him rolled into one. And now, coming upon the parking lot, and seeing a strange car parked there, he was really concerned.

A small group of people were standing around the car, Amy included. From where he saw them, it looked as if Amy was a queen and these kids were her guardians.

"Looks like she made friends," said Wendy.

"What the hell is going on here?"

His headlights flared over them, briefly lighting them in the bright beams. Two guys and three girls, counting Amy. He didn't get a decent look at their features, but he could tell that they were younger than her.

Gary stopped behind their Dodge and shifted the gear to park. Leaving the engine idling, he was out on the parking lot, the loose gravel slipping under his shoes, before Wendy had even unbuckled her seatbelt.

Amy dashed from the group and into his arms. They hugged. Thankfully, he'd gotten what he had wanted—a powerful first embrace, the kind that set in motion their reunion.

"Hi Gare-bear," said Amy, her mouth pressed into his chest.

His worries subdued.

The two young men watched Gary's movements like nervous dogs wondering if they could trust the human offering them a treat. The girls—probably their girlfriends—smoked cigarettes and watched him candidly. What did they fear he might do?

Amy pulled back and looked up at Gary. Even in the dusk, the rising sun had no hope of being brighter than her smile. He melted in her arms. He pictured Amy pulling back and screaming as his body liquefied into human pudding all over her pretty coat. "Are you okay?" he managed to ask.

Amy smiled, nodding her head back to the group. "Do you mean them?"

He nodded.

"I'm fine. They've been a great help."

"I bet so, especially since they're watching me likes snakes ready to strike."

"We don't know you from shit," said the guy with longer hair.

"It's okay. This is Gary, the one I was telling you about." That put the group at ease. They nodded, waved and said their hellos awkwardly and shy-like. Amy looked back at him, her smile growing even larger.

Then the sound of a car door closing resonated from behind them.

The mood died.

Wendy, stretching beside Gary's Jeep, looked at them and smirked.

The curly blonde leaned forward, whispered, "Is she the *other* one you told us about?"

Amy nodded.

Guess she's already warned them all about Wendy.

"So, what's going on," he asked, implying the entourage.

"Well, it's a bit complicated."

They all pitched in, getting Gary caught up on how they'd met, and what all she'd told them. Gary lowered his guard. These kids were friends. If Amy liked them then they must be all right.

"So, this is the famous Gary?" asked the quieter girl with dark hair.

"The one and only," answered Amy.

"Hi, I'm Mary."

"Nice to meet you."

Mary introduced him to the others. They exchanged their hellos. And Gary stepped closer to shake Jake and Steve's hands. "Thanks for staying with her until I got here. That was very nice of you."

"It was no problem," said Jake. "We're just glad we could help in some way."

"If you don't mind me asking, what *were* you doing all the way out here? This place doesn't strike me as a popular hangout spot."

Jake laughed. "No, it's not. We were coming back from the Kreator show in Strand County. About seventy miles from here, I think. There was an eighteen-wheeler that had turned over on 601, so we took the back roads to avoid it."

Mary quickly intervened. "Hey, this is just an idea. I'm sure everyone is tired and would like some rest. Why don't you guys follow us farther up the road a bit? We were on our way to the Sleep Tight Inn. The GPS on my phone said it was about another ten miles north. You guys could get a room too."

Gary thought it over. He'd wanted to stop *somewhere*, but he also wanted to be done with Amy's roadies. Not that he minded them hanging around, he was just scared they would slow them down. With Wendy's elevating mood, and Piper possibly on the prowl, they could do without that. Or maybe they could just sneak out early before the kids woke up. That way, feelings wouldn't get hurt.

Mary continued, "Then we could grab some breakfast before parting ways."

That shot his plan to shit.

"A very late breakfast," added Shannon.

"Sounds good to me," Amy said. "If it's all right with Gary and Wendy."

"Fine," said Gary.

Wendy glanced from Gary to Amy and back. Then she threw her arms in the air. "I don't want to be the bitch that ruins your plans."

The group must have taken her snide comment as a yes. They hooted and hollered, throwing high fives. To Gary's surprise, Wendy was actually smiling at their reaction. It even looked, God help him, like she was laughing. Maybe, there was a nice person entombed deep down beneath the eternally pressing darkness that was Wendy.

"All right," interrupted Steve. "If you guys want to trail behind us, we'll lead the way. Should only take about fifteen minutes to get there. Sound cool?"

"Yep," said Gary. "We'll follow you, and I'll pay for the rooms."

There were more hoots and hollers, and even harder high-fives. He glanced at Wendy and saw her smile had vanished. The happier version was short-lived, and the bitter-hearted bitch that was the true Wendy had returned.

PIPER

On the way to the bus station, traffic had been fine, but afterward it was hell, holding Piper up much longer than he'd expected. Amy wasn't at the station, but Piper hadn't expected her to be. Pretending to be working on a case, he'd asked as many of the attendants that he could if they'd seen her, flashing a picture of her, but none of them had recognized her. More than likely, she'd never been there. That bitch had pulled one over on him good, and he was pissed with himself for having allowed it.

Coming back on the 601 had turned into catastrophe. Stretches of cars, all standing still in single file, had kept him cemented in one spot for an hour. Finally, the traffic had sluggishly moved far enough for him to grab the next exit and hop on the back roads.

Piper lit a cigarette, using the lighter from the Bronco's console. Pulling the lighter away from the cigarette's head, a chunk of paper and tobacco stuck against the cherry red disk. He tapped out the crispy chunk into the ash tray.

Taking the back roads was a longer route, but there he could pick his own speed. Being nothing but farming land and privately owned fields, there wasn't much need for the police, so cops mostly stuck to the main roads. The folks in the deep country took care of their matters mostly by themselves and in their own ways. He could appreciate that. Not to mention, they wouldn't try to stop him from driving over a hundred.

But if they did, it would be their funeral.

Also, the long drive gave him more time to think about what he was going to do once he found them. He hoped he could beat them to Gary's house in Stone Quarry. That way, he could be there waiting for them.

He pictured himself sneaking up behind Gary while he took a piss, and whispering into his ear. "Surprise." Piper laughed, took another drag from his cigarette, and exhaled. He cracked the window to let the smoke out. Sweet autumn aromas drafted in with a touch of the neighboring pastures.

Through all of the crap he'd gone through tonight, tracking Amy down had actually been fun. The payoff would be that much greater when he actually found her and killed her. She *had* to die. It wasn't just that he *wanted* to kill her, he needed to. She knew so much about him and the things he'd done. She was aware of his side jobs—selling pot to kids at the high school and taking payouts from several members of the community to look the other way while they conducted their business matters in a way that the law didn't support. She never scolded him for it, but she knew about it, and that was enough. He didn't trust her to keep it to herself once she was on her own. Plus, it would be fun as hell giving her what she deserved. Piper heard maniacal laughter. Glancing at his reflection in the rearview mirror, he discovered it was his own.

Then he laughed harder.

GARY

Gary lay in bed, unable to sleep. The sun was up outside, but luckily the room had blackout shades. The inside had the appearance of the dead of night, even though his body wasn't being so easily fooled. It knew he should be up right now, drinking coffee and sitting in front of his computer, typing away.

Wendy had groused about Gary paying for four rooms, but when she'd realized that one of those rooms was for Amy, she'd dropped it. He assumed she was thankful in her own right that Amy wouldn't be sharing a room with them. And he also figured that Amy was probably appreciative too.

On his back, one arm under the pillow and his head, he looked around the room. It was really dark. More than night dark, it was deathly dark. The walls were painted in shadows. Gary felt as if he had opened his eyes in a coffin buried several feet underground.

Claustrophobia nibbled at him. He hated feeling like this. How much of this was because of the room, and how much of this was Wendy sleeping beside him while Amy was in the next room over?

A little from column A and column B.

Perhaps he was feeling this way due to Wendy's jealous hold that sheathed him like a tarp, darkening him like the blackout shades had done to the room. He couldn't shake the feeling he'd done something wrong, like he had some kind of secret relationship with Amy and was trying to keep it from Wendy. There was nothing more to them than there always had been, but Gary felt like there was. Sure, he'd dabbled with the idea of him and Amy in romantic adventures on a few occasions, but not once had he ever considered anything beyond that.

Maybe it was the fact he'd begun questioning everything again, like he always did when Amy and Piper had a fight and Amy told him she was done being Piper's punching bag. As much as he wanted to believe it was only that, he couldn't. Although Gary had not cheated physically, he already had emotionally.

Gary wasn't a churchgoer, but he believed in God and tried to live a good life that would satisfy Him. Yet knowing he was in bed with his girlfriend, the same woman that he assumed one day he would decide to marry, while the woman he cared about the most was only separated from him by a wall, wasn't a Christian-like thing to do. His guilt nibbled at him.

He began to sweat.

The air conditioner was off when they'd first arrived, and Gary had left it that way. With the sun up, the air in the room was thickening with heat. He felt it pressing on him like a solid mass. The air conditioner was only a tiny window unit across the room. Even though he'd gone to bed naked, he now wanted to cut on the air to help thin the stuffiness, and also put some kind of noise other than Wendy's whispery breathing in the muted room.

An idea to sneak out of bed, turn on the AC to shield his noises, and get dressed to go next door flashed in his mind. As tempting as it was to see Amy, he wouldn't. Wendy would surely catch him.

She was up late tonight, though. Maybe she'd sleep right through it.

Perspiration began soaking him, making the sheet cling uncomfortably to his body. As he was about to toss it aside and introduce his naked body to the darkened room, the sheet stirred. It was rising. A round shape slithered up his body like a python on a mouse. He felt a presence on his legs, warm breaths fanning over his penis. It began to harden as each warm breath wafted across it. Gently, a hand curved around the shaft, and began to lightly stroke. As hard as he was getting, it couldn't distract him from the rising fury inside that Wendy was seducing him. After all the nasty things she had said tonight, and with Amy in the next room, Wendy still felt it was required to fool around. This was a new kind of low for her.

He flung the covers away to expose her ploy and gasped.

The hand fondling his erection was Amy's.

"Surprise," she whispered.

Shocked, Gary nearly leaped out of bed. Her gentle tug pulled at him, keeping him still. He checked beside him one more time for Wendy but didn't find her there. *Where is she?* Amy's hand stroked up and down, gently gliding her palm over his penis. The tickling friction caused his legs to shudder. Goose flesh hardened on his skin.

"What are you doing?" he asked.

Her lips curved, forming a seductive grin. "Playing. Don't you like it?"

What kind of question is that?

"Of course I do."

"Then don't ask why, just sit back and enjoy it." Bending her neck, he felt the cool dampness of her lips sucking him into her mouth. Her lips expanded around the head, taking him deeper in. Her smooth tongue licked and rolled under the base of his erection. He was already awfully close to a climax. Tensing, he tried to contain it. It would take a fight, but he hoped he could last. "Where's Wendy?"

Amy snickered at the mention of her name, her warm breath tickling his manhood's indurate structure. Gary pondered a few things. Like how she'd gotten in the room to begin with, where Wendy had disappeared to, why was Amy doing this to him, and more. He didn't give a shit about any of the answers. He was content, and decided to just let what was happening, happen.

Oh God. Here it comes.

"I'm, almost—"

With this warning, she siphoned harder, forcing his release to come even quicker, as if she needed him to unload right now. The pressure was building, starting in his testicles, and rising higher. Soon, it was drafting upward through his shaft, building at the tip. He was ready to explode. The need became less for enjoyment, and more for necessity.

It must happen.

Now.

"What's going on?"

Gary understood Amy could not be speaking so clearly with her mouth obviously full. He wanted to fill it even more, but the strident voice had softened his erection a bit. Amy noticed. She pulled his penis away. It popped like a cork when her mouth set it free. "What's wrong?"

Confused, Gary didn't know how to answer. He'd heard a voice but couldn't find where it had come from. He looked around the room, only seeing an impassable darkness. His swollen testicles seemed to weigh ninety pounds.

"My, aren't you excited?"

Wendy?

Opening his eyes, Gary found he was still on his back, and staring at the ceiling. In the dark, the white paint on the walls looked like gray slabs. Amy was gone. Actually, she had never been there at all. She was just a wet dream. *Shit.* The blanket protruded to a point over his midsection. His unyielding erection stuck firmly in the air.

Beside him, Wendy had rolled over to her side, balancing her head on her hand and rubbing her finger bashfully up and down the bed. "I was beginning to think we weren't ever gonna get to make up tonight."

"W-what?" he said, trying to sound dumb.

Wendy was aroused. Evidently after waking from the noises he had made in his sleep, she'd found him with an erection that could burst through a cement wall. It had excited her. She pulled the sheet down to his knees, exposing its solid glory. Although he felt awkward like this, he did nothing to hide himself. "What are you doing?"

"Oh my," she said. "It hasn't been that hard in a *long* time. Jesus, look at it."

If Jesus was here to see it, he would surely be pleased. It was one to be proud of. But thanks to the dream, he wished Amy was the one complimenting it, and not Wendy. *Just a sex dream*, he tried convincing himself. But the truth was apparent. Amy was who he wanted. Until now, he had never allowed himself to acknowledge it.

Wendy was rising to her knees. Pulling off her night shirt, she was naked underneath. Her breasts swayed with each movement. From the shave earlier, there was a small white band between her legs where the hair used to be that was pale in the darkened room.

Noting his nudity, she said, "I see you're already dressed for the occasion as well." She giggled.

The dream had left him craving Amy more than he ever had before. He wished he could have her, but in this situation Wendy would do just fine.

Sex is sex in a time like this.

Doing this with Wendy right now would only add more confusion later when he dumped her. The realization that he no longer wanted to be with Wendy wasn't new, but now that Amy was single again he might consider it seriously for a change.

Wendy straddled him.

He gulped.

Last chance. Now or never. Tell her to climb off and go take care of it myself. Two minutes in the bathroom will probably save me from two months of agony later.

Gary admitted to himself that having sex with Wendy right now was much better than masturbation. *Might as well go out with a bang.* Give it to her like he never had before, and then when all this traveling was done and Amy was settled wherever she needed to go, he'd tell Wendy it was all over.

And it wasn't like Wendy was hideous to look at. She was sexy, smart and had several qualities about her that Gary found to be cute. He was certain that was mostly the arousal talking, but she could be quite enjoyable at times.

Knees bent under her, she reached behind her, and found his erection. Her fingers slowly curled around the lengthened staff, causing Gary to huff. She sucked in her bottom lip and grinned as she guided it to her wet hub. Then she eased herself down, enveloping him with her heat. She was wetter than he'd ever remembered her being before. It felt *good.* He would enjoy it for now, but knew that when it was done guilt would consume him, making him feel like he'd cheated on both her and

Amy. This was a callous thing to do, but at the moment he wasn't going to be bothered by it.

Wendy lowered all the way down, impaling herself, and taking him all the way in. As she began thrusting her hips, guilt was the furthest thing from Gary's mind.

MARY

Mary sat on the iron stairs outside of the hotel rooms, writing lyrics in a battered and beaten notebook with duct tape on the spine holding it together. She needed to replace it but wasn't ready to call this one done yet. She'd filled most of the pages, then had gone back through and written on the backsides and was now writing fresh lyrics in the margins with her fine point pen, scribbling her furious feelings over what Shannon had become onto the paper.

She squinted against the sun echoing off the white paper.

Her sleep schedule was all out of whack thanks to the previous night's festivities. Never being one to adapt to the third shift cycle, she was wide awake while the rest of the gang was sleeping.

Well, most of them.

For the last fifteen minutes she'd had the unfortunate pleasure of hearing Wendy's screams and moans coming from Gary's room. She had thought about moving to the other end of the building but decided not to. She was comfortable where she was, and the lyrics were pouring out of her. She didn't want to interrupt the flow she'd garnered. Plus, she kind of enjoyed hearing Gary make Wendy breakdown like that. In some morbid way, she hoped he was really giving it to her the way she deserved.

But the last five minutes had been quiet. Wendy must have had all she could handle and tuckered out. Mary had grown comfortable with their noise and used it as a metronome to keep her thoughts away from Shannon.

Shannon.

Why did she think of Shannon?

Why was she making this already weird situation even more bizarre? Mary had trouble accepting that Shannon may actually be in love with her. How could she be? They're both girls. Women. It wasn't natural. Plus, they had been friends for what seemed like forever.

She's confused. Things with Jake hadn't been so great lately, and she's turned to a friend, me, and gotten her emotions tangled in a web.

Mary also couldn't understand how Shannon had problems with a guy like Jake. He was as close to being the perfect guy as you could get. Open-minded, polite, brave, and he was also good looking and charming. Those were just a few of his impressive qualities.

Shannon may be reaching out to Mary for help. Could she be suicidal? It wasn't likely, but not doubtful either. Shannon liked to put up an adamant front to those that didn't know her, but Mary knew her better than anyone else, and she could recognize that Shannon was scared, confused.

And why was Mary thinking so much about it? Also, why did Shannon's touch affect her in a way that she *couldn't* stop thinking about it?

"Terrific," she muttered. "Where do we go from here?"

"You look conflicted."

Mary squealed.

Standing halfway out of her room, Amy cupped a hand over her mouth, laughing. "Sorry, I didn't mean to scare you."

"It's fine," said Mary.

Amy stepped out, closing the door behind her. She crossed the haircloth that tried passing as carpet, sat beside Mary and leaned her back against the wall. "Is this cool?"

"Sitting down?"

Amy nodded.

"Yeah, sure."

"I didn't want to bother you."

"Oh, no, not at all."

"You seemed like you were busy."

"Nah, just jotting down some uh, stuff."

Amy smiled. "Stuff?"

"Yeah," Mary said with a sigh. "I used to have a metal band back at home, but when I left for college, we broke up."

"You had a band? What'd you play?"

"I was on vocals." Mary shrugged. "So, I still write lyrics even though I don't have a band anymore. I don't know why, really."

"I think you're doing it with the hope of one day being in a band again."

"Maybe."

"Where's home?" Amy asked.

"Appleton."

"Oh, that's a nice city."

"You've been there?"

"Oh yeah, a couple of times," Amy said. "Gary's cousin Ashley lives out there. I've been there with Gary to visit her a few times."

"Oh, wow."

"Small world."

"Yeah, it is."

Mary rubbed her hand through her dyed-black hair and adjusted her thin, black night shirt. If the sun were to cast a decent amount of light on it, anyone could see she was not wearing a bra. Looking at her shorts, she realized they were quite short, hugging the lower curves of her buttocks. She suddenly felt underdressed. Her legs were bare and exposed. Seeing them this way, she couldn't help but agree with Shannon's claim that they were lovely. She rubbed her hand down her thigh and smiled. Suddenly, she hoped Amy hadn't noticed her becoming fixated on her own smooth legs, and quickly moved her hand away. "So, what brings you out here? Shouldn't you be getting some rest?"

"Shouldn't you?"

Mary smirked. "Touché. I should be, but I can't sleep." She almost slipped up and told Amy about the sex noises coming from Gary's room, but quickly thought better of it. She hadn't known those guys long, but it was obvious that Gary and Amy had feelings for each other.

Deep feelings.

Like Shannon does for me?

"I can't sleep either," said Amy.

Mary wondered if she'd been awake and heard the porno too. "Why not?"

"Well, I was asleep for a while, but I had a nightmare about Piper. I thought I heard screaming somewhere in my dream. It sounded painful."

You heard screaming alright.

"Anyway, I didn't want to go back to sleep. I came out here to take a walk, but I'm glad I bumped into you instead."

"Really?" Mary said.

"Yeah. Sometimes, I let things build up in my head, and I become a wreck. Talking to you will keep me from doing that. And you're good company."

Was that a come on?

Stop it! Shannon's got your head all messed up.

"Aw, thanks." Mary felt heat rising through her face and couldn't believe she was blushing.

"So, why are you conflicted?"

Mary laughed. "Conflicted doesn't even begin to describe what I am."

"Sounds like some deep stuff."

"Ocean deep."

"Shit, that's pretty deep," Amy said.

"You're telling me?"

If she only knew.

"Well," Amy demanded. "Tell me about it."

"It's complicated."

"And this isn't?" Amy held her arms out, indicating their present location.

Mary laughed. "I guess you're right. It doesn't get much more complicated than this."

"I *am* right," said Amy with a proud nod. "What's going on in your head should be a cake-walk compared to what I've gotten you wrapped up in."

Mary shrugged. "I think my best friend is in love with me."

Amy laughed, but sucked it back in. Putting a hand to her chest as if it hurt, she said, "I'm not laughing *at* you."

"Then why are you?"

"It's just that…we're in the same boat."

"We are?"

"Yes," said Amy. After taking a deep breath she explained, "I think my best friend is in love with me."

"Yeah," agreed Mary. "But my situation is different."

"How so?"

"Because I don't know if I'm in love with my best friend. It's obvious as hell you are with yours."

Amy gaped.

Mary chortled. "Did I forget to mention I'm brutally honest?"

Amy's mouth finally began moving again. "Seems like you did forget to mention that."

"My bad." Amy sat quietly for a while. Mary's candid accusation was probably swimming around inside her head. Her silence made Mary uneasy. "Hey, I'm sorry if I upset you."

"You didn't upset me."

"You're upset because of me, it's the same thing."

"No, it's not," Amy said. "I think you were the only one to have the balls to tell me what I was too afraid to admit myself."

"That you like Gary?"

"That I *love* Gary."

Mary laughed.

"What's so funny?"

"I can't believe you never knew that you were. It was obvious to all of us, and we just met you. I bet it's even obvious to his girlfriend."

"Think so?" Amy asked.

"Yep."

"Oh great. Do you think it's obvious to Gary?"

"Nah, probably not. He's probably too blind from his own denial to notice."

"Well, thank God for that."

"Why?"

"Because."

"That's the dumbest reason I've ever heard," Mary said.

"Why do you say that?"

"Because he's your best friend. He knows you better than anyone. And you love him. What's wrong with that?"

"What if it doesn't work?"

"It *will* work. He'll love you better than anyone has ever loved you before. I don't see the problem."

"Well, you must see enough of a problem not to commit to your own best friend. You're telling me all this shit, and you're going through the same thing. That's not what I call practicing what you preach."

This time, Mary went quiet. "It's Shannon."

Amy's eyes widened, then her defense dropped. "I'm sorry, I shouldn't have said that."

"It's okay."

Why am I so frightened that Shannon loves me?

Because she's a girl, that's why. It makes you uncomfortable to even consider it.

Maybe she should think about it.

What about Steve?

Steve. Did she love Steve? They'd been seeing each other formally for a few months. She cared about him, but was it love?

"Yoo-hoo, Earth to Mary."

"Huh?" Mary shook her head.

"Let's forget about it, okay?"

Nodding, Mary said, "Good idea."

"Gary *is* great though." Amy admitted.

"You seem to have a lot in common, just from what I've been able to tell."

"We do." Amy smiled while thinking about it. "We're both artists in our own right. I'm a sucker for photography and I can paint and draw pretty well, I guess. Gary says I'm really good at it."

"I bet you are. What's Gary good at?"

"Writing."

"Really?" Mary glanced at her notebook and pondered the idea of showing Gary some of her lyrics. None of the ones about Shannon of course, but maybe the ones that aren't so personal.

Who was she kidding? They were all personal.

"Yeah, he's got a book out."

Mary's mouth slacked open. "Nuh-uh, really?"

"Yep. Sold quite a few copies, and his new one comes out in the winter."

"Holy shit, that's awesome!"

"You might have seen it in a store or something. It's called *Shep*."

"*Shep?*"

"Yeah."

Mary's eyes brightened, her smile widened, stretching across the lower portion of her face was a grill of teeth. "Gary Butler?"

"You've heard of him?"

"Have I heard of him? I'm reading his book now. It's in my bag."

"No way."

"Yes way. Oh my God, that's great. The book's been great so far. He did a great job writing it from the dog's point of view."

"You know that picture of him on the back of the book?"

"Yeah?"

Amy pointed at herself, nodding.

"You took that one?"

"Yep."

"That's incredible! I can't believe I didn't recognize him. I knew he looked familiar, but I thought he just has one of those faces."

"Yeah, in the picture he isn't so scruffy. His hair is longer now, and he hasn't shaved in a couple days."

"This is unbelievable."

The goofy grin on her face should have been embarrassing but it wasn't. *An actual horror author.* Mary was ecstatic that she could say she knew someone famous. The backbone of the story made even more sense now: Amy was obviously the girl that Stan, the main character, let get away, and Wendy was the wretched wife. All of the elements fell into place. Mary's admiration for Gary grew even stronger.

Mary had often chewed over the idea of being a writer herself. She had even written a few short stories and some plays. Maybe with some advice from Gary, she would actually give it a shot. What could it hurt?

Amy groaned. "I just wish that I knew where to go from here."

"My bag."

"What?" Amy shot a puzzled look in Mary's direction.

"My copy of his book is in my bag. Do you think he'll sign it for me?"

"Um…" Amy seemed flabbergasted by the question.

"He probably gets asked that all time. I'm sure he's sick of it by now."

"Gary?" Amy laughed.

"Yes, Gary. What's so funny?"

"I'm just not used to this."

"He's a good writer."

"You're right about that. I mean, I'm just not used to him having fans. It's still new to me."

"It probably isn't to him. I'll just leave him alone about it."

"Are you crazy? Gary would be honored to sign your book."

"Do you really think so?"

"I know so. He eats that shit up."

They laughed so hard they woke up the rest of the group. As the minutes passed by, the others stumbled out of their rooms like dazed zombies in pajamas to see what the deal was.

Mary and Amy agreed to keep everything they'd discussed a secret. A bond had formed between them that was so apparent, Shannon watched them with animosity.

PIPER

Piper had lost count of how many hours he'd been on the road. The knot on his head made his memory fuzzy at certain parts, but he figured that it had been around five hours.

Maybe longer.

Piper had seen a sign two miles back for a hotel.

The Sleep Tight Inn.

It didn't look like much on the outside from its languished paint and splotches of mud across walls pockmarked with mold and mildew. The wood had warped near the gutters, but overall, it appeared stable. Sitting just off the road, all that bordered it was open land woods, and a gas station a few yards up. Good thing too. He'd have to gas up the Bronco before heading out. Now that he knew there was a hotel, he wished he had held out on taking a dump at that dingy store a few miles back.

The shithouse was one he would not soon forget.

The hotel would have a bed and shower, and that was all he needed. Then he'd be back to his old-self again. His bandage could probably use a changing as well.

He veered the Bronco into the parking lot. It wasn't paved, just old gravel and dirt. The way the pebbles cracked and popped under his tires and reminded him of some parking lots in Texas. Not many of them were paved either. At least, not in any of the areas he'd been to.

The office was located on the first floor of the hotel under the rooms. Two staircases on each side led to the rooms on the upper level. Not many, but judging by the few cars, there must certainly be a vacancy. Four, including his, were all that he counted.

Then he spotted a Jeep.

It seemed familiar. He wasn't quite positive as from where, but he couldn't shake the feeling he'd seen it before. *Could be anyone's.* How many people in Wisconsin own a Jeep? He figured a good many of them. But still, there was something about it that beckoned him, practically screaming at him to investigate further.

"I'm too fucking tired," he mumbled.

As much as Piper didn't want to admit that he needed a break, his body ached with exhaustion, a pounding head, and a pair of burning eyes. He needed some sleep in a bad way. He wished he didn't have to bother with checking in and could skip straight to the bed. He needed to recharge his batteries.

Piper shut off the engine and unhooked his seatbelt. He rubbed the sore spot on his shoulder from where it had been pressing against him for hours. It burned. He may have to put ice on it. Jesus Christ, he hated feeling like this. Weak. Worthless. He wasn't the one that was supposed to feel this kind of pain, but thanks to Amy, he did. He hated her for that. Amy's death would be slow, agonizing, and he can't forget painful, for all the misery she had caused him.

She deserved it.

More than that, she'd earned it.

He would also punish her for making him realize he was getting old.

Piper opened the door and stepped into the flaring sun. The ever-changing weather was a Wisconsin characteristic, never staying the same for more than a couple hours. Last night had been so cold, he'd worn his camouflaged hunting coat. Now, he would be just fine in a T-shirt. He removed the coat, chucked it in the backseat and shut the door.

The loose gravel slid under his boots as he traveled toward the office. Under the eave that wrapped around the building, there was a wooden bench with an ash tray on each end. On the other side of that was an older model Pepsi machine with the original logo. It'd been years since he'd seen one with Pepsi written between the red and blue swirls. His mouth watered. Not at the idea of a refreshing beverage, but at the long, slender legs standing in front of the machine, which were attached to a firm mold of ass. His eyes roamed the willowy pair, the velvety skin practically calling to him. What he liked most was the girl that the pair of legs belonged to wore knee high leather boots. Come fuck me boots, he liked to call them. He followed them up to a short black skirt, where behind the thin fabric was a perfect ass.

Piper felt heat rising in his pants, and it wasn't because of the sun.

She was reaching into the narrow mouth of the drink machine, obviously struggling for a drink that hadn't fallen through. Twisting her body sideways, she was able to force her arm higher inside the machine. Her tank top curved tightly around her breasts. The cloth was wrinkled at the slope, allowing him a good view of the creamy white flesh of her right breast.

No bra.

He liked this girl already.

"Shit," she said. Sticking out her tongue, she pushed her arm up as high as it would go, but the disgruntled look of defeat showed Piper she wasn't getting what she wanted.

"What's the problem?" he asked.

Looking over her shoulder, she shyly smiled. Her face went scarlet. Obviously aware that he was getting quite a view, she didn't bother—or care enough—to change her position. "The damn drink machine took my money."

"Aw, that's too bad."

"This always happens to me. *Ow!*" Her cute face wrinkled in pain. Her tongue twisted as her eyes squinted. "I'm *stuck*."

"Shit," Piper said. He trotted to her and wrapped one arm around her waist, his crotch pushing firmly against her rump. He felt her tight ass squashing against him. With his other arm, he reached into the machine, and gripped around her elbow. "Now, this may hurt, but only for a second."

"Okay," she said, breathing heavily. "I'm ready when you are."

The heat in his crotch grew to an inferno pitch. Her breaths tickled his neck and ear, sending chills down the small of his back.

Looking back at him through enticing eyes she said, "And I can feel that you're ready."

"Yes, I am." He clutched tighter. "Here we go." With one quick pull, he jerked her arm free. She stumbled against him, her buttocks rubbing back and forth against his solid erection.

A sixteen-ounce bottle of Pepsi was clutched in her right hand. "Ouch!" She grasped her foreman, dropping her head back against his chest.

Piper caught a whiff of her hair. It smelled inviting. From this angle, he could see over her shoulders and down her tank top. Her turgid nipples poked against the shirt in two points. Her breasts weren't as big as he first thought, but even heftier than he'd imagined them to be. She had a bit of meat on her, but she was nowhere near fat. She couldn't have been any older than twenty-one, and most girls her age were scrawny scaffolds of bones, and disgusting to look at. Girls like that wouldn't be fun in the sack with their jagged bones jabbing at him. She wasn't one of those girls by a long shot. Her breasts seemed unnaturally large compared to the rest of her body, and he guaranteed they were her own, and hadn't been doctor-produced.

"Did that hurt?" he asked, not removing his grasp around her abdomen.

"A little bit, but I'll live."

Putting his lips against her ear he asked, "Are you sure?"

She turned around, lips so close they nearly touched. "I'm sure."

"Does that mean you want me to let go of you?"

"I don't know... Are you having fun back there?"

"Can't you tell that I am?"

"Why, yes, I can. But I want you to let go of me now or you won't be able to have fun with that thing again."

If they weren't out in the open like this, Piper would have lodged his elbow against her smart mouth. But he couldn't. Someone would see, call the cops, and that would ruin his plans for the rest of the day.

She's damn lucky.

Reluctantly, Piper complied.

As if wiping away his touch, the tease brushed herself off with her empty hand. She turned around, her curly blonde hair bouncing, and said, "Thank you."

"Uh-huh," he said. His eyes squinted from the brightness of the sun. With his forefinger, he rubbed his bottom lip. "What's your name gal?"

Her arms froze in mid-brush, and she smirked. "Gal?"

"That's what you are, ain't it?"

"Who says gal anymore?"

"I do."

"Oh right, you would, Mr. Brick."

Piper laughed.

That was a good one. She's funny.

"Mr. Brick?" He glanced at the sky, playing the nickname around in his head. "That suits me."

"Then who am I?" she asked, placing a finger in her mouth, lightly gnawing at it.

Piper groaned. The tease was asking for it. He doubted that she had any intentions of going to bed with him and was just doing this to taunt him because she knew that she could. "Out of my league," he said and smiled.

"Wow, you're right." She took the finger out of her mouth, wrapped her moist hand around the bottle cap, and twisted open her Pepsi. It fizzed over the top.

Piper felt drops of the soda spitting against him. Smelling its sugary scent made him hanker for one.

"But you can call me Shannon." She offered her hand to him. Smiling, he stepped forward and took it. Shaking a normal greeting at first, he turned her hand and positioned it with her palm down. Lightly arching her wrist, he brought her hand to his mouth, and kissed it.

Her skin tasted like strawberries.

Shannon sucked her bottom lip between her teeth, the upper corners of her mouth twisted upward.

Taking his lips away from her hand he said, "I'm Piper Conwell, but Mr. Brick is fine."

Her hand tensed in his gentle grasp. She pulled it away, planting her fist firmly against her chest as if nurturing it. She stared at him like he was contaminated with a deadly virus. "What'd you say your name was?"

"Piper Conwell."

Shannon took a slight step back and quickly laughed an artificial laugh with no sign of sincerity. The look on her face read like someone had just informed her that her mother died. She was trying to come off as casual but wasn't very good at hiding her mounting tension.

Piper sensed her sudden discomfort.

"Oh?" she asked. Her hand trembled, causing some Pepsi to spill. It splashed on the parched dirt, sucking up the liquid as if it were dehydrated.

"Does my reputation precede me?" He studied her movements. She was nervous. Not just that, she was frightened. Saying his name was what had done it. He just didn't know why.

Laughing another bogus laugh, she said, "Of course not. We don't even know each other." As if trying to think of something to say, she tapped her foot on the ground, and jutted a hip out to the side. "It was nice meeting you."

"You too."

Shannon moved further back, putting a good distance between them as Piper only stood, watching through his narrow eyes.

"I better get back to my room. I'm sure my boyfriend is wondering where I am."

"Boyfriend? Funny, you didn't mention him before."

"I didn't?"

Piper slowly shook his head.

"Oh... Well... He gets extremely jealous, so I better hurry and get back."

"I bet he does when it comes to you."

Her face reddened. It wasn't a cute bashful shade, more of a self-conscious uneasiness. "Aw, thanks."

"If I was your boyfriend, I would worry that you would flirt your little ass off with the wrong kind of stranger and bring on all kinds of nasty trouble."

"Nasty trouble?" She gulped.

"The nastiest. There are some folks out there that would love to get their hands on a girl like you."

Her brow wrinkled, lips tightened. "I can take care of myself pretty well, thank you."

"I don't believe that for a second."

"Anyway, it was nice meeting you."

"The pleasure was all mine."

Shannon hurried away. Speeding up the stairs, she glanced over her shoulder every couple of steps as if she was expecting him to be chasing after her. He wondered if he should, but remained stationary, watching her retreat. At the top of the stairs, she marched to the fourth door. The number on front declared the room as number eight.

The door slammed. He saw a flutter of movement at the curtains. She was checking to see if he was still there. He made a mental note to catch up to her again real soon.

Then he glanced at the Jeep again.

This time, he wasn't so quick to brush it off as coincidence.

GARY

Gary sat on the edge of the bed, his head drooping over as if he had a hangover. Replaying last night and the earlier parts of the day in his mind, he felt as guilty as a devoted man that had cheated on his wife. The bathroom was opposite the bed and Wendy was in there with the door opened wide. Since her shower, she'd been standing naked and damp in front of the mirror humming. Her sodden hair hung in waves across her shoulders. She was handling the morning-after much better than he. Actually, he couldn't remember the last time he'd seen her so chipper. The sex last night was probably the best they'd ever had. She'd had three orgasms, and Heaven help him, Gary had a couple too. It had been brutal, intense and passionate, something that had been lacking in their relationship nearly since its commencement.

But as good as it had been, he wished it had never happened. He was in worse shape than before, and Wendy was the happiest she'd been in months. *Enjoyed it so much she's singing.* This would be so much easier if she was miserable.

Without taking her gaze away from the mirror she stopped singing and said, "I was thinking, when this whole thing blows over you and I should go on a vacation. Just the two of us."

Gary sighed. "I don't know. I've got so much work left to do on the new book before I turn it in. They want to rush the release for late summer."

"Thinking the sales are going to be big numbers?"

"Something along those lines, yes."

"Take your laptop with you, work on it at night."

"You hate it when I take my work with me."

"No, it never really bothered me."

Could've fooled me.

"Where would you want to go?" she asked.

"I…don't know."

Her humming rose in pitch as she mulled it over. "How about we leave the state? Want to go somewhere with mountains? Or a beach?" She turned around, thrilled over what she was about to say. "The beach would be fun. We could go and stay for a week or something…"

"The beach?"

"Yeah, somewhere private at the beach. Wouldn't that be fun?"

Actually, it sounded like a lot of fun, and that only made him feel worse. What was he going to do? Hearing her talk like this confused him more than he already was.

She turned back to the mirror, and stood facing him while she studied her profile. Gary enjoyed the view he received very much.

"I'm gonna work on things, Gary. I know I'm not the nicest person at times, but it's because I'm insecure."

She admitted it. He'd always assumed she was nasty to him because of how she felt about herself, but he never would have guessed she'd actually acknowledge it herself.

She kept talking as Gary listened to her in silence, keeping his eyes focused on the wall in front of him. "Sometimes, I get the feeling that you want to leave me. I don't want you feeling like that." She continued talking, but Gary could no longer hear her.

She's only saying this because she feels threatened. Once Amy is on her way, Wendy will be back to the stubborn, hateful bitch she always has been. At least, he thought so, anyway. What if everything she said was true? What if he could have a good relationship with Wendy? He was sure he could as long as Amy was no longer in the picture.

When Amy wasn't in the picture?

Amy *had* to be in the picture. He couldn't give up on her. If he turned his back on Amy she would crawl right back to Piper. Where they went after that would probably kill her.

He also knew he could never forget about Amy, even if he asked her to leave him alone so he could focus his energy on his relationship with Wendy. The guilt he'd have because of that would ruin him, and it would also ruin whatever hopes of a decent life with Wendy he might have.

Amy wasn't going anywhere. He was convinced he wanted her to be in the picture. The wet dream, as odd as it was, had opened his eyes to a realization. They should be together. He was pretty confident that Amy felt that way too.

The sex last night had left Wendy in euphoria. Once it wore off, she'd hate him once again.

"You're not saying anything," said Wendy, breaking his concentration.

"What?"

"Were you even listening?"

"Yeah," he lied. "I heard every word."

Finally Wendy diverted her attention from herself in the mirror, and focused on Gary. She crossed her arms over her bare breasts, mashing them under her forearms. Her piercing eyes made him uncomfortable.

Here it comes.

"Do you have something you want to tell me?" Her voice trembled.

Gary groaned, looked at the ceiling for a moment, then back at her. She could read it in his eyes.

Everything he wished he could say was projected across his dumbstruck face.

Her lips quivered.

This is not going to end well.

Gary took a deep breath. "We really should take some time later to talk about some things."

"What *kinds* of things?" Her voice was shaky, as if fighting back tears.

He opened his mouth to answer, but the door rattled violently against its hinges from the shock of someone knocking outside.

Wendy gasped. "What the hell is going on?"

Gary leaped off the bed and ran to the bathroom. "Stay here." Then he shut the door.

"Gary? It's Shannon!"

Sounds urgent.

His trot turned to a run. He turned the deadbolt to the left and unhooked the chain. The door was shaking so vigorously that he had trouble grabbing the knob to open it.

"Shannon, stop!" he shouted.

The hammering ceased, allowing him a chance to unlock the knob. Before he could open it, the door flung wide, and Shannon charged in.

Running full speed, she didn't notice the bed, tripped over it, and landed on the other side with a thud.

Gary grimaced at the sick noise her body made when it landed on the unforgiving concrete floor. Sure, there was carpet, but it was a thin sheet that could hardly cushion Shannon's fall. "Shannon? Are you alright?" He took small steps forward. Shannon sprung up from the other side and grabbed the mattress, panting.

"Hold on…got to catch my breath…."

The bathroom door lashed open. Wendy, fully dressed, stormed out, brushing her hair. "What's wrong with her?" she asked, more amused than concerned.

"I don't know, she can hardly breathe."

"Where's Amy?" Shannon managed to ask.

"Not here," said Wendy.

Shannon heaved as if she was about to throw up.

"Don't puke on the bed!" shouted Wendy.

"We have to get Amy…" stated Shannon between huffs.

"I'm not sure where she is," said Gary. "At breakfast, she mentioned something about going to take a shower. I guess she's still in her room."

"She didn't come to the door…"

A tingle of fear tickled Gary's chest. "Maybe she didn't hear you."

If she had banged on the door the way she had his, there was no way Amy could have missed it. *Unless she was in the shower still.* From the heavy currents of a hotel's shower, he could believe that.

Wendy walked over to Shannon, sitting next to her and patting her back. "What's wrong?"

"I just met Piper."

Five minutes later, they were packed. Gary took the bags down to the Jeep and sat them on a tarp in the back. He'd put it there to keep the upholstery from being scratched and the carpet from being pricked. It'd done a good job so far. He wondered if he should use it to cover their luggage, then realized how stupid that would be.

Gary scanned the parking lot. No sign of Piper. His Bronco was there, which meant he was nearby. How had he found them? Gary had assumed Piper would come looking for Amy, but he was not expecting to have to deal with him until they got back to his house which would be safer because they could get the cops involved if needed. He wanted a cigarette now more than ever. His nerves felt as if they had been put through a blender. Maybe he'd ask Mary for one. *She doesn't know about the secret pact he'd made with Amy.*

But he couldn't do it.

Amy had been finally located and it was just as Gary predicted. She'd been taking a long shower and hadn't heard Shannon's knocking, which surprised Gary because it looked as if Shannon might have put a dent in the door with her fist.

Wendy was the first one down the stairs. She wore her heavy sunglasses and sunhat, Khaki shorts, and green tank top. The hat and glasses did a good job of shielding her face. If he didn't know her really well, he probably wouldn't realize it was her.

Gary looked down at himself and frowned. He wasn't wearing any type of disguise. If Piper was to come outside, he'd spot him right off the bat. He wanted to kick himself for not putting on his own hat and sunglasses. It wouldn't have hidden much, but something was better than nothing.

Jake and Shannon appeared from their room. Shannon was empty handed, but poor Jake appeared to be carrying their whole set of luggage. He struggled with the stairs, taking them diligently one step at a time.

Gary passed Wendy and trotted to the stairs. Stepping to the side, he allowed Shannon room to go by, and then took one of the heavy bags from Jake.

"Thanks man, you're a life saver."

"You looked like you were having some trouble."

"I damn near fell and broke my neck."

"Good thing you didn't."

"Yeah, I know. Who would Shannon get to carry all this shit if that had happened?"

"Probably me, which is why it's a good thing you didn't."

Jake laughed nervously.

Gary let Jake walk ahead. When they reached the car, Shannon already had the trunk opened for them. She was lighting a cigarette when they chucked the bags inside. The smell of burning nicotine made Gary's skin tingle. He was so close to relapse.

Maybe Amy would understand, given the situation.

No. I will not smoke. I will not smoke.

Steve came out of his room. Mary's book bag was draped over his shoulders, and in one hand he carried a small suitcase. In the other hand were their coats from last night wadded together in a ball of black fabric. Gary wondered if Steve remembered to grab Mary's copy of *Shep* that he'd signed for her at breakfast. It was probably somewhere in her stuff, but if not, he'd sign another for her. Hell, after all of this, he'd send her one regardless. Not to mention, an advanced copy of his next release, *Night Fear*.

Steve took the stairs confidently, and with ease. Jake leaned against the car, out of breath, watching him with envy.

Where's Amy?

Gary pictured Piper storming into her room while they were down here waiting for her. They wouldn't be able to hear the noise. Piper could be doing all sorts of things to her right now.

Amy was fine. Mary was up there with her. Piper was strong enough to take them both on, but not without a fight. One of them could certainly get away and let them know if something had gone wrong.

Gary combed the parking lot, but he still didn't spot Piper.

Maybe he'd already checked in and was in his room asleep. Their window of opportunity was narrow, but if they played this right, they'd be long gone before he realized they were even here.

Mary finally emerged from her room, and she wasn't alone. Another girl was with her. Her hair was dark, with a single blue streak running the length of it, and she was dressed in a black leather skirt, boots, and a long-sleeved fishnet shirt with a tight black halter top under it. She wore a leather choker around her throat. Her lips had been painted jet black. The makeup around her eyes was an identical blue to the streaks in her hair.

She was sexy.

Gary had always had a thing for Goth girls. Not the emo-kids that he'd seen making a travesty of the scene, but a true Goth girl. And this one with Mary was the hottest he'd ever seen.

Mary led the way down the stairs, and as they neared the bottom, Mary's friend began to look awfully familiar. She smiled at him. As they came closer, he recognized the smile as belonging to Amy underneath all the makeup and black clothes.

He was instantly rock-hard.

My God.

Mary smiled at the group. "What do you think of the new and improved Amy Stone?"

Jake and Steve smiled, nodding with approval.

Shannon lightly clapped.

Wendy rolled her eyes.

Gary couldn't move. In a trance, he stared at her in awe.

"Great disguise," said Jake. "I couldn't even tell it was you."

Neither could I.

Mary put her hand on Amy's arm. "So, if anyone happens to peek out through a window or something they won't find Amy Stone."

Shannon laughed. "Guess that's what you get for having such a distinct look."

"It's the eyes," said Amy.

"And the skin…hair…everything!" said Mary.

Amy stepped over to Gary. "What do you think?" She tugged at the bottom of her skirt as if hoping to lengthen it some.

He'd never seen her wearing anything so short and doubted that she ever had. Her legs were caramel-colored and shapely. Hints of muscle lined her thighs and calves. "Your smile gave you away."

She laughed. "Do you like this getup?"

"I do."

"Really?"

"A lot."

"Oh?" She pulled her bottom lip under her teeth, nervously gnawing at it. Then she pursed it back out, wincing. "Yuck, I hate the taste of makeup."

"Where to now?" Jake asked them.

Amy's smiled dropped as she turned around. "No. You've done enough. I think this is where we need to go our separate ways."

Shannon appeared disappointed. "Are you kidding?"

"No, I'm not."

"We're going where you go," said Jake. "That's all there is to it."

"I don't know," said Steve. "This is getting a little dangerous. Maybe we should split up now."

"Fuck that," said Jake.

Gary stepped forward. "Look guys, we appreciate all that you've done so far. But this is the real deal. We can't have you getting mixed up in this. It's too dangerous for you all."

Mary laughed. "We're already mixed up in this, whether you like it or not."

Gary sighed. Her rebuttal was precise. There wasn't much left that he could say.

Mary added, "We'll follow along behind you and make sure you get to where you're going safely."

"Mary?" Steve started, but she made a face that shut him up.

"Shouldn't you be getting back to school?" asked Wendy.

Gary wondered if she was only trying to sway them from tagging along, or was genuinely concerned about them missing school.

"It's cool," said Jake. "We're on fall break."

"Yeah," added Shannon. "We don't have to be back for another three days."

They weren't planning on giving up, Gary realized. If they kept arguing like this Piper was sure to bust them and they'd all be dead meat, then.

"Anyway," Jake added, "we'll follow you regardless of you wanting us to or not."

"Okay," said Amy. "If you're going, that's fine. But we need to get moving. Now."

Jake all but leaped into Steve's car, Shannon followed.

Mary and Steve remained.

"Where to?" asked Steve, halfhearted.

"I was thinking about that," said Gary. "We'll probably head up to the crossroads, then take 70. There are some heavy woods out there, and a lot of farmland. I saw it on the map."

"Sounds good," said Steve.

"We'll basically be taking a very scenic route to Stone Quarry. Hopefully, we'll stay off of Piper's radar that way."

"Whatever works for you guys," said Steve.

"Should we call the cops?" asked Mary.

Amy grimaced. "No, that's the last thing we want to do right now."

"Why?"

"Piper's the Sheriff back in our hometown of Petersburg. He'll hear it on the scanner. Calling the police will have to be the last resort for now, at least until we get back to Gary's."

Mary frowned, her complexion whitening as reality sank in. Gary wondered if she was really as gung-ho about all of this as she had led them to believe. For the first time she was showing fear. It didn't fit her well. Gary liked the other Mary better, the brave one. This Mary looked sick and puny. Steve took her by the arm and led her to the passenger side of his car.

"Do you guys need to get gas?" Gary asked.

Steve shook his head. "No, we're good."

"All right, just keep up."

Steve nodded.

Jake hopped out of the backseat. "Hold on a second." He pointed to the Bronco. "You said that's his ride, right?"

Gary nodded.

"Perfect." He grinned, showing a grille of white. Hunched over, he snuck to the Bronco, and crouched next to the rear driver-side tire.

Gary nearly gasped. "What are you doing?"

In his hand something shined. In the glare of the sun, it appeared to be a silver blur. When Jake pressed the object to Piper's tire, Gary realized it was a hunter's knife with a blade longer than any he'd ever seen. He'd written about blades that big but had never thought they actually existed. The blade disappeared into the tire's sidewall. When he ripped it out the tire hissed as it quickly began losing air. Then Jake hurried around to the rear of the Bronco and stabbed the mounted spare tire on the back gate as well.

"Let's go!" said Jake, running back to Steve's car.

"Are you crazy?" cried Steve.

"Yep!" Jake hopped into the back seat.

Steve and Gary shared the same look of panic before they ran, piling into their separate cars. With Gary in the lead, they evacuated the hotel in a mad dash as if Armageddon was coming. They didn't know just how close to that concept they actually were, and not just from Piper, there was something waiting for them.

And they were heading straight for it.

GARY

Gary steered the jeep off the road just past a sign that read: *Now leaving Doverton.* He put the car in park and leaned back in the seat. The air felt stuffy, so he adjusted the air conditioning to high.

"I'm going to freeze," said Wendy. Goose bumps were already dimpling her downy legs.

"Sorry, just let it run for a few minutes at least. I'm sweating."

"Fine."

He looked in the rearview mirror to check on the others. He could see them, a skulking smear on the road behind him. He figured they must be gazing at the scenery the same as he had on his way past.

They had been driving, following the map and the GPS navigation through a town called Doverton. Rather, what was left of it. The town was void of all human and animal life. They'd passed deserted farmlands, vacated houses and farming equipment that looked to have been ditched in the middle of a job.

Gary had heard the small towns were hit the hardest during the recession, but he had no idea it was this bad.

Doverton was nothing more than a phantom community, a ghost town.

"Where to now?" Wendy asked, rubbing her legs.

Gary turned the air back down below halfway and sighed. "Amy, what have you found for us back there?"

"Do you guys want to stop at a lake?"

"A lake?" Wendy sounded as if she had never heard of such foolishness.

Gary glanced in the rearview mirror again. Amy, sitting in the backseat, had the map she'd picked up at the hotel unfolded across her lap. It was so big it looked like a blanket. Her index finger rested on a spot.

"Yeah," she said. "I was reading the map, and there's a place called Whisper Lake. It's about four miles up between Doverton and Littletown. We've been in the car for about two hours. I was thinking we could all use a break."

"By stopping at a lake?" She spoke as if Amy was stupid.

Amy wasn't blind to it. But being Amy, she was able to take it in stride. She smiled. "If it's okay with you two."

"It's fine with me," said Gary. "I'd like to stretch my legs."

"Whatever."

That was Wendy's way of answering in a language that she thought only Gary could understand. She would be pissed whether they stopped by the lake or not.

"Amy, does it show where any gas stations are on that map? We're going to need to fill up soon." The gauge in the instrument panel had dropped below half a tank.

"Uh…I see the symbols on the side of the map here…let me see if I can find…Yes!" She tapped the paper. "There's a rest area coming up soon and looks like they sell gas."

"Perfect." He glanced in the rearview mirror and saw Steve's car was closing in the distance between them. "Here come the others. I'll run it by them."

"I'm sure *they* won't mind," said Wendy, coldly.

Steve rolled up beside Gary. Mary had the window down, a pale look on her face. Apparently, the forsaken town of Doverton hadn't set too well with her, either. Steve leaned over her to talk to Gary. "What's going on?"

"We're trying to decide if we want to take a break before continuing any further."

Wendy rolled her eyes and shook her head.

Jake leaned up, shouting past Mary. "Sounds cool, what did you have in mind?" Mary flinched. "Sorry."

Nodding, she plugged a finger in her ear, and jiggled it.

"There's a lake a few miles up." They were happy to hear that. Smiles filled the car from front to back. Gary took that as a yes and waved. "Just follow us."

"You got it," said Steve.

Gary sat back, shifted the car into drive and eased out. He still had trouble focusing on the road. With Amy in the backseat looking the way she did and wearing a skirt that was practically the length of a dishtowel, he wanted to keep his eyes on her instead. He felt like a dirty old man for sneaking so many peeks at her slanted legs in the mirror. Her hips were turned with her knees pointing toward the door, which gave him a nice shot of her legs from the thighs down. The skirt had pulled back, nestling on the seat just over her rump. It looked as if she were wearing high-cut shorts. She'd always been a beautiful woman and her new look was working delightfully.

The urge to take another glimpse was overwhelming, but he resisted the temptation. Last time he'd peeped, she had busted him. Even though she'd smiled shyly at him, he didn't want her to know he'd been gawking at her for the last several miles.

As they exited Doverton's city limits, lake bound, Gary couldn't stop thinking about that place. It looked like something out of one the *Phantasm* movies. It was creepy. The houses and farmland were specter foundations, structured aimlessly without occupants to fill them.

Wendy sighed next to him as she stared out the window. Her arms were crossed, her firm breasts rested on them.

This sucks.

He was torn between two women that he kept on two totally different pedestals. Should he dump one, and go with the other? What if Amy rejected him? Then what?

Gary had never considered that possibility, because he'd never been tempted to try it, but now he could easily picture it. Dumping Wendy would be a brutal obstacle. She'd probably cry and scream, and definitely fight it every step of the way even though, before today, she'd never acted act as if she really wanted to be with him. She had always acted like she had settled for him. Finally, after Wendy was gone from his life, he would crawl to Amy and confess his newly discovered feelings for her. She would reject him, saying it would ruin a wonderful friendship, and she wouldn't want that to happen.

But either way, it *would* be ruined just by him saying something.

Damned if you do, damned if you don't.

If he threw himself at her, she could easily swat him away. Then the awkwardness of her knowing how he *truly* felt would drive a wedge between them. That would hurt more than the actual rejection.

Now, he debated telling her anything.

Okay, if you don't say anything to Amy, what will you do about Wendy?

Wendy was high maintenance in appearance and personality, the exact opposite of Gary. Wendy needed to go out, go to expensive restaurants, enjoy the night, and Gary was perfectly happy with staying at home.

Wendy also had a large group of man-hating girlfriends whose idea of a good time was going to bars, picking up strangers and taking them to bed. After a fun night of sex and debauchery they'd kick the poor sap out of their bed having only used them for an orgasm. These women who Wendy called friends had been pushed to this point because of poor choices they'd made with men, much like Amy had been doing with Piper.

Gary shuddered to think about it. One day, Wendy would be like that, and there was a possibility that even Amy could be. If he ever married Wendy, she would turn that way a few years into the marriage. Then they would divorce. If it was later in life when it happened, and it *would* happen, he may be too old to find another companion. His hair could have receded, his stomach could have succumbed to the dastardly *writer's gut*.

It may be too late for him at that point.

But if he dumped her now, she'd turn into one of the pack right away.

No one to blame for it but himself.

Damned if you do, damned if you don't.

Screwed any way he measured it.

Gary sighed. He was in bad shape. His mind had been set at the start of the day. Driving these back roads in the sticks, with nothing around to stare at except trees, he'd allowed wariness to clog his head to the point of exploding. The uneasiness he'd felt in Doverton hadn't helped, either. The desolate town still nagged at him, still had a chill lodged in his bowels, and he didn't know why.

He really wanted a cigarette now.

And to get the hell out of this car. What was I thinking bringing Wendy along?

How different would this trip have been if Wendy had stayed home? He tried not to think about it.

Wendy sighed again.

Amy adjusted herself in the seat. "Are you sure you want to go to the lake?"

"Well, if I say no, I'll be the biggest bitch around, wouldn't I?"

"Not the biggest," Amy said, "but close to it."

Oh God.

"Excuse me?"

It was happening. He'd expected it to come at some point, but he'd hoped it would have been later. He grimaced, preparing himself as it began.

"I didn't stutter, Wendy."

"No, you didn't, so I guess I heard you correctly."

Dear God, let me live through this.

"Do you have a problem with me?"

Don't ask her that Amy, are you crazy?

Gary saw a wooden sign on two posts. Carved in the lumber was a marker for Whisper Lake.

He had a mile and half to go before he would be free. It was a mile and a half too long. He'd probably be dead by then.

"Do I have a problem with you?" Wendy shook her head. "No. I have *several* problems with you."

"Oh really? Like what? I'm just curious."

Amy's voice hadn't risen higher than casual chit-chat. Wendy was already yelling. Before long, she'd be screaming.

"For starters, it bugs me that you keep putting yourself in these goddamn situations."

Good point, but a horrible way to express it.

"*Putting* myself into them?"

"Yes," said Wendy, throwing her hands in the air. "Either you like it, or you're too fucking stupid to realize that these men you end up with are piles of shit."

"Okay…"

"And I also don't like the way you always call Gary when you're at rock bottom."

"What do you mean by that?"

"Wendy–" Gary tried to intervene, but Wendy countered it with a flat hand in front of his face. He shut up immediately.

"Before last night, when was the last time you'd spoken to him?"

Dammit Wendy, stop it.

"It's been a while."

Wendy laughed a throaty, cold chortle. "Yeah, you can say it's been a while. Gary said something the other day about how he hadn't spoken to you in…two months? Was that it, Gary?"

He didn't answer. Just gripped the steering wheel so tight, his knuckles were white. Keeping them at ten and two, he couldn't reach over and punch Wendy in the jaw.

"Well, he's not saying anything, but I'm pretty sure that was it."

"I'd love to speak to Gary a *lot* more."

"I'm sure you would, especially if you need to mooch off of him for something."

"That is a lie. I do not *mooch* off of him."

"Look around you, Amy." Wendy pointed out the windows, then behind Amy to the following car. "If Gary didn't come out here, where would you be?"

"I…don't know."

"You'd be fucked, that's where you'd be. Gary goes out of his way for you any chance he gets, and you can't call him in two months?"

"It's not as easy as you make it sound."

Don't do it, Gary. Do not throw Wendy out of the car.

"It's not? Why isn't it as easy as I make it sound?"

"For starters, there's Piper."

"Oh yeah, another one of your award-winning boyfriends. Do go on."

Amy showed her first signs of frustration. She whipped her head to the side and took in a deep breath. Slowly exhaling, she said, "And then there's you."

Fuck me. Why? Why am I being put through this? Did I do something so wrong in a past life that this very moment is my punishment?

"Me?"

"Oh yes, you. Actually, it's *mostly* you. I haven't called Gary in two months, but what's stopped him from calling me? I'm willing to bet it's you."

"No, it's not."

"Yes, it is. You take great pride in controlling his every move like he's a puppet dangling on little strings attached to your fingers. Thing is, Gary's too nice of a guy to snap back at you for it. If it weren't for me rooting him on, he never would have finished that book that bought that house of his, you know, the house you're always crashing at."

Wendy tried to say something, but Amy kept talking, not giving her the chance.

"I've heard you tease him for writing in the past. Now that he's successful you want to be near him and the money. I've known Gary for years. It's something he's always been good at, and always enjoyed. But if you're around, he's not allowed to enjoy anything other than you. Eventually, he would've given up on writing like he gave up on me. And it would have all been your fault."

I didn't give up on her, did I?

Yes!

Wendy made a coughing sound in the back of her throat. "My fault? You're serious. You think I'm to blame for the way Gary is?"

The way I am? What does that mean?

Wendy continued about Gary's theoretical poor health. "Gary has a lot of issues, but I'm not the reason for any of them. I'm trying to help him. I worry about him all the time."

Now, I have issues?

"No, you worry about how he's going to make you look to everyone that can see you. Your heart isn't big enough to care for anyone but yourself."

"You *bitch!*" Wendy had her seatbelt off, turned around, and was leaping over the seat before Gary could react. Thankfully the headrest was too high, denying her room to get in the back. With it blocking her, all she could do was blindly swing her fists at Amy.

Amy threw her hands up to block. She caught Wendy's left arm but couldn't stop the right. It connected with a few blows, but Amy fought back, punching Wendy any chance she got.

Wendy's nose was bleeding in seconds.

Gary was shocked, but not over the actual fight. That had been brewing for over a year. What surprised him was that Amy was actually fighting back. She wasn't one to back down, but Gary had never seen her enraged enough to physically clash with anyone. In some way, he was honored Amy cared enough about him to fight.

And then, Wendy's hip bumped against Gary, making him swerve the car to the left.

STEVE gasped, pumping the brakes.

Mary leaned forward, as if being closer to the windshield would somehow grant a complete view to what was happening in the Jeep ahead of them.

"What the hell's going on?" called Jake from the backseat.

Shaking his head, Steve said, "I don't know, they're swerving pretty bad."

"Keep it up and they'll crash," Shannon added.

Mary could see the dark shapes of people struggling through the glass on the Jeep's back gate. Two of them. Female. Both wildly attacking each other. She continued to watch. When she spotted the girl in the backseat pinning the other's head to the roof and throwing disorderly punches at her face, she started laughing.

Jake leaned up next to Mary's head. "What's so funny?"

"It's Wendy and Amy."

"What?"

"They're *fighting*."

There was a brief pause of silence in the car. Then the four of them erupted in cheers, rooting for Amy to kick Wendy's ass.

Steve honked the horn each time they enunciated the words, *"KICK HER ASS! KICK HER ASS!"*

GARY could hear Steve's horn. Obviously, he was worried about the Jeep's swerving. He probably could see the girls fighting, all of them probably could. He was willing to bet they were cheering Amy on, hoping she beat the hell out of Wendy.

Holding the wheel steady with his left hand he reached out with his right, and hooked it around Wendy's waist. He pulled. She fought him, punching down on his shoulder like an angry kid, but he was stronger. Finally, she gave up, and fell into the seat. Her hair hung in her face like a curtain, blocking the infuriated stare she was probably giving him. During the struggle, her shirt had been torn, leaving her upper chest bare. The top slopes of her breasts were visible. Her purple bra had been pulled down enough to reveal the dark coin of her right nipple.

"What the fuck, Gary?" Wendy shouted, adjusting her bra. "What did you do that for?"

"That's enough!" he shouted. "Both of you!" He tried telling himself to just stop right there, he'd made his point, but his temper disregarded the warnings.

"Wendy, you've got a lot of nerve going after her like that! Using *me* as an excuse to attack her? And Amy, through all of Wendy's bitching, she made some valuable points, but neither one of you bothered to ask me what I thought about all of this!"

"I'm sorry," said Wendy.

"Shut up! I'm not done talking!"

Wendy pulled her hair out of her face. Her eyes were wide, round, and watery. Her mouth was agape; his outburst had stunned her.

Last chance. You could stop now and be all the better for it.

He continued, "The reason I came all the way out here to get Amy is because I love her. That's right, I *love* her! I always have. I've never acted on it because I feared what she might think about it. I also love you Wendy. I never thought there was any kind of future with Amy, but I wanted so badly for there to be one with you and me. And *that* has me confused more than a son of a bitch, because you treat me like shit, and make me hate myself more than you already seem to. If we stay together one of us will snap and start a killing spree."

What are you doing man? Shut up!

"G-gary?" said Wendy, her lips trembling, eyes swelling red.

"You don't love me. I can't even think of the last time you actually said it."

"I tell you that I love you…"

"When? Tell me the last time!"

She turned away, perhaps trying to remember the moment. Then she looked back at him, confessing her guilt with silence.

"I didn't think you could remember either, because I sure as hell don't. But it's just as much my fault as it is yours. I should've broken this off a long time ago instead of allowing it to go on and on. Now, we're both damaged goods!

"Look at me now," he continued. "Just *look* at me! I'm *really* bad off. I'm in love with my best friend who probably wants to remain *only* friends, but I also love my girlfriend who likes to take cheap shots at me any chance she gets. If you weren't already fooling around with other guys, you were sure to start soon."

Wendy quickly looked away.

Gary took that as another admission of guilt. "So, that's that." He groaned. "We're almost to Whisper Lake, and I'm going to stop there, because I've got to get out of this fucking car, stretch my goddamn legs and kick my own ass for even admitting any of this, because I am totally fucking goddamn asshole stupid!"

After that, they drove the rest of the way to Whisper Lake in silence. On a beaten road through the woods, the car bounced and shifted over each nook and bump. They arrived at a small, dirt clearing that Gary guessed was meant to be a parking lot. The sun sparkled off the lake's rippling waves and the water looked clean and cool. If he hadn't been so hopping mad, Gary might have found the scene to be beautiful and something worth writing about in a story.

As Steve parked his car, Gary was already out of his and marching into the woods. He wanted to get as far away from the others as he possibly could.

Finally, after a long hike through the woods, he found an old Oak tree with withered branches that hung over as if offering a hug.

Gary had gone far enough.

He sat under it and wept.

AMY

"Did you find him?" Jake asked, standing ankle deep in the lake. He'd rolled his pants up to his knees and kicked off his shoes and socks shortly after getting out of the car. Since then, he'd been stomping and splashing in the shallow water.

Wendy shook her head as she exited the woods. She kept her eyes aimed at the ground, walking along the shore. She picked a spot away from the group and sat alone. Out of respect, everyone had decided to give her some space. She was obviously hurting too.

Amy sat on an old, warped pier with loose boards, kicking her feet in the water. At first, the water had been so cold it hurt, but it didn't take long for her feet to adjust to the temperature. Now, it felt wonderful.

Whisper Lake was a gorgeous, private area. The water was bright and nippy. The surrounding woods were thick and alive with the sounds of nature. Across the bank of water was more land and all she could distinguish from that distance was that it was covered with a vast field of corn stalks. She'd noticed several cornfields along the way, full of dying stalks and ready to be harvested.

Farming had always intrigued her, just not enough to attempt it herself. But she'd often imagined having a house with a decent-sized garden. It would be fun planting rows of tomatoes, squash, corn, and watermelons. She loved watermelons. With her feet in the water, cold splashes licking her legs, she thought about being outside on all fours, picking vegetables while Gary sat at his desk, typing away on his latest book. She'd look over her shoulder, see his frame through the window, and hear the steady clacking of his fingers on the computer's keys.

The fantasy made her smile.

Gary.

Did she want that kind of future with him? She could have it if that was what she truly wanted. It felt like she did. There was always something just under the surface of their friendship that she'd tried to ignore, basically because she had never believed he cared about her in any other way.

There was one instance where she'd almost kissed him. They had gone to dinner at their favorite Mexican restaurant, followed that up with a movie, and when he had taken her home, Piper was out of town hunting, so she had the house to herself. She'd invited him in, and although she told herself it was just for some coffee, she knew deep down that she wanted him to go to bed with her.

She'd fought her urges with everything she had, and probably would have succumbed to her temptation no matter how hard she struggled not to, but Wendy kept texting him, so he finally left because he was tired of her annoying him. That was the first night she truly realized that without him she was alone.

They needed to talk.

Wendy's attempts to find him had been unsuccessful, but Amy doubted she'd tried very hard in her search. She was only gone maybe five minutes. Plus, Gary probably didn't want to be found by her.

Maybe Amy would have better luck.

What if he doesn't want to talk to me?

She hated to think that but couldn't keep herself from doing so. She imagined finding him dumbly wandering the woods like a bear looking for honey in beehives. Wanting to hold him, she'd go to him with her arms held out, and he'd push her away.

Her eyes watered at the thought.

She backhanded the fresh brew of tears, and remembering her makeup, looked at her hand. A moist, black, trail of gunk was smeared across the back of it.

"Fantastic," she muttered.

Got to get this shit off of me.

Amy scanned the area for Mary. She quickly spotted her lying on a blanket with Steve. On their backs, eyes shielded by sunglasses, and their noses pointed at the sky.

Probably sleeping.

As much as she wanted to return to her regular style, she hated waking Mary to help her get the makeup off. From what Mary had told her earlier, she hadn't slept at the hotel. Amy wanted her to have what little rest she could get while they were here. They'd be leaving soon. She assumed it would be dark in a few hours, and they'd have to be on the road by then. She wasn't exactly sure how long of a drive they had ahead of them.

She sighed, deciding to let Mary be.

"What's up lemon cup?"

Amy jumped, surprised by the voice. She looked behind her and found Shannon approaching, wearing only her bra and panties.

"Shannon?"

"Sorry I scared you. I have a knack for doing that to people."

Probably the shock of you being half butt-naked.

"Aren't you a little under-dressed?"

As if not knowing why she asked, Shannon looked down at herself. "This?" She pointed to her bra, waving her finger up and down from bra to panties. *Her thong panties.* A matching black, nylon set. "I was about to take a swim. Don't have a bathing suit with me."

"Ah," said Amy. "I'm surprised you bothered wearing anything at all."

Shannon laughed. "Would you rather I hadn't?"

Standing up, Amy said, "Don't strip for my sake." Amy brushed the seat of her pants then stretched. It felt good. Her stiff muscles loosened after the long car-ride and from no sleep in a lumpy hotel bed.

"I don't mind, actually. I was thinking about diving in the water in nothing but my skin suit. It's just that I imagine some of the group would take offense." Like a hitchhiker, she pointed her thumb in Wendy's direction.

"Not to mention, Jake."

"What about Jake?"

"I'm sure he wouldn't appreciate everyone seeing you naked."

Shannon shrugged. "I don't think he'd mind."

As if to confirm her comment, Jake yelled from the water, "Take it off!"

"See what I mean? I love him, but he's only got two thinking methods."

"Which are?"

"Eat and fuck."

Amy's laughter bellowed a lot louder than what she had expected. Not knowing Jake that well, she still believed it. "You're lucky, normally I get stuck with the men who eat and eat. No fucking involved."

They both laughed. Amy felt guilty for laughing while Gary was out in the woods somewhere, alone and upset.

"I should've worn something thicker though," said Shannon. Cupping a breast in each hand she shook them. "That water's gonna be cold, and my headlights will be shining bright for sure."

Amy could not understand these kids, though she liked all of them. *Kids.* Listen to her. She was only a few years older than this bunch, but she felt as if she was twenty years their senior. Their opinions on sex and decency were so different than her own had been when she was their age. She would have never gone swimming in her underwear around a group of people, alone or with a lover, maybe, but not a group. And she would definitely never go swimming naked. No way.

Maybe if she had the body Shannon did.

I do.

Her body was just as solid as Shannon's, but with some age and strength added on. Shannon's body was also one to envy. Not chunky, but thicker than some girls. Her stomach was flat, hips curved like an hourglass, and her thighs were meaty. If she kept a close watch on her body and maintained that size, she'd be set for life. Her round and melon-shaped breasts were large enough to be fake, but Amy doubted they were. The way they bobbled with each step she took, they had to be real.

Amy glanced up from her breasts and found Shannon watching her. Her mouth formed into a sly smirk.

Had she noticed me staring?

"What are you doing?" Shannon inquired.

Yep, she did.

Amy hurried to switch the point of the conversation. "Oh, I was thinking about waking up Mary so she can help me take this shit off my face." She hoped that would convince her she wasn't staring. All she needed was for Shannon to get the wrong impression, especially after what Mary had told her.

"I noticed you're a little smeared there." She raised a finger to her face and wiped crumbs of eyeliner away. Amy tried not to flinch from her being so close.

"Yeah, plus it itches. I just want it off. Then I'm going to go look for Gary."

"Might not be a bad idea."

Amy stepped past Shannon and took the unsound pier back to the shore. It swayed and teetered with each step. Shannon trotted up to Amy, breasts bouncing so hard Amy wondered if they were going to knock Shannon in the jaw.

"I'll clean you up."

"All right," said Amy. "But you have to get some clothes on first."

"Don't flatter yourself," said Shannon. "You're pretty and all, but you're not my type."

Blushing, Amy said, "I don't want my nose buried the entire time between those two beasts you call tits."

It was Shannon's turn to blush. Her light-colored skin turned crimson. The dimples of her buttocks looked like blossoming roses. "I'll throw on a shirt."

"Thank you."

"But you're going to upset poor Jake out there. You know how sensitive he is."

Amy turned around and laughed at what she saw: Jake, oblivious to all around him, was stomping through the water like Godzilla. Grinning ear-to-ear with his legs stiff and bent at the knees, he raised one out of the water, then slammed it down. The lake swashed, spraying water high into the air. He repeated this a few times before raising his arms into the air like a ghoul.

Shannon laughed softly. "See what I mean?"

The two of them stepped onto the shore. The sand felt soft and warm under Amy's bare feet. It was harder to walk on, and the way it slipped out from under her caused her to stumble, but it also massaged the soles of her feet, so she'd deal with it.

In the parking area, they approached Steve's car first. Gary's Jeep was parked on the other side. Shannon opened the driver side door and bent over. Halfway in and out, her smooth rump jutted up in the air. The thong string disappeared between her buttocks, looking like a jellybean eating a piece of black spaghetti.

Amy quickly looked away.

Don't want her to catch me staring, again. Wait, why am I staring?

"I've got makeup remover in my kit."

She heard a thump, and then the trunk popped open. Shannon stood up straight, holding a shirt in her hand. She grabbed the bottom, and let it drop. It was too long for her, so it must have been one of Jake's. She pulled the shirt over, pushing her head and arms through the holes like a turtle coming out of its shell. She tugged the bottom and straightened it out. Its length stopped just below her buttocks. It was sleeveless. Through the holes under the armpits, Amy could see the white inclines of her breasts.

The shirt hardly covered her body. It helped Amy's awkwardness some, but not much.

Shannon politely smiled at her. Amy went around and joined her as she sifted through the mess in the back. Hoping to avoid staring at Shannon's rump, she scanned the woods instead, trying to concoct a plan. Finding Gary wouldn't be the hard part. It was talking to him that seemed impossible.

What would she say? How should she say it when she did think of something?

Why was the back of Gary's Jeep open?

Too many questions.

Amy shook her head, not knowing where to start. She scratched her head, hard. Her hair barely moved at all. When she pulled her fingers out of the block that was her hair, her fingers were sticky with hairspray and gel.

Then a thought returned to her, something she saw a moment ago wasn't adding up.

Was Gary's Jeep open?

Amy stepped around to the other side of Shannon and studied the Jeep. The front and back doors were shut tight, but the back gate was yawning. The tarp

Gary kept back there lay on the ground in a crumpled pile.

Amy's bowels tightened. Her stomach felt as if she'd swallowed a bucket of ice.

"Found it," said Shannon. She stood up, dangling the small vinyl bag like a freshly caught fish. "You could probably sit in the passenger seat, and I could sit in the driver's." She noticed Amy's diverted attention. "What's up?"

Amy knew Shannon was talking but had no idea what she had said. "Look at the Jeep."

Shannon turned around, staring a moment before she spoke. "Even better, you can sit in the back of the Jeep, that'll be a lot easier."

"No, that's not what I mean."

"What *do* you mean?"

"It's open."

"I see that."

"Who opened it?"

"I don't know. Did you?"

Amy looked at her like she was an idiot. "No, I didn't open it."

"It must've been Gary or Wendy."

"Gary took off as soon as we got here."

"Okay, then it was Wendy."

"Maybe." She didn't think so. Right after Gary, Wendy had leaped out of the Jeep and chased after him. But she was wearing sandals and had come back to change her shoes. She could have opened the back gate then, but it didn't seem likely. She tried remembering if Wendy's bag was one of the many she was sitting beside, or if they were all Gary's.

No, one of them had pink edges. That was Wendy's. The map was sitting on top of that bag. It was a small one, but certainly big enough to carry a change of shoes.

She thought about asking her.

Then she glanced over to where Wendy sat smoking cigarettes. *Yeah, right.* Wendy would love Amy asking anything, even a simple question like that, Wendy would doubtlessly bludgeon her with a rock in response.

Thanks, but no thanks.

"Why does it matter?" said Shannon, breaking the silence.

"Why does what matter?"

"Why does it matter who opened the gate?"

"It doesn't, I guess."

"You're spooking me girl." She laughed, nudging her arm with her elbow.

"I'm spooking myself."

They walked to the Jeep. After giving it a good look-over, Amy sat in the back, dangling her feet over the edge. Shannon stepped between her spread legs and removed a sponge. She dabbled it with liquid remover and then got to work.

Amy realized she hadn't checked under the Jeep before sitting down. She imagined her feet hanging down with something ready to grab her ankles from underneath. But what? What could possibly be under there?

Nothing.

She failed to convince herself there was nothing out of the ordinary going on, and that it was only a feeling she had, although she couldn't explain why. She regretted her feet hanging there like that. Susceptible to anything that would want to take a bite.

Or grab.

Or stab.

Amy shivered. Goose bumps dotted up her arms, sides, and legs.

Shannon noticed and laughed.

FROM the woods, Piper watched the girls for a long moment before leaving to find Gary.

GARY

Gary glanced at his bare wrist and remembered his watch was in his suitcase back in the Jeep. He couldn't check the time on his cell phone either. It was in the glove compartment. After his hundredth time checking for a signal, he'd tossed it in there, giving up on ever getting one.

How long have I been out here? Twenty, thirty minutes?

He was certain his editor would be calling about his latest book today, so he should get back to his phone at some point. If he didn't answer, then she'd think he was avoiding her because he didn't have the work done.

He *didn't* have the work done, but he wouldn't avoid her if she called.

After hearing him out, surely Deborah would understand why he was behind. He had expected to finish up his polish on the new manuscript today, but his plans had changed. He'd tell Deborah the truth. He doubted she'd be too pissed about it.

She was strict, yet patient, and a peach to work with. He trusted her more than anyone else when it came to his writing and took her advice like it was the gospel. So far, she hadn't steered him on the wrong path. Doing what she had suggested on *Shep* helped get him where he was now.

And where was that?

Stuck in the goddamn woods behind a tree sobbing for the past several minutes. He'd finally stopped the tears, but he was still an emotional wreck. Another crying spell could come at any moment.

He wondered what Deborah would advise for this.

Take it easy Gary. No harm no foul. Everyone needs to let it out now and then. You did it almost perfectly. The one thing I would suggest is less self-pleading, and more groans and grunts. That would get the point across better if you were crying so hysterically that you couldn't speak. Plus the paragraphs would be shorter. It might need a new title though.

He rested his head against the tree behind him. It was hard and uncomfortable, but he didn't care enough to move.

How much longer should he stay out here? *After making an ass out of myself at the lake, I think I'll stay here as long as I can.* He was embarrassed over how he'd acted, and if that meant snuggling against the tree for two weeks, then he would gladly do it.

Gary folded his arms behind his head. It still wasn't comfortable, but it was better than getting pricked by the notched tree bark. He took a long, deep breath, held it in for a moment, and exhaled. He closed his eyes and could already feel his heartbeat calming. His hands weren't shaking as badly as before.

The trees above him were tall, acting as an awning, and covering him with a blue blanket of shade. In the slots between the limbs, sunlight shined through in glittery ropes. When the breeze picked up, the light flickered against the shadows like fireflies.

He loved the outdoors. Growing up in the country, he'd learned how to appreciate the comforting peacefulness of the woods. He'd grown to love its sweet, crispy smell of pine. Most people figured he would've moved to the city at his first chance, but he proved them all wrong by remaining in the small town where he was raised.

Since the minimal success of *Shep*, he'd been treated like a big-time celebrity there. He was far from actually being one, but he enjoyed the special attention from time to time. Occasionally, but not often, people resented him for his new career. They accused him of arrogance and of thinking he was better than everyone else in town. Gary understood where their jealousy stemmed from, but if it got any worse, he'd probably just move. He'd been looking at a house in Deer County that wasn't too far from civilization. All the malls, grocery stores, and gas stations were well within driving distance, and it would also be a great place to raise a family.

A vision of Amy flashed in his mind, fluttering his heart as if a small current charged through. It'd be nice living together and raising a family with her. He could imagine them doing husband and wife things like taking vacations, yard work and going for checkups after she became pregnant.

The fun stuff. A perfect life for a perfect team.

Something pushed against his head and slid down by his ear. It settled there, making a home in his wavy hair. A bug? A leaf? Too hard to be a leaf, a bug maybe. He sighed. The one thing he didn't like about the woods was all the bugs and ticks. He should've brought a can of bug spray with him. Once one bug showed up, a million followed. If his mind had been stable when they'd arrived, he would have grabbed some repellant.

Gary swatted at the bug in his hair, striking something solid, cold, and firm enough that he could wrap his fingers around it.

Metal?

Using his index finger, he traced the length. It was long, cold steel.

"Oh, shit…" He managed to say before his finger was gripped and snapped back. The bone cracked, splintering as the tip of his finger touched his wrist. He yelled, jerking his hand away. While caressing it with his left hand, he whipped around and fell onto his back.

"Did I wake you?"

Gary's eyes widened. "Piper?"

"Surprised?" He stepped out from behind the tree, pointing a gun at Gary. The barrel was aimed at his head. The gun was a large-caliber, police-issued hand cannon.

"Piper? How…"

"How did I find you?" He laughed. "I would like to say it was because of my excellent detective work, but no. It was just dumb luck."

Gary attempted to get on his knees, but Piper stepped forward, cutting him off with his gun drawn.

"Huh-uh. No sudden moves. Just stay right there."

Gary froze.

If only he had one shot at taking Piper down. He pictured himself jumping to his feet, charging him and wrapping his hands around his throat. His crotch tingled over the vision because he wanted it so badly, but he knew it wouldn't work. He'd be shot before getting on his feet. As much as he wanted to fight him, he was helpless.

"I know that look," said Piper, referring to Gary's pig-headed expression. "You feel like a horse's ass. Am I right?"

Hit the nail on the head with that one.

"You want a piece of me, don't you?"

Right again, Piper ol' chump.

"It's not going to happen. I'd plant one between your eyes before you got your wits about you."

Three for three!

"Just stay right where you are so I don't have to shoot you before I plan to."

Gary noticed the brown-stained bandage taped on Piper's head. A trickle of blood had escaped down his cheek. He hadn't bothered to wipe it, so it had congealed on his jaw line.

Piper was hurt, but Gary wasn't sure as to what extent. If Piper was a hundred percent, he'd be wailing Gary's face to a bloody pulp. He must be too hurt to do so, or too afraid that he was to try.

That was one thing Gary had in his favor.

"Since the little spat you guys had in the car, I imagine Amy will come looking for you, so I'll wait. Kill two birds with one stone. Well, one gun I should say."

How'd he know about that in the car?

Piper smiled as if reading his thoughts. "Whoops, I guess I said too much, huh? If you're wondering how I knew about the spat, I was hiding in the back." He laughed harder. "Under the tarp."

The tarp. If I would've just taken the damn thing out like I'd originally planned to, this wouldn't have happened. Gary wondered if Piper would allow him to stand long enough to kick his own ass for not checking before they left. He'd looked in every corner, nook, and cranny before leaving, but the one place he did not check was the actual place Piper had been hiding.

His own car.

"Dammit," said Gary.

Piper laughed. "After meeting Shannon, I put two-and-two together. I called in your plates and got it confirmed. So, I just picked the lock and climbed in. You really should learn to set your alarm. It was a long shot, but it looks like fate is playing in my favor, huh?"

Gary hated to agree with him, but he had to. Piper had a lot more fate on his side than he did.

"Now, let's get comfortable. We'll just sit here and wait. She'll be along soon enough."

Gary hoped she wouldn't come, but stubbornness was a characteristic that Amy lacked. She'd come looking for him. No doubt about it. Just a matter of when.

Probably already on her way now. Any moment she'll come around the tree and walk straight into an ambush.

Holding his breath, he listened carefully for the sound of Amy's approaching footsteps but didn't hear any. As a matter of fact, he didn't hear much at all. The woods, so animate a few moments earlier, were now tranquil as if holding its breath. Waiting.

Something was coming. Gary could feel it through every shivering inch of his body.

AMY

Amy ducked under a stray branch. Leafless from rot, it hung limply like an old man's penis.

She laughed at the similarity. "Looks like Piper's," she muttered, then laughed again. The giggle was short-lived when she thought about the monster Piper had become, though. She supposed he'd always been a monster, but he had done a very good job of hiding it in the early stage of their relationship.

Like Bruce Banner, he had probably once been mild-mannered, but had grown to be a beast. As opposed to the *Hulk* comics, Piper never changed back. She was stuck with the Hulk, and never saw Bruce Banner again. She grew to learn that was just how Piper was. Whether it was legitimate shyness or not, she was certain that he'd staked out the relationship to see what kind of woman he had, then when he learned how far he could take it, all bets were off. It seemed the only time Piper could get aroused was if she was either in tears or in pain, or both. The first time sent up a red flag, but either out of denial or just plain stupidity, she chose to ignore it as rough sex play. What she should have done was beat her feet against the concrete and never look back.

When her mother passed away, Aunt Sherri had phoned to tell her the heartbreaking news. She went delirious. Before she was off the phone, Piper's hand had snuck under her shirt, and squeezed her breast.

He didn't stop there.

Soon, she was forced down on the bed with Piper's hand around her throat. It was off kilter for him, but she kind of liked it. He'd never been aggressive. She'd often wondered if he was frightened of intimacy. That was the first time. Later, she realized, he was just bored with it. If she would have known a trend of violent sex would follow, she would have refused. At the time, he was still withdrawn, or pretending to be, and when he discovered she was one to submit, it changed him.

Or set the real Piper free.

Then he took her all the time. Even if she wasn't willing to submit, he'd make her. Her stomach sank, daunted by the memories of everything he'd done to her. Why had she stuck around so long? And for god's sake, why would she defend him when someone pointed out the type of person he was?

I never have been one to do what makes sense...

Take Gary, for example. She could have been with him all this time if she would have just opened her eyes and seen that he was the one for her. Never knowing Piper Conwell would have been a blessing. Gary was her twin flame. She'd read enough about the theories of soul mates and twin flames that she should have known a long time ago.

Amy hopped over a small creek that zigzagged through the forest. Not much water in the rivulet, but it flowed vigorously. She wished she had time to stick her feet in it.

Find Gary first. Talk to him, get this right. But what about Wendy?

She hadn't thought about Wendy's reaction to all of this, but she figured it would be the same as Piper's.

Violent.

They still had a long car ride back to Stone Quarry and plenty of chances for Wendy to lash out. She had to get things with Gary where they needed to be, but he had to hold off telling Wendy until they had gotten back to Gary's.

Maybe I should ride back with Mary.

Though she didn't want to, she figured it might be for the best. As much as she wished she could ride with Gary alone to Stone Quarry and discuss where they were going to take their relationship from here—if anywhere—she knew Wendy wouldn't give up her seat and ride back with the others. She would have to be the one to sacrifice Gary's time to help keep the peace.

How will you fit? Their car is awfully small, and awfully full.

She thought about it a moment. *We'll make it work. I could squeeze in between Shannon and Jake if I have to. Maybe one of them will be nice enough to switch cars, especially after the ordeal between Wendy and me.* Amy laughed as an idea came to her. Put Shannon in the car with Gary and Wendy. Let her rub her breasts all over Wendy and see how she liked it.

Hell, Wendy might even enjoy it.

Amy came to a slight incline. At the top of the hill, the woods seemed to stretch on forever. Being this deep in isolation made it easy to forget a real world existed beyond the trees.

Amy smirked.

The real world, what's that?

Taking the incline one step at a time, she leaned forward, putting more weight on her knees and less on her back. As she neared the top, she noticed a large oak tree just a little farther up and woods as far as she could see beyond it in all directions.

In the small clearing, opposite the oak tree, she saw him.

Gary.

Sitting with his legs folded, his hair was a mess and matted down with sweat. He clutched his finger, nursing it in such a way that it appeared to be injured. *What's going on? Why is he just sitting there like that?* She wondered if his legs were hurt too. The way he rocked on his knees, they looked to be broken. Slowing her stride, she tiptoed forward. She stepped to the tree in front of her and pressed her chest flat against it.

Then she eased her head around the tree to spy.

Why doesn't he move?

Staring haplessly at the ground like a child put in time out, he hadn't noticed her. He snuggled his finger against his stomach, and she could see him wince with the slightest movement. She switched her weight to her right foot and bowed at the hip. Leaning over even more, she could see all the way around the tree. In front of it, a man stood with his back turned to her.

He had a gun aimed at Gary.

Gary was a hostage.

What happened?

She didn't recognize the man from behind. He had dark hair and was wearing a T-shirt and cargo pants. She scanned him, looking him up and over, but nothing stood out to her. Then she observed the gun closer.

It was stainless steel with an ivory-colored grip. She immediately realized what kind of gun it was: a .357 caliber, steel-plated pistol.

Piper's pistol.

Her bowels ached. The muscles of her legs felt soft and stringy. Looking at the man's backside, she couldn't believe she hadn't recognized him. Somehow, Piper had found them. Not only that, he was holding Gary prisoner. Amy had no idea how this had happened.

She needed a weapon. It would be hard finding something nearby, and harder to do it without being seen or heard. She looked around from where she stood, hoping to find something. Old, broken tree branches were everywhere. Those could help, but more than likely they would break in mid-swing. No good. What else was out here? Leaves, dirt, grass. It was disheartening.

This is the woods, for Christ's sake, where's a bear? Piper is strong, but he can't stop a bear.

Feeling helplessly defeated of coming to Gary's rescue, she noticed something jutting up through the mud by her feet. She nudged it with the toe of her shoe. It was hard and jagged.

A rock.

How big is it? Can I lift it?

She crouched down to the buried object quietly and carefully and dug her fingers into the soft mud around it. The rock wasn't very wide. She could probably lift it with one hand, but it would take some effort to dislodge it.

She finally found the bottom and cupped her hands around the rock. It was the size of a grapefruit. It wasn't very big, but it was thick, and could cause some serious damage.

I'm going to get us both killed.

Gary had spent so many years helping her out of positions she should've never been in to begin with that it was time for her to pay him back and show him how much she cared. But did she care enough about him to get killed for him?

Hell, yes.

Her mind made up and the rock in her hand, she stepped to the left hoping to ambush Piper from behind. She hoped he remained distracted by Gary long enough.

Please, don't let him turn around.

GARY

Keeping his head hanging low, Gary peered up at Piper. Over the last few minutes, Piper had been quiet. Gary figured he was trying to hatch out a more thorough plan than the one he had now. So far, Piper had been going by the seat of his pants. He'd been lucky so far, but that would run out eventually.

Gary hoped for sooner rather than later.

He wanted to catch Piper at the exact moment his luck dried up. He'd have to act quickly, and it had better be good. If he got the opportunity at all, he likely wouldn't get another opportunity again.

I'm dead if I fuck up.

Piper raised his head, tilting it so his ear perked to the side. He was listening.

What does he hear? Gary focused his attention on the surrounding woods but heard nothing other than the rasping of leaves as gentle breezes drifted through the woods.

His heart raced. Unaware of *what* was about to happen, he could feel it coming.

Then it happened so fast he would have missed it if he'd blinked.

Piper whipped around, blocking Gary's view so that he only saw the quick stroke of a rock rising and slamming down.

Piper avoided the attack, catching Amy by the arm.

Amy? What's she doing here?

Saving my ass, or at least trying to.

Piper squeezed her forearm. Amy tried holding the rock, but her grip loosened, and she dropped it.

Now's your chance Gary, his luck can't save him from the both of us.

He jumped to his feet, charging at Piper full steam. Piper flung Amy to the ground. She landed so hard that she bounced. Before he could turn around, Gary leaped upon his back, and wrapped both arms around Piper's neck, putting him in a chokehold.

Wrestling in high-school and most of college, he'd learned some pretty powerful moves. Even though he never once thought he'd have to use them again, he was thankful that he'd never forgotten them.

Piper swung his arms madly, a few blows connected with Gary, but they weren't hard enough to make him drop his hold. Gary squeezed tighter. He heard Piper's wheezing breaths and saw his ears were turning red. His face was probably even redder. His struggles lessened and then his legs buckled. Piper collapsed to his knees, but he didn't fall over.

Piper wasn't making this easy. He continued to fight with what he had left.

"Gary? Let him go!"

Amy's voice sounded like it had come through a funnel, and everything looked as if Gary were viewing it through a red filter. Rage had consumed him. He wanted to make Piper pay for everything he'd done to Amy. He deserved every bit of the punishment Gary could give him.

Gary wanted him to die.

"Let him go. You're going to kill him!"

Piper's arms dropped, dangling by his sides. His unflinching fingers scraped the dirt.

Gary let him go.

Piper fell forward, landing on his stomach with a thud. The little bit of air left in his lungs huffed out. His left arm was bent at the elbow in front of him and the right was straight down by his side.

Gary shook all over. He felt as if he was trapped in the snow in his underwear, but at least he was no longer scared. It was only his adrenaline pumping so vigorously that was making his knees clack together.

Amy grimaced as she looked him over. Gary imagined he wasn't a pleasant sight to behold. He felt guilty knowing she'd seen him react in such a way. He was no better than Piper, attacking like a madman.

Takes one to beat one.

His legs were unable to support his body any longer and he sagged to his knees. He held himself up with his uninjured hand, mortified and unable to look Amy in the eyes. He tried convincing himself that it had to be done, but it didn't make him feel any less ashamed of himself. He was impressed that he'd won the fight, but his guilt surpassed the victory.

For a few moments, he wondered if he'd killed Piper, but eventually heard him breathing. He couldn't deny the disappointment he felt at that.

"Are you okay?" Amy said, her voice shaky and her lips quivering.

Through his tears, Amy was hazy and blurred, but he could tell she'd taken off the makeup. No longer masked by black and white paint, she was her normal, beautiful self once again.

How'd she get the blue out of her hair?

"You look different," he spoke through heaving breaths, as if he just ran a mile.

"What?" She blushed a little, twisting a lump of hair around her finger.

"The makeup, you took it off."

"Ah, yeah. Do you like this look better?" She pulled her finger away from her hair, and pulled it back, exposing all of her lovely face to him.

It felt good seeing it. "Much better. Not that there was anything wrong with the other look."

"Maybe I'll dress up like that again sometime."

"I'd like that."

She raised her shoulders, crunched her neck, and grinned. Her face was as red as an apple.

"How'd you get the blue out of your hair?"

"Oh, that? It was just a clip-on that Mary cut to fit the length of my hair." She laughed.

Gary realized they were ignoring the fact that Piper lay sprawled on the ground between them. He had always been between them.

"So." Amy stopped, as if waiting for him to say what she wanted to hear.

"So, what?"

"How about that kiss?"

"Kiss?"

"Yeah. Our first one. I think now would be the perfect time for it, don't you? A victory kiss." She smiled.

Gary's worries over whether or not Amy cared for him the way he did for her rocketed away from him. He knew he should be thinking of how Wendy would respond to this, but his mind couldn't grasp a single thought about her beyond that. He glanced at Piper's body that lay prone on the ground between them.

"Who knows when we'll have this chance again?" she urged.

In unison, they stood up. Gary felt like he was walking through jelly. Unable to find a total balance, he managed to stagger toward her like he'd had one beer too many.

Amy laughed.

He glanced at her and said, "I see. Laugh at an injured man."

"No, I'm not laughing." She laughed again.

"Yeah, yeah. Kick a man when he's down too."

"You're not down, you're up. And you're walking like a toddler taking his first steps." She bellowed with laughter. He shook his head, trying to compose his stride better.

It didn't work.

They met at Piper's boots.

Gary was taller. He looked down at her round, almond-colored eyes, which were nervously darting back and forth and up and down as they studied him. He loved the way it made him feel.

"Hi," she said.

"Hi."

"Here we are."

"Yep."

She gnawed at her bottom lip. A nervous habit of hers that Gary had always adored. "I've been so blind…"

"Not now. We'll talk about all of that later." With both hands, he caressed her face. Using his left and careful of his broken finger, he rubbed her bangs of hair out of the way. The soft fragrance of her delicate, caramel-like skin combined with the natural aroma of the woods to make him dizzy. "So, you planned to repay me for being your hero with silly insults?"

Smiling back, she answered, "No, I planned to repay you with this…"

As he leaned down, she came up to meet his lips. They lightly brushed. Gary felt a gentle push of softness from her mouth.

Then a succession of howls erupted from the woods.

The trees rocked. Birds screeched as they took flight. The leaves rustled so hard foliage rained all around them. Amy stepped back and looked up, gasping. Gary spun around, stepping in front of her like a shield. She reached under his arms, hugging him from behind, and poked her head between his arm and side.

"What's happening, Gary?"

He had no answer for her. He gawked upward and saw what at first glance appeared to be the trees shedding a massive amount of leaves, but when they struck his body they were much too heavy to be only that. They felt as if they had been packed with bricks. Gary cried out as he was covered. He was quick to shove Amy away from the downpour, hoping to spare her from it. Then the additional weight on his back became too much and he dropped down, vanishing under a mountain of green.

Amy screamed.

Under the pile, Gary slapped and elbowed against whatever was forcing him down. He could hear miniscule squeaks and grunts in his ears that sounded like mice or ferrets. A hand no bigger than an infant's pushed into his mouth. He felt it at the back of his throat. Then he couldn't breathe. The way it was lodged had blocked off his air entirely. It didn't take long before his head began to pound, his eyes to blur. His lungs began to burn.

The need to escape had become even more desperate.

Thrusting backwards, he knocked several of the little critters away. They shrieked as they tumbled from him. He crouched, having managed to get his knees off the ground. He could do more damage from an upright position, but it seemed that with each success more and more replaced them. A fresh batch of the creatures hastily re-covered him after he'd dislodged the others.

Gary grabbed the one on his face with both hands and pulled as hard as he could. It tore free, bringing something from the back of his throat with it. His tongue. Its plump, slushy shape sagged in the little one's minute hand. Holding the tiny creature in front of him, he only got a quick peek of its features before the little bastard punched both of its fists into his eyes. The last image Gary saw was Amy kicking at the critters as she tried to make her way to him.

She was probably trying to help him but was too late.

Gary only managed to grunt at her before his eyes were torn from their sockets. He tried convincing himself that this was only temporary, and his vision would return, but even he wasn't dumb enough to believe that. It all had happened so fast, that he only briefly considered the oddness to it all. Creatures had dropped from the trees and were killing him. Soon, they would probably do the same to Amy. It didn't get any wackier than that. He had managed to defeat his arch nemesis, Piper Conwell, but could do nothing against this assault. Not only was he outnumbered, but he was inexperienced and way out of his element.

His feet kicked something solid, and it rattled as it rolled away. *Piper's fucking gun.* Something sharp pierced his side, then his back. Another punched him at the nape of the neck. He was being penetrated like a pin cushion.

God, it hurts! I'm dying!

He wished he'd thought to grab Piper's gun after he'd taken him out. That would have been wise. But it was too late.

Suddenly, explosions erupted all around him, ringing in his ears. He could smell the rotten-egg odor of gun smoke. Amy must have gotten the gun. *Way to go!* The little things shrieked and hollered. He felt more blades ripping through. Somewhere, through his wailing eardrums, he swore he heard paper tearing, but realized it was only his flesh.

Amy's screams for him were hollow and ghostly.

Then he heard nothing at all.

AMY

Gary was dead.

It had happened in a matter of seconds. Ambushed and taken by surprise, he hadn't stood a chance against them. Now, he was gone. Amy stared as the little leaf monsters swarmed over him like ants on a dropped piece of cake. She pointed the gun at the teeming crowd but couldn't keep her hand steady enough to fire again. If she were to miss and hit Gary, she would just die inside. Though it wouldn't hurt him, she didn't want to add any additional inflictions to his already mangled frame.

His intestines were strewn out in front of him like rope with two of those things fighting over them, each tugging at one side like it was some kind of sick game. Where his gorgeous brown eyes used to be were now cavities brimming with thick, syrupy blood.

A few were tying Piper up like a hog while the others fought over Gary's parts.

Watching them lit something inside of her that burned like acid. Unable to shoot the gun, she did the only other logical thing she could think of. She screamed at them. "You sons of bitches, I'll kill every one of you mother fuckers!" Such words had never left her mouth before, and, she had to admit, it felt good saying them. But maybe she shouldn't have. The only thing that this outburst had accomplished was to stop what they were doing and focus their ravenous attention on *her.*

A dozen or so petite heads, blood smeared around the boundaries of their mouths and little shreds of flesh caught between their rotting teeth, grinned in synchronicity.

Some stayed on Gary, but the others charged. *How many are there?* It looked as if they were coming from everywhere. Maybe they were. They yipped and howled, a leafage army aiming to infiltrate Amy's innards. Not caring what she hit, she fired four rounds into the throng. Two dropped. The rest stopped to check on their comrades. This gave her a narrow window of opportunity and she took it.

Amy turned and hauled ass, screaming as she fled.

MARY

There were disputes over what they'd heard before, but nothing could convince Mary that last sound had not been a scream. And if that was so, then those other noises had to have been gunshots. She looked at Steve. His face had lost its color as he stared at the woods. Wendy opened her mouth to say something, but nothing came out.

"That had to be a scream," said Shannon, confirming what everyone was thinking.

"And gunshots," said Steve blankly.

No doubt. It was a scream. *Amy's* scream. The one that had come before it sounded like a man. Gary. In the last few minutes, they'd heard Gary and Amy screaming from the woods, followed by a rapid chain of gunshots, while they had all just stood on the shore doing nothing. Mary was tired of doing nothing. She wanted to find them. They could be in trouble. *Could be?* With racket like that, they were most likely being killed. Mary's stomach felt as if it was being clutched by frigid hands. "We've got to go get them," she said.

Shannon nodded even though Mary assumed she hadn't done so intentionally.

Jake stepped forward. "I agree. Something's going on out there."

Mary continued, "And it doesn't matter what it is, they need our help."

Jake reached into his back pocket, removing his folded blade. "I've got my knife. Does anyone else have anything?"

At first, no one said anything. Then Wendy nodded excitedly as if she suddenly remembered something. "I do. It's in my bag."

"What is it?"

"A gun my dad gave me. He wanted me to carry it around after my sister was raped last year."

Ignoring the remark about her sister, Jake said, "A gun?"

"Yeah, it's only a .22. That's hardly a gun."

"Better than nothing."

"I'll go get it."

Wendy ran to Gary's Jeep. Mary noticed how wobbly her legs were. She wondered if it was from fear, worry, or both.

"I'll go with her," said Shannon. "No one should go off anywhere alone."

Jake nodded. "Good thinking."

Shannon kicked up clouds of dirt behind her as she trotted after Wendy and caught up to her by the cars. Mary watched her standing over Wendy's shoulder while she dug through the Jeep.

"Maybe we shouldn't go out there," said Steve in a low voice, trying to keep his words between him and Mary. "Let's *all* go back to the cars. We can call for help."

Mary scowled at Steve. "From what? I didn't see any pay phones out here."

"No dummy, our cell phones. We've all got one."

Mary went to say something, but Jake stepped in front of her to intervene. "Do you have a signal this far out in the sticks? I sure as hell don't."

Steve glanced at the sky as if all his answers were shaped in the clouds. He stuttered a few syllables before Jake stopped him.

"I didn't think so, none of us do. Now, shut up." He turned around to face the woods. Then, with a sigh, he let his head drop.

Wendy and Shannon returned, and as Shannon stepped up behind Jake, she wrapped her arms around his stomach, and rested her head against his shoulder. "Do you think they're alright?"

"I hope so," he said.

AMY

Amy was lucky to be alive.

Yeah, real lucky.

Keeping her back to the tree, she pushed with her feet to stand up, wincing as the bark tore at her shirt and scraped her skin on her way up. She felt trickles of warm liquid on her back. She'd fled the chaos, and for the moment, had escaped. She wasn't exactly sure where in the woods she was. It all looked the same to her.

Amy reexamined the route she'd taken in her escape. The clearing was several yards back. She should have crossed over the creek by now, but she hadn't. She'd gotten completely turned around.

If only she had a compass.

I can't even read those goddamn things.

Amy heaved an annoyed sigh as she leaned against the tree and replayed what had just happened in her mind. It didn't seem real. Like some kind of horror movie, she had watched and should be discussing with friends at dinner afterward. Or a nightmare. One she should have awoken sweaty and whimpering from. As ludicrous as it all had been, the most ridiculous part was that it was real. Not a movie nor a dream. She had witnessed it and had somehow survived. But that would change if she didn't get back to the lake where the others were. Right now, they were probably wondering what was going on.

She inspected the gun and brushed it clean against her hip. She stuck it between the waistband and small of her back where it held, but not tightly. The band wasn't strong enough and if she were to run, it would surely fall out. Keeping it there would have to do for now, though. There was nowhere else she could put it, and her arms were too pathetic to carry it.

If Piper hadn't fired any shots himself, she should have six or seven bullets left. Maybe eight. Either way, she had a few to spare if she happened to come across more of those things, but once the clip was empty, she was fucked beyond words.

Farther west, she could see distinct shapes among the myriad colors. Tree branches swooped over three objects. They were large. She squinted her eyes. One was brown, the other two grayish white.

Cars.

Old ones, probably eighties models, and all abandoned and corroded. Just seeing the metallic shells made Amy uneasy. She wondered how long they'd been there, and how they had gotten there. Were those same creatures responsible? Had others decided to head to the lake for a day of fun and sun only to be waylaid by those minute trolls? It was depressing knowing they had been out here for all this time, and no one had discovered them. She couldn't help but fear that may be her fate as well.

Amy broke down, her tears ambushing her.

She'd gotten Gary killed. She shook uncontrollably as she realized that.

If she hadn't called him to come pick her up…

If those damn kids hadn't suggested stopping at a hotel…

It was my idea to go to the lake. All of this could have been avoided if I had kept my mouth shut about Whisper Lake.

But she knew that at the lake, she would have the chance to talk to Gary one-on-one. She'd gotten her moment alone with Gary all right, and now he was dead.

Gone forever.

She cried harder.

Her body trembled. She leaned over, put her hands on her knees, and took deep breaths. Then, she noticed something chunky and filthy on her boot. She backhanded her wet eyes and bent her leg, raising it to see what she'd stepped on. At the bottom of her boot was a brown substance covered in strawberry jelly. She leaned forward, hugging her boot closer. Her thigh burned as she gauchely twisted her foot to the side.

Brushing off some sodden dirt, she realized the substance was an eyeball. And the jelly substance was actually coagulated blood.

Her stomach sprung to her throat so fast she barely had time to turn her head. The vomit was immense as it exploded from her mouth, spattering the dirt in thick, sloppy chunks. The earth swashed it up.

"Oh, God!" she bawled.

Knowing it was Gary's eye made it worse. Puking until she dry-heaved, she continued to gag and hack, only spitting up phlegm.

Amy finally stood up straight on legs that could barely support her. Her head was swimming and it nauseated her more. She tried to contain the heaves as she began to walk north.

MARY

At the back of the line, Mary walked alongside Steve. Jake led the troop through the woods, only pausing long enough to hold a limb out of the way so the others could pass through without getting whacked.

No one had spoken.

While Jake maintained the front, Shannon nipped at his heels in a tight second. Wendy walked in front of Mary and Steve, her eyes glossy but intent. She was with them but didn't seem to really be anywhere at all.

After Wendy had gotten her gun, they'd quickly changed their clothes. It was surprisingly warm out, and Mary had convinced them that the ticks would be bad. They wore shorts, T-shirts, and tank tops to spot them better if one happened to latch onto their legs or arms thirsty for blood. Deer ticks were common, and the group wasn't taking any chances. Wendy had taken turns spraying them all with insect repellant, but in woods this deep, and as much as they were surely to sweat, it would only last for so long.

Mary hated ticks. Why had an atrocious insect like a tick even been created? It didn't make sense. Neither did mosquitoes for that matter. Two insects that could kill you with a meager bite from all the bacteria they carried around.

Gross.

She could go on for hours about diseases, and now wasn't the time. They had a job to do.

"How far out do you think they went?" called Jake.

Mary spoke up. "I don't know. Probably a little ways to go yet. Those screams sounded pretty distant."

"And gunshots," added Steve.

Mary had tried forgetting about the gunshots. It was bad enough they'd heard the screams. The gunshots made the circumstances feel even more threatening. Neither of them had left with a gun, so why would they have heard gunshots?

Something bad had happened.

Mary shuddered to think about it, but she had nothing else to go on except for that assumption. She didn't want to presume anything at this point, but the gunshots made it hard to avoid.

"What are we going to do when we do find them?" said Shannon, slapping her arm. A flattened mosquito dropped off her skin.

"*If* we find them," added Steve.

"Nice," said Mary.

"I'm just saying we may not find them."

"Don't talk like that!" Shannon shook her head. "Idiot!"

Jake shot a hateful sneer over his shoulder at Steve. It was enough to shut him up. Looking at Shannon, he said, "To answer your question sweetie, I guess what we do depends on what we find."

"Depends how?" said Steve.

Jake didn't answer.

"Weren't you told to shut up?" snapped Shannon.

"Let's not fight guys," said Mary.

"We should go back and get help." Steve repeated his argument.

"We're not going anywhere until we find them," said Mary. "It wouldn't be right if we left them alone out here."

"One of us should, at least."

Mary had never seen this side of Steve, and she didn't like it. He was practically begging permission to go to the car. And if he did go back, could he be trusted to stick around and wait for them? She doubted it. She felt a hollow place somewhere inside that hadn't been there before.

Wendy sighed. "Before you two go on any farther debating the importance of going back to the cars, what needs to be said but you all are too scared to say it is. Everything we do depends on whether or not they're *dead*!" Wendy's words stuttered together toward the end of her sentence, and she was crying before the last word poured from her mouth.

That silenced the troop.

They marched on through the uncharacteristically still woods, as Wendy continued to sob with each step she took.

PIPER

Piper opened his eyes. It hurt doing so. Trees zipped by in green blurs, and he could feel himself moving at a steady pace as his back bounced over uncovered roots, rocks, and mounds of hard dirt. Some fire ants clung to his skin; they clamped and pinched, their bites feeling like bee stings.

He'd been bound and was being dragged on either a tarp or blanket.

By whom, he didn't know, and to where, he had no idea. All he could comprehend was that he was being taken away by multiple people. He'd heard more than one voice. Although they were very similar, with the same squeaky tones, he was able to slightly differentiate them. He wished he could raise his head and see what they looked like but doing so seemed impossible. It hurt too bad to move his neck, and his head seemed too heavy to try.

That fag, Gary, was a tougher opponent than he'd originally given him credit for. He was impressed. Pissed off, but impressed. He'd really given him a hurting. It'd been a long time since someone had gotten the drop on him like that. But that was the sort of shit that could happen when you let your guard down. People can surprise you and catch you when you least expect it. Gary had managed to spring on him at just the right moment.

That had been a good plan.

Piper had a plan of his own. It was a simple one. He'd wait for his chance to strike back. When it came, God help those that had put him in this predicament, because it was only temporary. He'd be free at some point.

And these fuckers would pay.

Then it was back to Gary for a rematch.

MARY

"Look there!" said Jake, stopping. He raised his finger and pointed.

The group gathered atop a hill, staring down on a stream that snaked through the woods. On the opposite side, on her knees and cupping handfuls of water into her mouth, was Amy. She hadn't noticed them. Her attention was drawn to the cold flow of the stream.

Mary's mouth watered looking at the gushing water. It was a small current but would feel and taste so good right about now. All she had was lukewarm bottled water in the carry bag strapped to her back. And cigarettes. Lots of cigarettes.

Mary watched Amy put both her hands together, letting them fill with water before she splashed her face. She kept her eyes closed as the water dripped down her neck and chest. Beads of moisture reflected the yellow rays of the sun, making her look as if she were sparkling. A puddle had formed in the curve of her collarbone. Mary's eyes traveled to Amy's knees. They were scraped and red. Seeing the abrasions and chewy pieces of serrated skin made her stomach roil. Then she caught the glimmer of something metal. On the ground by her feet was a gun.

We did hear shots.

She also noticed none of the group had yet spoken to Amy.

It felt like they were eavesdropping.

Mary pushed her way through to the front of the group and called, "Amy?"

Startled, Amy snatched the gun from the ground and fired without looking. The bullet went wildly astray, ricocheting deep in the woods somewhere. When she realized what she had done, she dropped the gun and cried.

To avoid falling, Mary carefully trotted down the hill. It was slick and loose under her shoes. At the bottom, she found Amy had fallen with her back against an incline that climbed up into the woods. Her head was buried in the fold of her arms and muffled her sobs. Mary took a step back, and then jumped over the creek. She felt dots of water splashing her calves in flight. Her feet slapped the ground, trying to slip out from under her, but she caught herself and managed not to fall.

She stepped over to Amy and squatted down next to her. Patting her gently on the back, she said, "Amy? It's me, Mary."

Amy jerked around, latching onto Mary's tank top as if she were about to fall. It was the same top she'd worn to the club. It stretched under Amy's tow, revealing the smooth, pale slopes of her breasts. She kindly removed the shirt from Amy's hands and guided her closer.

They hugged.

Amy buried her head on Mary's chest. Mary could feel her warm, rapid-firing breaths against her skin.

"What happened? We heard shots."

"Piper's here!"

Amy's voice was barely audible against Mary's breasts.

"What?"

"He attacked us!"

"Where's Gary?"

Amy started to say something, but only cried even harder. Her shoulders bopped up and down so harshly it looked as if they might lop her head off.

Mary knew the answer before Amy spoke the words.

And finally, Amy shrieked, "Gary's *dead!*" She pounded her fists against Mary's shoulders.

"What?" cried Wendy, charging down the hill. At the bottom, she also slipped, and, just as Mary, was lucky not to fall. "What did you say!"

Amy tried to speak, but it was difficult understanding her through the babbling sobs.

Wendy pointed her gun at Amy, clutching it with shaky hands. She pulled the trigger. It clicked. "Shit."

Wendy lowered the gun and fumbled with the safety. Before she had another chance to aim, Jake had rushed down the hill and grabbed her from behind. She fought him at first but was quickly subdued.

He held her back against him.

Shaking her head skeptically, she bawled too. "Oh God… Gary…"

Jake shook her lightly. "It's okay It's all right."

"We have to get out of here," said Amy, choking on her wails.

"Is Piper after you?" asked Mary.

She shook her head. "I don't know where he is. I think they took him. They were tying him up when I ran."

"*Who* took him?"

"They're in the trees. Those disgusting things. They'll be here soon."

"You're not making any sense, Amy."

She shook Mary. "*They're coming!*"

Wails that sounded like kids at a birthday party erupted all around them. Bundles of leaves began to leap from tree to tree. No way could they be moving on their own, yet they were, and not only were they mysteriously animated, but the leaves were laughing. From the trees up the incline, they were coming closer, and gaining fast in an undulating torrent of green.

Jake pushed them all toward the hill. Clods of dirt slipped out from under Mary's feet making it difficult for her to climb, but she managed to make it to the top. She turned back as Jake was trying to induce Wendy into following, but she wouldn't move. Her eyes remained fixated on the trees behind them. Finally, she snapped out of her trance and darted up the hill.

At the top, Mary watched as bands of leaves detached from the trees, hopping to other limbs on opposing trees.

The mobile leafage pursued them, trailing steadily behind.

JAKE

They charged through the woods in a mad dash, not avoiding the limbs this time. Steve was the first to flee, and he'd left them far behind. Shannon stopped to wait for them, but Jake sent her after Steve. He was now making sure Wendy kept going and didn't lag behind. They closely trailed Mary, who was guiding Amy.

He hoped Mary remembered the way back to the lake, because he had gotten confused as to where they were.

Then, Wendy took a shot across the throat from a thick branch hanging too low in her path. It stopped her in place, hoisting her feet in the air. She cut a barrel and flipped sideways, then landed hard on her stomach. The air in her lungs huffed out.

Amy and Mary tried helping her up. She was coughing, and her eyes were glazed over. Jake dropped to the ground next to her and helped her sit up. She gagged, choking on air that was frantically trying to force its way into her lungs. She was also empty-handed, having dropped the gun somewhere during the collision.

Turning to Mary, he yelled, "Get out of here. We'll be right behind you!"

"Are you crazy!" Mary said.

Howls reverberated from behind them. The trees rustled as if from an oncoming hurricane.

"Just go. I'll help Wendy. You two get to the cars and don't let Steve take off without us!"

"I promise!"

Mary tugged Amy by the forearm until she finally moved her feet. Jake watched them cut around a tree, where he could no longer see them at all. He left Wendy alone for a moment to search for the gun. After kicking and pawing through branches, pine needles and leaves, he gave up on finding it. All they had to protect themselves with was his hunting knife. It could slash tires, but he wondered how good it would be against a forest that had suddenly come alive.

The howls were getting closer. Not far behind now. He threw his hands up in the air in defeat and snatched Wendy by the arm, drawing her to her feet.

Dragging her behind him with her free hand grasping her throat, they ran.

Ahead of them, four knee-high bushes jumped out from behind the trees. Two skinny, twig-like arms protruded from the sides. Clutched in their petite hands were spears the size of yardsticks. They shrieked at Jake and Wendy while hopping up and down as if part of a bizarre ghost walk meant to frighten them.

It was working.

Wendy opened her mouth to scream, but all that came out were dry wheezes. Jake tugged her to the right, but they were soon cut off by more leafage plummeting from the trees. The creatures blocked their path in that direction, too, swinging tiny blades the size of pencils at their ankles. Jake jumped around the attack and circled back to face Wendy.

Gripping her by the arms, he yelled, "Fuck, they're surrounding us!"

Wendy shook her head, clearly unable to comprehend what was happening.

"Come on!" He yelled, guiding her back the way they had come.

"No," she groaned. "We can't go this way." Her voice sounded as if she'd been gargling glass.

"It's okay. We'll cut to the left. It'll take us farther up the lake, but we'll get there. I promise."

Their feet slapped the dry ground, flapping dirt against their shins. The harder pieces stung like little bites where they nicked their legs. Dashing into thicker parts of the forest, they were lashed repeatedly by sagging branches. Jake held his arm out to shield them the best he could, taking many of the hits against his forearm. It kept Wendy from getting whacked again, but the impact was beating his arm senseless.

Wendy stopped running and pulled back against him. His weight shifted, but luckily, he didn't fall, although he'd come close.

"Look," she said.

Jake saw it too.

A shack.

It was a crooked structure, gaping with missing boards. A rotted door hung loosely on corroded hinges. Ivy and vines grew up and around the dilapidated erection as if trying to pull it under the ground. What was left of the roof had been raped with holes.

"We can hide there," she said. Her voice was no longer husky and now sounded like a teenage boy hitting puberty.

"No," he said through hefty breaths. "We'll be sitting ducks in there. Besides, I want to get back to the cars. I don't trust that Steve will wait for us."

"I don't either," she said. "If he leaves, I know where Gary's hidden key is, but we're a moving target out here!"

"At least we'll be moving. In there, we'd be a *sitting* target. Trapped. Nowhere to go."

Wendy looked around, munching on her lip nervously. Behind her, the green flood was coming toward them. Grass. It looked like a blob of grass. She stepped behind Jake and hugged against him. Jake gasped. The tops of the trees on their other side were exchanging clutters of leaves with one another like athletes tossing baseballs back and forth. But he knew that the ground wasn't moving and that the leaves weren't being passed from tree to tree. They were alive, and that left Jake and Wendy with nowhere else to go except to the right.

To the shack.

MARY

Shannon was first out of the woods. She flopped down on the flat land; her mouth smacked the sand and swallowing grits of it. She pushed herself to her knees and coughed a dry, broken cough. With the back of her hand, she wiped her tongue as clean as she could.

Steve hurried out from the woods, frantically looking over his shoulder. Mary was next, leading Amy by the hand. They spotted Shannon on the ground and went to her. Each one of them grabbed one of her arms and scooped her up in one quick motion. Her feet dangled in the air a moment before slapping down on the ground.

Shannon looked around. Panic was a mask on her face, her blue eyes wide and darting. "Where's Jake?"

They didn't see him.

Mary tried to say something but couldn't make herself.

"What happened to Jake?" Shannon grabbed Steve by the shirt and shook him. "Did you see Jake?"

Amy gawked at the woods, sweat stinging her eyes. She expected that at any second, Jake would rush out with Wendy close behind. It didn't happen. Looking back at Shannon, she said, "He was just right behind us with Wendy. He told us to catch up to you two. I don't know what happened!"

The sand under Amy's feet shifted. She bounced and swayed as it wobbled. Minuscule hands jutted up from the sand grabbing for her. She screamed, stomping at them as they pawed at her feet. A pair of the teensy digits latched onto her left ankle and pulled it under until it disappeared into the sand. Grasping at the air, she tried grabbing onto anything that could stop her from sinking. Her round eyes stared at the others, pleading for their help. Mary was quick to respond. Steve and Shannon only watched in shock, unable to move.

"Help me!" Amy cried. "It's got my foot!"

"Mary, come on, we've gotta get to the cars!" shouted Steve.

Crouching down, swatting at the molesting hands, she spoke to him over her shoulder. "She needs our help!"

Steve's hands clenched into fists. "*Come on!*"

"*No!*"

Steve pushed his hands into his short hair and latched on. He looked as if any moment he may start to cry. He turned to Shannon. "Go get Mary! If we don't get to the cars now, we might never make it!'

Shannon nodded. She charged past him, bumping his shoulder so hard he spun around. She fell to her knees and slid to a halt beside Mary. Instead of pulling her away so they could make a break for it, she did just the opposite.

Hands balled into fists, she punched at the tiny, nabbing paws.

Her act of heroism was pointless; there were just too many scrawny hands to hit, and not enough people doing the hitting. As the girls struck, punched and pulled, others appeared, outnumbering them by many. Before long, Amy was knee deep in the sand and plummeting deeper.

Steve let go of his hair and stood frozen. He watched through the lenses of his crooked glasses. Using his middle finger, he pushed the frames up his nose. "I'll get the car! You take care of her, I'll be back!"

Steve turned and ran, leaving them behind.

"You *asshole!*" shrieked Shannon.

Mary worried about his safety only for a moment before her anger made her blind to it. Disgust outweighed her fear, which allowed her to think clearly for the first time since this had begun. The cotton-like fog had lifted. *Steve's not just an asshole, he's a scared asshole.*

And that left Amy's life in Mary's hands.

Planting her feet sturdily on the ground, Mary rose to a squat. She latched onto Amy's right arm with both hands and heaved. At first, Amy didn't budge, but slowly she began to rise. Soon, she was only ankle-deep.

A faint whistle sounded, becoming louder as it neared. Something thudded against Mary's shoulder and burned as warm liquid ran down her arm. Then her neck and shoulders went hot, scorching hot. Her arm became weaker, making her unable to hold Amy. She glanced at the searing place on her shoulder and gasped.

An arrow was jutting from the knob of her shoulder.

Short and thin, it didn't look like any arrow she'd ever seen before. This one was much smaller, and probably homemade. Another one shot straight through her hand.

She released Amy as she fell and rolled.

Her back now faced the other two. She could hear Amy pleading with Shannon to pull harder as Shannon cried and shouted right back with her attempts to free her. Mary grabbed the shaft of the arrow that was pierced through her hand just below the pointed tip. She yanked forward, knowing that if she pulled it out the other way, the tip would make the wound bigger.

It ripped free without much effort, but the pain was tremendous. She hollered, hugging her hand to her chest. Gripping the wrist of her injured hand she slowly straightened her fingers wanting to see how bad the wound was. It hurt. A lot. With her hand extended palm side up, she could see the ground through the hole. No wider than the end of her pinky, it throbbed, pulsating with each heartbeat.

Behind her, Amy's cries became muffled.

Mary rolled over. Amy's head, mouth gaped open and begging, disappeared under the sand. Shannon continued tugging until Amy finally jerked from her grasp.

The sand gurgled a moment, then didn't move at all.

JAKE

There wasn't much inside the shack that Jake could use to barricade the door. All he and Wendy had found during their frantic search was some old, fallen pieces of wood from the ceiling. They piled what they could in front of the door. It would hold up for a while, but not long. Plus, the creatures could come in from any one of the dozen melon-sized holes scattered across the ceiling with no problem. Fortunately, there weren't any limbs sagging over the roof that would assist them in getting on top of the shack.

Strike that as one for the good guys, but it wasn't much to celebrate.

Jake wished they hadn't trapped themselves in this death-hole.

Wendy's eyes had been glued to one of the slits between the wall boards. On lookout, she constantly updated him on their assailants' every move. The last bit of information she'd given him was they had seemed to be moving on as if oblivious to their hiding spot.

Jake looked at himself in his knife's blade. He didn't recognize the person twisted in the silver shaft staring back at him. His reflection looked more like the Wildman of the Wisconsin forests.

I could come to be, if I don't ever get out of this damn shack.

"I don't see them anymore," said Wendy. She pressed her face closer to the wood. "They're gone."

"We'll wait."

"I'm telling you, I don't see them. At first, they were running around out there like crazy, but now they're gone."

"I'm telling *you*, we'll wait a little longer just to be sure."

She groaned and stepped away from her post. "Okay, if that's what you want."

"It's not what I want, but it's what we should do."

Wendy crammed her hands down into the pockets of her shorts and walked over to where a pile of junk—old blankets, hubcaps, and other clutter—was centered on the floor. Everything was useless and taking up way too much space. She nudged the pile with her foot and quickly snatched it back with a sour look on her face.

"Gross."

"What's wrong?"

"Those blankets, they're wet."

He laughed softly. "Yeah, probably gets rained on so much they never dry."

"And all the little animals out here like to use it as their litter box, I'm sure."

"Yeah, that too."

Wendy made a face.

He laughed a bit louder, but quickly hushed it.

Sighing again, she looked at Jake. Her mussed hair hung around her face like a sweaty hood. Her head was slouched, and when she looked up at him, her eyes were white spheres amongst the tangled, brunette locks.

"Thank you."

The nape of his neck warmed. He tried hiding his obvious blush. "No problem."

"No, really, *thank* you." She prodded the toes of her sandal across the slanting floor. His eyes panned up her dainty ankles, to her calves, and up legs that tapered to glistening thighs. Her skin was lightly misted as if she'd been caught in a soft rain. Under the thin layer of moisture, she was dark and golden. *Stunning.* He hated thinking like that in a time such as this, or at all for that matter. He figured it was better thinking about *her* than the unreal reality that pursued them outside the curdled walls.

"Anyone else would've left me back there," she continued. "*You* didn't."

"No, that's not true, Mary and Amy stopped."

"How much help would they have been, really?"

He shrugged.

"*You* saved me. Even if we get killed in here, *you* still had the balls to stop and save me."

"Yeah, well…" His mind returned to what she'd said. *Even if we get killed in here.* A chill pranced up his spine, lodging like jagged ice between his shoulder blades. If they were to die in here, then everything he had done up to this point would have been for naught.

The soft sound of whimpering pulled him away from his thoughts, and back to the shack's interior. He looked over to Wendy. Her hand was flat over her eyes, blocking then from his view. They'd both had time to gather their emotions, and Jake figured she was just now letting it sink in that Gary had been killed. He hadn't known the guy all that long, but even he was affected by his death. He imagined that Wendy was crushed.

"I really did love him you know…"

"I'm sure you did." He tried to imagine himself in a similar situation with Shannon, but it was almost impossible. Wendy loved Gary but Jake wasn't sure if he truly *loved* Shannon. He cared about her, sure, but he wasn't convinced it was really love.

"I just couldn't show it. I wanted to but didn't know. It wasn't something I was raised in. I wish I just would have told him more that I cared."

Jake nodded but remained silent. He really didn't know what to say.

"And now, I'm probably going to die in this goddamn shack. You were right, we should have just kept running. Maybe we could have gotten to the cars, but even if we didn't make it, dying out there doesn't seem as bad as dying in here." She sobbed some more.

He wanted to hold her.

Should he try?

What would she think if he walked over there, took her in his arms, and held her? Would she think he was making a move?

Am *I making a move?*

Of, course not. She's scared, I'm scared, and it's a natural reaction to hug, to console each other. Plus, she could use one.

Jake had to admit, he could also use a hug, to feel arms holding him in a tender cuddle. He gulped, much louder than he'd expected, and slowly walked over to her. She lowered her hands as he approached. Tapped with tears, her eyes were shiny, spilling creeks of salty warmth down her cheeks.

Her eyes were a lovely set. Jake's chest caved just looking at them. It was no wonder Gary couldn't pull himself away from her. She was hauntingly gorgeous.

As she backhanded her tears, she forced a smile. "I bet I look a mess, huh?"

Afraid his voice might betray him and go shrill, he only shook his head. He took hold of her by the hips and her eyes flashed down to his hands. The glance was so fast, he considered removing them, but he didn't. Her eyes returned to his, confused at first, but then they began to warm. He felt a tepid tremor of stimulation lope through him.

Soon, her eyes were sparkling, but then she closed them, and he could no longer see their worldly gaze.

She stepped into his hug.

Slowly, he glided his hands up her back, rubbing her tense muscles, then wrapped his arms around her. The knife was still in his left hand, but he was careful to keep the blade pointed away. He raised his other hand to the nape of her neck and massaged it. Her head fell against his shoulder, giving in to his touch. Her breasts pressed against his chest, and he could feel their plump shapes through his shirt.

A reaction occurred in his shorts as she nestled tightly against him. He was terrified that she would feel him hardening against her. Hell, she probably already had. But what else was he to do? He didn't want to stop holding her. It felt good, in such a chaotic time as this, to have just one pleasant moment.

Wendy curved her leg around his, her sandal dropping off her foot. Her bare foot rubbed up and down his calf muscle. The unclad skin felt warm and soft on his exposed leg. He knew she was in a vulnerable state, and this hug and whatever else that might possibly follow was thanks only to the confusion, hurt and unabated loneliness she must be feeling. He was using her, and he was pretty sure she was using him. This might be her final contact with a man.

Jake didn't care.

She tipped her head back and licked her moist and juicy lips, staring at him like an anxious girl begging to be kissed on her first date.

She's cashing in her pity card. She'll resent you later, but right now, you're all she has.

It was a self-diminishing thought, but a true one. He swallowed the thick lump in the back of his throat. His heart drummed so rapidly he feared it would burst and kill him before he kissed this woman.

Woman.

Kissed this *woman*. Wendy was a grown woman, not some college girl. She was mature and not confused about who she was.

Not like Shannon.

Pushing his guilt aside, he lowered his head. His lips pressed against Wendy's welcoming mouth. Her tongue forced its way into his mouth. His hardness pushed like iron against her stomach. He was afraid he might skewer her. She writhed against him. He slid his empty hand down her back and under the band of her shorts. He felt the silky firmness of her rump and squeezed. She gasped in his mouth. Her breath was warm.

Then the pile of junk beside them launched open.

A bush carrying a scythe crawled out of the homemade trap door as it dropped over on the floor with a loud crash. The bush was a disguise, and it worked. Wendy pulled away from him. He stepped in front her, still feeling the tingle of her lips on his. Jake wanted to slap himself for not checking the pile thoroughly. He'd focused his attention on Wendy instead of securing their hiding spot like he should have done.

Some hero. Way to fuck this one up. Too busy copping a feel like the worthless shit that you are.

It had been a trap all along.

During the commotion, he'd nearly forgotten about his knife. As the bush swung the scythe at him, he bent back, just avoiding the slash, and brought his knife up in a blind strike. He wasn't expecting to actually stab the thing, but he hoped at least to scare it enough that he'd get the chance to move in for an accurate blow.

Instead, and much to his astonishment, the blade slammed deep into the bush, embedding itself where a head should be. Jake hoisted the knife and the impaled creature into the air where it dangled like a piñata. He doubted it weighed even twenty pounds.

The shrub convulsed, writhed, and then finally doubled over. Runnels of red spurted out from under the leaves, dousing Jake's arm with sticky heat. He tilted his knife down, letting the limp hedge slide off the blade. It thudded when it hit the floor.

Jake crouched over the immobile shrub.

"No!" cried Wendy. "Don't touch it."

"I think it's dead."

"How can you be sure?" She hopped to her shoe and slipped it back on.

"I don't think a bush bleeds." He gripped the top of the bush and pulled it free from the rest. Holding a hood treated with leaves and twigs, he realized it was actually no more than a mask. He tossed it over to Wendy so she could study it too. "It's camouflage."

She looked confused at first. Then her face smoothed out as she grasped what he was telling her. "Something's wearing these?"

"Yeah, something like this." He stood up and pointed down at the dead mini-human with his knife.

Wendy gasped.

Jake's knife had punched under its chin, going straight up through the mouth.

It looked as if he'd slaughtered a two-year-old child. Once Jake studied it more closely, he noticed the stubby, crescent shape of its head, which reminded him of the old dolls his mother collected. It appeared male, with a thin beard, scraggly hair, some stress lines, and even crow's feet around the eyes.

"Looks like a shrunken old man," Jake said.

The arms tapering out from the leaf suit were as thin as pencils, and although he couldn't see its legs, Jake imagined they were probably similar.

"A dwarf?" asked Wendy.

"Even smaller than that."

The shack thundered. The walls shook.

Wendy, screaming louder with each quake, staggered around out of balance. It seemed as if a giant was pounding on the door.

Jake dashed by her to an opened space in the wall. He peeked out. What he saw was a line of them, twelve easy, using a cut log like a battering ram. In unison, they revved back and then ran forward, smashing the lumber against the decrepit door. It wouldn't be long before it was battered down.

"They're trying to bash in the door!"

Wendy shook her head. "I can't be in here. I've got to get out of here!"

He started to remind her it was her idea that had put them in here to begin with but stopped as he thought of another way out.

The ceiling.

"If I hoist you up through the roof, can you get back to the cars on your own?"

"I'm not going out there by myself!" She stepped backward, shaking her head, then dropped down out of sight as if the floor had opened its mouth and swallowed her.

"Wendy!" He ran away from the door as it splintered apart. Their feeble barricade of rotted wood was now all that kept it braced.

Jake stood over the trap door. Looking down, he saw a vast hollow of black like a hole to the center of the earth.

He shouted, "Wendy!"

She leaped out of the blackness and grabbed his leg. He screamed in alarm, his bladder nearly emptying itself.

"Come on!" she shouted. "It's a tunnel."

"Underground?"

"Yeah, looks like it goes straight. There's more that crisscross in other directions. It's our only chance!"

If they ran into those things down there, that would be it for them. He wanted to be down there even less than he wanted to stay in the shack. But Wendy's pleading eyes made the decision for him.

He followed her down.

STEVE

Gary's Jeep had been razed. The windshield was smashed and both doors were hanging open. The suitcases were strewn about in severed portions, and articles of clothing had been scattered over the ground like litter left on a highway. There wasn't a tire that hadn't been flattened, the rubber left hanging like ribbons around the rims.

Steve's spine felt like it was being scoured with icy nails. It took his breath. Unable to run from the pain in his back, he bent over, putting his hands on his knees, and tried to catch his breath. He was close to shock, and he knew it. If only he could get his heartbeat to slow down.

As he neared Gary's mangled Jeep, he hoped to God that his own car was unscathed. He'd had the best intentions in coming to get the car. By the time they got here, he'd have it cranked, and backed up to the edge of the sand with the doors open, ready to peel out once they got inside. He was thinking ahead. Better than what they were doing, which was nothing but panicking. He was on to phase two while they still struggled with phase one.

They'd thank him for it later.

Yeah, right.

He remembered the look Mary had given him before he ran away.

Left. He'd left, not run away.

The expression on her face read of desertion and disdain. It haunted him. Steve hoped it wouldn't be his last memory of her sweet face. He suddenly felt sick to his stomach. Even if he saved them all, Mary would never look at him the same again. He would be the coward who had retreated and deserted them when they needed him to stay and fight.

She knew what I was when she started dating me. I like computers and video games. I hate sports for Christ's sake. I've never been a person to welcome confrontation. This shouldn't surprise her at all.

Steve stood up straight.

His stomach felt better. It wasn't cramping nearly as bad. He couldn't decide if it was him growing comfortable with the guilt or knowing that he'd be able to live with it no matter what Mary thought of him.

"I can handle it," he muttered.

If they survived this, she could look at him however she wanted. He couldn't care less.

When he stepped around the rear of Gary's demolished Jeep, he discovered that the condition of his car was not as bad as Gary's… It was even worse. The windows had been smashed from front to back and the tires had been slashed, torn and shredded. The body was dented and crinkled, which he assumed had been done by someone kicking it. Someone small. Everything, except for what Mary took with her on her back, had been scattered about the shoreline.

Steve walked over to the trunk. The lid had been left open, and the interior rummaged clean. Nothing had been spared, not even the tire jack or the tire iron. The only things in the car he could have used as a weapon were gone, stolen by whatever it was that had been coming after them.

How many are there? He thought about it. *More of them than there are of us.*

Those odds did not bode well for them. They needed to get as far away from this place as possible, and fast. He turned around and gazed at the woods. From where he stood, he couldn't see much. It was at least a hundred yards to the woods, and he would have to walk back there before he could see if anyone was left to save. And by doing that, he may come across more of those things.

He shuddered, recalling how Amy had been pulled under the ground and the fearful look in her eyes. He did not want that happening to him. He'd wait. But if no one showed up in five minutes, he was leaving. He'd drive his car on the rims if he needed to, let them take him as far as they could. When they couldn't go any farther, he would walk, and be damn sure he stuck to the main road.

Steve searched the ground for a heavy rock or a thick stick that he could use to defend himself. There wasn't much to choose from. All the rocks were either too small to do any real damage, or too big to lift. What sticks he found were thin, and barely long enough to hold.

He was screwed.

Steve groaned. His heart didn't seem to be beating, and his stomach was bubbling from his anxiety. He wondered if he was having a heart attack. There was great pain in his right arm, his vision was blurring, and the landscape seemed to be rocking back and forth.

He lurched to the car and leaned against it. He stared at the ground, taking deep breaths to give his head time to clear.

How am I going to get out of here if I can't see straight?

Steve wanted to cry. He had not felt this helpless since he was nine years old, when he'd had nightmares about monsters under his bed. He would wake in the middle of the night crying for Mama or Daddy or both, but usually he begged for Mama. Those few seconds seemed like hours, waiting for one of his parents to rush into his room while he shivered completely helpless under the sheets. He hoped someone would come save him now, but this time he could only do it for himself. Mama had passed away, and Daddy was in Vermont with a girl only three years older than Steve. They surely wouldn't be coming to his aid anytime soon.

Trapped on his bed in the dark all those years ago, he'd only *felt* alone, but out here in the luscious countryside of Wisconsin, having left his friends and the girl he loved behind, he was *truly* alone.

The grip he felt on his ankles was firm and the jerking motion was quick.

His feet went out from under him as something wrenched them under the car. The ground came up to meet him so fast he didn't have a chance to catch himself. His body smacked the solid ground, knocking the breath out of him. Steve clawed and scraped at the ground as he was dragged under the car by a pack of little hands that slapped and pawed him. One hand slipped under his shorts, between his buttocks and probed at his anus as they searched for anything to latch on to. The fingers tore through the seat of his shorts and found the small hole to penetrate. It clutched, and then pulled.

Steve screamed for his mama.

MARY

Mary and Shannon waited for Steve to come back with the car.

He never did.

The rumble in the woods had calmed to an eerie serenity, but Mary assumed it was only a temporary break from the carnage.

She saw the ground moving again, and then the sand parted, caving in on top of itself. A large figure emerged from beneath. Mary pulled back, burying herself in Shannon's arms. She knew she should run, but her legs didn't want to move.

The figure, browned with dirt, collapsed onto the ground in front of them, gasping for air. Sand rained off his body like a powdery storm.

"Help me guys," he said.

Mary recognized the voice, although who it had come from looked like a creature from deep within the earth.

"I've got to pull Wendy out."

It was Jake!

"You made it?" Shannon sounded surprised.

As was Mary. She'd almost given up on him.

"I did, but Wendy won't if we don't pull her out."

"How did you get under there?"

"It's a long story, help me get her."

Shannon crawled to the sand pit, kneeled beside Jake, and dug her hands into the sand, mimicking his movements. They delved down deeper until they excavated Wendy from the ground. Dirtied like an ancient relic, she looked even worse than Jake. Her eyes were crusted shut from a combination of sweat, tears, and sand. Her hair, matted with grime, clung to her head in a nappy mess.

Jake turned to Shannon. "Get the water out of Mary's bag, we've gotta wash this shit out of her eyes."

As Shannon dug out a bottle of water, Mary informed Jake and Wendy about what had transpired in their absence and Jake chimed in with bits of information on their escape. He was using the bottle of water to rinse out Wendy's eyes when Mary let him know about Amy.

"Pulled under?" he repeated, his face wincing as if it hurt him to ask.

"Right from where you two crawled out of. Did you see her?"

Jake shook his head. "No, we didn't. But there are tunnels going every which way like fucking burrows. They could've taken her through any of them."

Attack of the mole people, thought Mary. It would have been funny had it not been so damn scary.

"Hard to breathe under there too," said Wendy.

Jake nodded, agreeing with her. To Mary, he asked, "And Steve just took off? Leaving you two alone?"

Mary nodded.

"I wonder where the bastard's at now."

Sitting on the shore caressing her hurt arm, Mary realized she hadn't wondered that herself. Claiming he was only getting the car, a job that should have taken two minutes tops, he'd actually be gone longer than ten.

Either he'd bailed, or he was dead.

Mary grimaced.

Noticing, Jake said, "Do you think he's all right?"

"I don't know," she said.

"What should we do?" said Wendy. Now that her eyes were clean, they beamed with worry. "Should we go to the cars, or should we look for Amy?"

"I vote the cars," said Shannon. "I mean, Steve could be there waiting for us."

"Or he could've fled," said Jake. "I never would have taken him for such a spineless douche bag."

Neither would I, thought Mary, but said, "He was scared."

"We *all* are!" Jake shouted.

Mary flinched at his voice.

Taking a deep, steadying breath, he said, "I'm sorry, I shouldn't have yelled like that. What I mean is, we're all scared, but none of us are doing what he did."

"Some people handle it better than others," said Mary.

"Then I must be handling it peachy-keen." On that note, Jake walked over to the sand patch and stomped his foot on it. It clanged. Metal. A trap door. He whipped his head around, spotted a large rock nearby, and went to it. He hunched over it and pushed.

The heavy stone didn't budge.

"What are you doing?" asked Mary.

"Making sure this thing stays closed tight. I don't want more of them coming out and surprising us."

Wendy joined him.

With her help, he was able to roll it over to the trap door and position it on top.

"Where are they now?" asked Shannon.

"The ones that shot me," said Mary, "must've taken off in the woods."

Huffing, Wendy said, "Probably looking for us."

"Yeah," Jake agreed. "I don't think they were expecting us to find their tunnels, but we did. I'm guessing they shot Mary to immobilize her until they could get back. They must want her alive for some reason."

"Me too," said Shannon. "They left me alone."

"You're probably right," Jake agreed.

"Perfect," said Wendy. "And I lost my gun in the woods."

"What happened to Amy's?" said Jake.

No one seemed to have a clue. They just stared at each other dumbly, waiting for someone to answer.

"Well, we've got my knife."

Wendy laughed. "Wow, one knife against an army of those fuckers!"

"It's done a good job, so far."

Wendy shrugged, "Yeah, but it can't save us every time."

Nodding, he said, "I know. I wish we had Amy's gun."

Leaning up, Mary said, "She must've had it on her, when…" Her lip trembled and her eyes drenched up.

Shannon put an arm around Mary, and said, "It's okay."

It felt good having Shannon so close, even if her words did little to comfort her. "No, it's not. I let her go."

"You had to, just look at your hand and your shoulder."

As if to remind her that she'd been injured, her body shot quick jolts of pain to her brain. She winced and pulled away. Holding her hand, she sighed. "It's hurting again."

"How about your shoulder?" said Wendy.

"It's not so bad."

"It can still get infected." Jake groaned. "Let's get to the cars. I might have an old shirt to bandage it with."

"Those vet classes are paying off," said Mary, smiling.

"Shit, they better. They're costing my folks a shitload of money."

Wendy snickered. "I never would have pictured you as a lover of animals."

"I'm a lover of everything."

His joke caused a much-needed laugh from all of them. They continued to guffaw, not wanting it to end. When it actually did, they would be right back to where they had been all this time.

In danger with their lives on the line.

Shannon helped Mary to her feet. Jake was the first to move. They followed behind him with Wendy trotting by his side. Every so often, one of the group would glance back, expecting for something to leap out at them at any moment.

IN nothing but her shorts and bra, Mary crouched in the nippy lake water. Jake used handfuls of water to rinse the wound and then squirted dabs of hand sanitizer in the hole on her shoulder. It burned like acid. Mary gritted her teeth to keep from screaming. He tore off a piece of his old Napalm Death T-shirt and folded it into a pad. Then he tore another strip and used that to tie the jerry-rigged gauze on her shoulder.

Her hand was much easier to treat. After the sanitizer, he tore off another strip of shirt, looping it around her hand several times, and knotted it on top. It wasn't too tight, but tight enough so it wouldn't fall off. The incessant blood had turned to a trickle but hadn't stopped completely.

"Thanks," she said.

"Don't mention it," he told her, and smiled.

Nice guy. All this time, Mary had him pinned as a jackass, when in reality, Steve was actually the jackass. She resented Shannon a little for that. She really had a good, completely decent guy here. When push came to shove, he'd shoved with force. She hoped Shannon realized that Jake was a catch, and she'd better not let him slip through her fingers. *How'd she end up with a guy like him anyway?* Mary could feel the hot coals of jealousy on her neck.

"Your shirt's hanging out of my back pocket. I'll turn around so you can get it and put it on."

"Thank you, Jake, again."

"Oh–and don't worry, I won't peek. Too much." He winked. Then he turned around. She was glad he couldn't see her cheesy smile because it was inappropriate in a time like this.

And why was he looking away now? He must have gotten a good look already.

That was different. He was helping me, now he's being a polite gentleman by not gawking. Just another side of Jake that she'd never realized existed. She had been so wrong about him. Mary kind of hoped he would sneak a peek, and then she felt her skin scorching with a blush.

Hanging out of his back pocket was her tank top, the one she had been so nervous to wear at the club the night before. Seeing it there, crumpled in his pocket like an oil rag, she wondered what had been so lurid about the garment to start with. Why had Steve been unable to keep his eyes and hands off her? Sure, it had felt good knowing that last night, but now it made her feel cheap. She stretched out the shirt and then rolled it up in her hands. Surprisingly, the bandage didn't get in the way; it hardly hurt her at all to use the damaged hand. She pulled the shirt on, and then straightened it. It didn't look as stunning as last night, but it still clung to her breasts.

Her mind kept returning to Steve, wondering what had happened to him and why he wasn't there. An image of him being sucked under the earth like Amy flashed in her mind. If she wanted to be honest with herself, she could figure out what had happened to him—they all could—but none of them were willing to say much about it. It was as if they didn't want to know the truth, because that would mean they were down another person.

When they got to the cars, they found them wrecked, smashed and battered, but Steve wasn't there, and there wasn't a sign he ever had been. All Mary could find were hundreds of petite footprints.

They were too small to be from adults. They were infant-sized, maybe a bit larger, but not by much. The footprints in the dirt reminded Mary of the plaster cast of her foot that her mother kept on the mantle back home. She'd had it made when she was just six months old and had kept it proudly displayed on their mantel, making sure to tell all her friends the story of how Mary pooped so much during the process that it had leaked out the sides of her diaper.

She'd even told Steve that story, and he'd laughed so hard it brought tears to his eyes. *Jerk.* They were just friends then, nowhere near what they would eventually become, but that didn't matter. He'd laughed at her, and she'd been more embarrassed than she ever had been. Steve was supposed to have been special. It angered her that her mother told him that story, but it angered her even more that he'd found it so funny. Now he was gone, so Mom would have to tell the story to someone else someday.

And she'd have to relive that mortification all over again.

Then she wondered if she'd ever get to hear the story again at all.

Jake groaned, exhaustion clear in his tone. "We better see if we can salvage anything."

Nodding, Mary said, "Okay." She stared off, her body there, but her mind was roaming far away.

"You all right?" he asked.

Mary nodded. "Okay."

"I need you to stay strong with me, Mary."

"Huh?" She blinked rapidly, trying to bring herself back to the lake.

"I said I need you to stay strong with me."

She turned around. Looking up at him, he stared down at her with his piercing, green eyes. They were weighty and intelligent.

"Wendy is doing all right for now, but who knows how long that'll last? And Shannon, she'll break down at any moment. But not you. You're tougher than them. I'm keeping a decently level head about all of this shit, but it might not last. I know you can do better than me."

"I'm trying, Jake. It's just all so fucked up."

"You're doing fine, and I need you to keep it that way. You've got to have my back, because no one else will. And if God forbid, I lose *my* shit, you'll have to pick it up for me."

He was right. No one else was reliable enough to handle all that. Especially not Shannon. At school she had a tougher than nails attitude toward life and most people found Shannon intimidating, but Mary knew the truth. She was just as frightened of herself as the others at school were of her. She wondered if Jake had any idea of Shannon's feelings for her.

Probably. He's smart. Wouldn't take much for him to figure it out.

And if not, it was not her place to tell him.

I do have to have his back, she realized. *I think he's saved my butt twice now.*

"I've got your back," she said.

"You promise?"

"Cross my heart."

"Coming from you," he said, "I believe it."

It felt good hearing him say that. She wondered if her face was turning red from the rush of heat fluttering through her body.

"Come on," he said, holding out his hand.

Taking it, they walked out of the water together. It splashed against her bare legs, the coldness of the water a welcomed chill from the heat. They held hands back to the cars.

When Shannon saw them, her face wrinkled. "All better?"

"For now," he said. "Those dressings aren't exactly what I call a health standard."

Shannon nodded. Mary could read behind her masquerading act that she was furious they'd been holding hands, then she realized they still were and quickly snatched her hand back. Jake hardly seemed to notice.

"What do we do now?" said Wendy.

Jake scraped his bottom lip across his teeth and shrugged. "We've got to try and find some help. A house. Or maybe go to the road and see if we can flag down a car, or something."

"Look where we are. I doubt there are many houses." There was whine in her voice.

"And," said Shannon, "we all saw that town and how it was abandoned. What if all the houses and towns around here are like that?"

Wendy sighed. Obviously, the thought hadn't crossed her mind, but now she looked smothered by it.

"Then we stick to the road," said Jake.

"No, I don't think that's a good idea either," said Shannon. "They're probably watching the roads."

"Good point," said Jake. "They knew we were here."

"They're probably watching us right now," Wendy added.

No one said it, but Mary was sure that they all agreed.

"That doesn't leave us very many options," said Mary.

Another pint-sized arrow whisked past her head, tussling her hair before it slammed into Steve's car just above the rear windshield.

They all yelped as one.

Turning around, Mary saw a pack of little bushes charging out from the woods, a throng of miniscule warriors running wildly and screaming. Mary realized that they were dressed in rags dyed green and brown. Leaves had been attached to the burlap. Since they were so tiny in size, she understood why she had thought that they were bundles of foliage.

The men, if one could call them that, were no taller than a two-year-old and skinny and frail. Some were holding miniature spears over their heads, ready to throw them. Two stopped running. One of them held a bow loaded with an arrow. The other was pulling an arrow out of a bag on his back to load into his empty bow.

He must have fired the last shot.

And missed.

He wouldn't miss again.

"Get in the water!"

From the squeals and shrieks coming from Wendy and Shannon, Mary had hardly heard Jake's order. She turned around. Jake was dragging Shannon by the arm, struggling to get her in the lake. Wendy darted past them not bothering to wait, and probably not caring to either.

Shannon fought Jake, pleading him not to make her.

"It's the only way," he yelled. "Maybe they can't swim!"

Yeah, right. Mary was sure they could. There might be more of them in the water, treading below the surface ready to snatch them by the ankles and pull them under. Maybe that was the plan. She realized if she kept standing there she'd never know, because she would surely get struck by another arrow. She ran to Jake, ready to assist him with Shannon. "Come on Shannon, it's all we have left. The water or them!" She pointed to the stampeding brownies with bloodthirsty eyes and foam dripping from their mouths.

Mary ran to the edge. The water splashed her feet. She debated leaving her shoes, but figured she'd need them later. If there was a later. She checked on Jake.

He wasn't any farther along with Shannon. The munchkins from hell were going to get them for sure if they didn't hurry.

They're so skinny. They look like they're starving. She realized they probably were. She'd rescued a few starved and abused animals in her day, but they had never looked as famished as these little things.

Jake's shouts cut through her thoughts. "If we stay here, we're dead. At least in the water we have a chance."

"A chance to what? Drown?"

The munchkins hooted and howled like leprechauns finding gold. They were much closer now. The two lagging behind shot their arrows high into the air. Mary watched them soar. She felt herself shrink inside as they rose higher and, as if gravity jerked the wind out from under them, they suddenly plummeted.

They'd over-shot her, Jake and Shannon. She turned around and saw Wendy treading water, waiting for them. The arrows were about to rain from the sky right above her.

Wendy!

"Look out!" Mary called.

Wendy looked up, spotting the plunging arrows. Screaming, she quickly ducked under water. Her feet shot up, kicking the air as she plummeted under. The arrows struck the water where her feet had just been, barely making a splash and went under after her. The water bubbled and rippled, then smoothed out. Mary was certain that any moment she would see Wendy's lifeless body floating to the top, face down, arms and legs straight out.

Two arrows in her back.

The dead man's float.

The minuscule men were very close now. Their lank legs were small, not allowing them a large running span. Thank God. If they were able to move any faster, they'd all be dead by now.

Mary could see their faces plainly—grimy, smudged and filthy. They looked as if they hadn't bathed in a long time. Snarling, she saw that their teeth were yellow and brown.

Mary felt like she was being pulled in three directions. One was to the water and swimming, getting as far away from the shore that she could. She also wanted to make sure Wendy was all right and knew that was where she *needed* to be. Where she *wanted* to be, though, was with Jake and making Shannon get in the damn water. She remembered Shannon wasn't a very good swimmer. She could, but just not well. In the pool at school, Shannon always stuck to the shallow end. If she trudged to the deep side, she'd use the pool walls for assistance. She wasn't confident enough in her ability to swim without at least some kind of support.

Finally, Jake scooped her off the ground, obviously tired of fighting with her, and threw over his shoulder. He hauled Shannon like a wounded soldier as he sprinted for the water. He looked at Mary and yelled, "Go!"

Mary was running too. She was knee-deep in the lake before realizing it. Farther out, something bobbed up and down, waving at them. Wrinkles of sunlight sparkled off the rippling water made the lake look as if it was glowing. She couldn't make out who or what it was waiting for them.

One of them?

Jake galumphed into the water, not slowing down as the water climbed up his body. As it wrapped around his chest, he grabbed Shannon and heaved her forward. She landed on her back with a huge splash.

What are they doing? Don't they see what's waiting for us?

Mary wanted to shout a warning, but the wet turf slid out from under her. She lost balance and crashed. The cold water that sheathed around her was agonizing at first, but it quickly became tolerable.

She looked back at their pursuers. They had climbed to the roofs of the cars. Mary saw them just as they chucked spears into the air. The spears fell short of her. The arrow men darted around to the front of the car and knelt. Mirroring each other, they both produced more arrows from the sacks draped over their backs. A scrim strap came down their chest and knotted around a rope that was being used as a belt for their burlap pants.

Something in the water or not, she had to swim. Those arrows would have no trouble hitting her. She wasn't far enough out yet to be safe.

Jake was up ahead, one arm wrapped around Shannon, lugging her like a drowned cadaver. She was gawking at Mary, eyes wide and blank.

"Come on guys!" The voice came from a female waiting for them up ahead.

The rippling water cast the sun's blinding glimmer in Mary's eyes, but Mary knew that voice. It was Wendy. Those arrows didn't get her after all. She was alive and safe, trying to guide them.

An arrow splashed the water ahead of Mary. Another grazed her left shoulder, leaving behind a tight, red line before it spiraled in front of her, skipping across the water like a flat stone. The slice wasn't as bad as the others, but it stung like hell. It slowed her down, but it didn't kill her, for which she was grateful.

We're going to make it.

Wendy pointed at the opposite shore. "A cornfield! We can go in there!" She paddled, leading them to the other side.

PIPER

Piper opened his eyes. Everything was fuzzy and it took some time to adjust. How long had he been out? He'd conked out again in the woods while being dragged, so he had no idea where they'd taken him. One thing he noticed right away was his position. Cramped. Scrunched up. Hugging his knees, his head was pressed into the fold between his thighs. He wanted to straighten his legs but couldn't. There was also pressure against his arms. Walls? No, too flimsy to be walls. Nudging it with his elbow, it moved, but not much. He struck it harder. It clamored, vibrated. He raised his eyes, peeking over his doubled forearms.

Some type of cage.

Oval at the top, it curved down to the ground where it had been crudely buried and cemented. Actually, it looked as if the *cement* was really just hardened sand. Whatever it was, it did the trick. The contraption had been set up like a large bird cage and constructed out of some wire-like mesh and what looked to be cornstalks tied together to make bulky beams. Not a cage exactly, but more like a kennel or a coop. That was more like it. A coop.

And it had been designed for someone much smaller than him.

It reeked out here, smelling of rotten food, decaying meat and something else. *Urine?* It was stale, but potent enough to aggravate his sinuses.

Paper lanterns dangled from the nearby trees, illuminating small puddles of light in a flushed ellipse throughout the heavily shaded area.

He looked around the best he could, although he couldn't move his head much, but the minimal amount of freedom allowed him to locate other cages like his spread out and around. Unlike his own, they looked empty.

Except for one.

Amy.

Rage crushed down on him harder than the unyielding beams of his coop. He wiggled but couldn't move an inch. There was no escaping his coop. It didn't appear to be reinforced very well, but the way he was folded up inside of it, he couldn't get the leverage he needed to break out.

Piper wanted to break down the coop and grip his hands around Amy's throat but could only sit and yearn about it. He scanned the other cages—those he could see—but didn't spot Gary. Could he be dead? Piper assumed that he was, or he'd probably have been locked up too. He smiled, though he felt a pang of regret that he wasn't the one who'd ended Gary's life.

"You're awake now?"

Piper cringed at the sound of Amy's voice. "Figured that out, huh?"

"You bastard. This is all your fault."

He wished he could grab her. "How do you figure that?"

"I left to get away from *you* and this happened to us. Gary's dead because of *you*."

"So, they did get him?"

She was silent for a moment. "Yes."

There was so much hatred in her voice. He wanted to find it amusing but couldn't.

"Well…" Piper didn't really know what else to say about Gary, so he opted to change the subject. "Have they been back since locking us up?"

"No."

Great. The one-word treatment. Whenever she was angry with him at home, she punished him with her one-word responses. He hated them then, and he really hated them now.

"Any idea why they didn't kill us too?" he asked.

"I have no idea…but I wish they had."

"You wish you were dead?"

"Me?" More silence. "I don't know. You? Definitely."

"You've always been such a whiny bitch, Amy. And if all of this *is* my fault, then I'm fucking flattered."

"Bastard." Her voice had lost its edge.

He'd done it again. Even locked up like this he'd succeeded in mentally crushing her. Not that it was ever a hard thing to do, but this time it had been too easy. He didn't feel the same satisfaction he usually did.

How he wished he could have seen Gary being killed. He'd probably gone down screaming and crying. Yes, he was envious, but it was also one less body he'd have to worry about, which was good. If he played his cards right, he could use this unexpected twist to his advantage. Blame whoever had gotten Gary for what he'd planned to do to the others.

It was a sign from above.

Someone up there was looking out for him after all.

Those kids would have to die too. They'd interfered. Especially that blonde. What was her name? Shannon? He couldn't exactly remember. The ache in his head was making it harder to concentrate, but he couldn't forget how she had teased him. The philandering whore would suffer before he finally allowed her to die.

At least he had survived the ambush in the woods. *Why did they let me live?* Apprehension sputtered in Piper's gut as several reasons trampled around in his head, none of which were good thoughts.

From somewhere out in the corn or surrounding woods came a distant chatter, more like a cackle. His back went taut as if being twisted by icy hands. The hints of fear fluttered into full-blown dread, and for the first time in years, goose bumps pimpled up his arms.

Piper couldn't even remember the last time he'd ever been scared, and now he was absolutely terrified.

MARY

Mary crawled out of the water, and collapsed onto her stomach, her panting breaths puffing the sand. Her hand throbbed. Her shoulder radiated sharp jolts of pain into her chest from under the provisional bandage. She didn't care, though. She was alive. She looked over her shoulder. Where they'd left the cars looked to be miles away. She couldn't believe how far they'd swam. It was a miracle they'd made it across the lake. The need to live had been the perfect motivational tool to keep her going.

Now, she was exhausted and didn't think she'd ever be able to move again.

Wendy lay on her side, her wet hair plastered across her face like a drenched rag. Her breaths came out in heavy huffs.

Shannon sat cross-legged on the sand staring across the lake to the other side. She'd informed them the munchkins had stood by the cars, watching them until just recently. Shannon hadn't given them any new updates after informing the others that the munchkins had left.

Jake was the only one standing. His soused shirt draped heavily on his shoulders. Mary watched him as he checked that he still had his knife—he did—and began to pace. He dug into his sagging shorts and hauled out his cigarettes. They were ruined.

"Shit," he said, turning the pack upside down. Water chugged out from it like a jug. He dropped them and stomped the soaked pack into the sand.

Shannon looked back at him, her face wrinkling. "Can't smoke them?"

"Nope." Jake said.

Slapping the sand like a kid ready to pitch a fit, Shannon said, "Is anything going to go right for us?"

"I have some in my bag," said Mary. She pointed with her thumb over her shoulder.

"Bag?" asked Jake.

"On my back."

"You don't have a bag on your back."

"Yes, I do."

"Trust me, you don't."

Sitting up, she reached behind her, frantically feeling nothing but slick skin between the straps of her tank top. Jake was right. There wasn't a bag there. It must have slipped off during their getaway and was probably at the bottom of the lake by now.

"Goddammit." Mary felt defeated. She grabbed handfuls of her hair, wanting to scream.

Shannon began to cry.

"It's okay," said Jake. "They'd only slow us down. Our lungs need to be as clean as possible. I imagine we'll be doing a lot more running."

"No more running," murmured Wendy. Grits of sand stuck to her lips like flaky lipstick. She pushed herself up to a sitting stance and sighed.

Jake swatted at a mosquito and said, "I don't like it any more than you do."

"I'm done." She wiped her mouth with the back of her hand. It did nothing to clean it, and only added the sand that was on her hand to her lips. She grimaced, spitting what she could out of her mouth.

"All right," said Jake. "Let's get moving. We'll *walk* through the corn. For now, anyway." No one disputed the idea, but Jake was quick to add, "We have to keep moving or our muscles will stiffen up."

The girls groaned, but slowly began to stand. Mary first, then Shannon, with Wendy coming up last.

"This cornfield has to lead us somewhere, maybe to a road, or even a house. We'll go through, get some help, and some damn cigarettes. Sound good?"

The girls didn't agree or disagree. They simply followed him when he said, "Let's go."

The corn stalks towered over them, concealing their position from any plane or helicopter that could be looking. That worried Mary a bit. They'd have no way of attempting to flag one down for help.

The field reeked of dead corn. The dried, fragile leaves rubbed against Mary's arms as she walked through the narrow paths between the rows, causing her to itch all over. Also, her nose was running and not just from the tears. When she pushed through the stalks, a visible cloud of pollen was freed from under the ears. She inhaled them as she walked.

She could even taste it.

Enveloped by the abyss of corn, the rest of the world seemed fictional. The stalks' thicknesses choked off all outside sound. She could hear the others' breaths as if they were her own. Mary remembered summers at Grandma's, picking and shucking corn as a kid. The fields had scared her then too. She was always afraid something would come out of the shadows and snatch her. A few times, she thought she'd heard something following her, creeping close to her as she ventured deeper into the fields. The difference was that back then, there wasn't any real threat, no real danger except maybe of the reptilian, slithering variety. Monsters hadn't been stalking her in Grandma's cornfield, and they definitely hadn't been waiting to gobble her up.

But now, the imaginary threat she had felt as a kid had become all too real. There *were* things that go bump in the night. Unexplainable creatures *did* exist. And most importantly, there *were* things out there that wanted to gobble her up.

Parents spent half their lives convincing their children that there wasn't really anything evil lurking out there. That nothing prowled in the shadows, lying in wait for the right moment to attack.

Mary wondered how parents could be so naïve.

Disoriented by her thoughts, she hadn't noticed that the line in front of her had stalled until she bumped into the back of Wendy, who whipped her head around, scowling.

"Sorry," she whispered at the girl rubbernecking her way.

Wendy raised a finger to her lips. The fear in her eyes was wide.

Mary mouthed, "What is it?"

Shaking her head, Wendy pointed at Jake. He stood at the front of the line with both arms straight out to block them from moving forward. His head was raised and canted to one side. Mary suspected that he had an ear pointed at the sky so he could listen better. She wondered how he'd been able to hear anything at all in this damn deafening corn. He turned his head to the other side, repeating the tilt and lift, then he slowly lowered his head and faced them. His eyes were wide and round, and his lips were pressed so tight they didn't seem to be there at all.

Behind Mary came the scurrying of little feet.

Fear snagged in her throat. Slowly, she stole a peek over her shoulder.

Two of them crossed the path in a jog, coming from separate isles of corn. They disappeared into the opposite sides. Mary was reminded of Scooby-Doo cartoons, when the monster would be chasing the gang and they'd cross paths in the ghostly hallway of some old mansion.

"Run!" Jake shouted.

No one moved, not at first.

"*Run!*"

This second outburst flicked an ignition switch inside of them all. They dashed past Jake. He chased after them through the corn.

Mary glanced back, seeing Jake brandishing his knife. There were brown stains that looked to be blood spattered along the blade. From his left, one lunged from the neighboring rows and latched onto his leg.

Jake planted the blade through the top of its burlap hood. As he ripped the knife free a line of red fluid came with it. The miniature body dropped off, its lifeless carcass rolling and bouncing along the dirt. Jake didn't stop to admire his work.

Mary had slowed to watch, but now she was moving again. Jake neared, his long legs making great distance in their extended strides. He grabbed her wrist as he passed, towing her.

Something screeched. Or *Some things.* Plural. Their cries reverberated all around them. Mary flinched. The stench of decay filled the air like a poisonous gas. The heavy odor made her eyes water, and her head go light.

A trample of footsteps rushed behind them. Mary wanted to peer over her shoulder and see how many there were but didn't dare attempt it. She was afraid she'd lose her footing and fall, bringing Jake down with her and have those little things swarming all over them. They were ahead, and she wanted to keep it that way.

"Keep going!" someone shouted.

It was Jake. He was still clinging to her, still holding on, and it helped Mary feel somewhat protected in all this lunacy. With him by her side, she felt stronger and braver. If Jake was going to handle this like a pro, then by God, she would too. Back at the lake, he'd said he needed her to help him. No one else, just her. She was special to him. She didn't know why, but she liked that he thought of her that way. Thank the Lord he'd told her that. She didn't know how she'd be handling things at this point if he hadn't.

The stalks beside Wendy blasted apart and another small body soared through the air, latching onto her back as she ran by. Two scrawny arms, browned with filth, clung to her shirt. Although she screamed riotously, she didn't stop running. The elf-thing bounced on her back, trying to climb up and failing. It tumbled off her back and screamed, not in attack but in panic. Shannon trampled it, pushing the minute body deep into the soil. Mary and Jake did the same.

Mary worked up the nerve to dare a peek at their pursuers. There were just four more, but the distance was growing between them and their attackers. They would probably lose them soon if they kept this pace going.

Shannon passed Wendy, ducking her head with her arms straight out in front of her. There was a wall of corn stems that crisscrossed like a barrier trying to keep them inside. Shannon burst through, disappearing on the other side.

Wendy followed.

Now, it was Mary's turn. She closed her eyes and prepared herself for whatever awaited on the other side. Tearing through, the ground leveled under her feet. She didn't feel the slapping leaves or the blunt, dehydrated stalks anymore. She opened her eyes and saw green. Grass. She'd never been happier to see grass.

She and Jake stopped running.

Shannon and Wendy stood in a field of shin-high grass. Shannon was crouched over, bracing her hands on her knees and panting. Wendy stood straight, her left arm draped across her cramping abdomen.

Mary looked at Wendy's shirt. It had been torn from front to back. Drooping low on her arm, the incline of her right breast had been exposed. It was pale and glossy with sweat. If the shirt slipped even an inch, the dark coin of her nipple would show.

Mary examined her own body, noticing shallow, nicks and scrapes from the stalks' leaves. Her sweat made each little abrasion burn and sting as if she were swabbing them with rubbing alcohol. She scanned the others and saw none of them had escaped unscathed.

Jake stepped away from the girls, not taking his eyes from the field they'd exited. Mary expected the little things to emerge from the corn at any moment, continuing the chase, but they never did. She was confused. What happened to them? Were they still in there watching them? She looked at Jake. He must have been thinking the same thing because he took a few steps toward the corn.

"Where are they?" Mary asked.

"I don't know," answered Jake. "They're in there somewhere."

"What should we do?"

Jake shook his head, backstepping away from the corn. Finally, he allowed himself to look away, but his guard was still up. He walked ahead of them and stopped. He observed their surroundings with his hands on his hips.

Mary did the same.

The maize split at the field, continuing on each side like a cross. The grass had browned in places, still feeling the effects of the previous summer's drought and the nearing winter. The warm weather during the days had helped keep some of the grass alive, but the colder temperature of the nights had been making it hard for fresh grass to grow, and the nights would only get worse as the weeks progressed.

"I think they're too scared to come out," said Jake.

"Why?" asked Wendy.

"Because we could easily take them out if they did. There was only what? Three of them left?"

"Then they probably went back for reinforcements."

"Maybe."

Mary lifted her hair off her shoulders with both hands. Cool air brushed the back of her slickened neck. If felt good. Jake stepped up behind her, rubbing his hands up and down the curve of her sore and damp back. His hands moved up to the nape of her neck. She felt her arms pimple up with gooseflesh. It calmed her. He massaged her shoulders a beat, then squeezed.

They heard high-pitched laughter. They turned around and found they hadn't lost the little people after all. Three of them stood in the corn, just at the launch of the field, where they watched the group and snickered amongst each other.

"Why aren't they coming after us?" asked Shannon.

"Don't question it stupid," said Wendy. "Just be glad they aren't."

The trio waved at them, turned around and dashed back into the corn.

"They left?" asked Mary, puzzled.

"Maybe Jake was right, and they don't want to risk trying to attack us," Wendy offered.

Shannon grabbed Jake's shoulder. "Let's get out of here before they change their minds."

"Good idea," he said. Walking rearward, his eyes on the corn, he returned to the girls. "We should get going."

"Why?" asked Wendy. "If they're staying in there, then let's stay here, someone has to come by eventually."

Mary said, "Just because those things haven't come out, doesn't mean they *won't.*"

Wendy didn't retort.

Jake looked around. "This has to be private property. If we keep moving, we're bound to stumble across the owner eventually."

"What if we don't want to find the owner?" asked Shannon. "What if he's one of them?" She nodded at the corn, referencing the little things.

"That's a chance we'll have to take," answered Jake.

"That's a chance *you'll* have to take," said Wendy, pointing a finger and placing the other hand on her hip. "You don't speak for me, pal, or anyone else. Who gave you top rank?"

"No one."

"Exactly. No one. But you act as if we have. Telling us where to go and what to do. What gives you the right to do that? You're just a goddamn stoner, anyway. Probably lead us straight to our deaths."

Jake laughed. "This damn stoner has saved your life how many times?"

Smirking, Wendy crossed her arms. "What happened at the shack gives you no damn right to be my guardian."

Jake hissed through gritted teeth. Eyes scrunched tight, he looked away.

"Wendy," Mary began, "he took charge because no one else was willing to. You should thank him for it because I definitely don't want to be in his shoes."

Nodding at Mary, Jake thanked her with the simple gesture.

He faced Wendy. "I'm not telling you what to do or trying to speak on your behalf. If you'd rather go off on your own, fine. But I'm going this way." Pointing forward, his direction was aimed up the field. "Can you see that small line at the end of the stretch?"

The field protracted through the maize like a road. At the end it split in two directions. The line he'd mentioned was hardly noticeable, and beyond it were more rows of dead corn.

"Barely," said Wendy.

"It's a barbwire fence. If we follow right along beside it, we should come up on a house, or a barn, or something. We're on farmland. That's probably why those things aren't coming out here because they're not allowed to. Someone owns this land."

It made sense to Mary. If the corn was being used for seclusion, then those things wouldn't risk being caught out in the open. Someone could see them and kill them.

"And," Jake continued, "we need to find something before the sun goes down. I can already feel the temperature dropping. It's going to be another cold night. I, for one, don't want to be caught in the cold wearing what I am."

Mary added, "And those things might not be so afraid to come out at night."

Shannon shivered. "I'm sure they can see better in the dark than we can."

"You guys can come with me if you want," Jake said. "I'd rather that you did, because believe it or not, I don't want anything bad to happen to any of you."

What weariness Jake had displayed earlier was gone. His complexion was bronze again. His green eyes fluttered with sparks, and he looked ready to take on the world.

"I'll go with you," said Mary.

He looked at her somberly. "Thank you."

Shannon quickly spoke up. "Me too."

"What if you're wrong?" asked Wendy. "What if we follow that fence and it leads us straight to hell?"

"Well, then I guess I wasn't the hero I wanted you to think I was."

Wendy stepped over to him, wrapping her arms around his neck. Mary followed, doing the same. Then Shannon joined them, finishing the group hug. They were sticking through this, staying together, Jake and the girls.

Jake pulled them closer and held them tighter.

MARY

The barbwire seemed endless, combing farther through hilly fields of tall itchy grass than any of them had anticipated, and, as an added bonus, the field was littered with holes. The shallow orifices were like little mouths nipping at their feet and a perfect way for someone to strain or twist their ankle.

Mary kept tripping over them, buckling at the knees as her foot suddenly dropped into the ground. Each time, her mind would immediately flash back to when Amy was pulled under the ground and Jake informing them of the tunnels he and Wendy had found. She just knew that the next time her foot sunk into a hole it wouldn't quit falling.

Then she thought of Steve and wondered if he was all right.

Wendy staggered and plunged as she tripped over her third hole. She stood up, cussed, brushed off the seat of her pants and slid her breast back under her shirt. It had plopped out three times already, so the shock of seeing her bare breast was done.

Mary figured they'd all fall at least once during this venture.

They'd been hiking for at least an hour and the sun was dropping behind the trees fast, casting the sky with orange and yellow puddles. Soon it'd be flooding with purple and then deluged in black. If they didn't find a house, barn, or some kind of shelter soon, their survival would rely on nothing but hopes and prayers.

It already does, Mary thought. Finding a house would help matters and give them at least a shimmer of hope in what appeared to be a hopeless situation.

A shimmer of *anything* would be welcomed right now.

"I can't go on like this," complained Shannon. Her steady walk had turned to a drag. Her feet kicked through the weeds instead of marching over them. A hole nabbed her foot and she dropped, disappearing into the weeds.

Jake trotted to where she sat crying.

Wendy stood at the front, shaking her head as if asking, *What now?*

Mary went to Shannon and knelt down by her. She patted her back, lightly rubbing it up and down. Her backbone jutted like shells in sand through the soggy shirt. Mary pulled her damp hand away and flicked Shannon's sweat into the grass.

"We don't have time for this," said Wendy.

"Back off," defended Mary. "She needs a break. We all do."

"I don't. And in case you've forgotten…" she pointed at the setting sun, "…we don't have *time* to take one."

"I know," said Mary. "Just give her a minute, would you?"

"I'm going ahead to see if I find something."

Jake looked at her over his shoulder. "You *will* come back and tell us if you find something, right?"

Wendy seemed hesitant to answer, but finally said, "Yeah, sure." She turned around, flipping back her head. Her wavy hair bounced behind her, the loose breast swaying this way and that as she strutted forward. She followed the fence up to where it turned left and kept going without looking back.

"Just go with her," said Shannon. "If she does find something, I'll be surprised if she comes back to tell us."

"No," Jake said. "You either go with me, or I stay here with you. It's that simple."

"I'm with you too," said Mary.

"Why?" Shannon sounded annoyed that they were willing to stick by her.

Shocked by the question, Jake said, "What do you mean *why?* You're my girlfriend, that's why."

"Oh, please, some girlfriend I've been."

"Don't say that."

"I'm not worth any of this. You'll get yourself killed trying to protect me."

"And if I do, I do."

"Plus, I've been trying to fuck Mary." Her eyes misted up with another breakdown coming. "I'm a lousy girlfriend." She buried her head into her palms, sputtering unrecognizable syllables and sobs in her hands.

Mary's chest felt as if it had been hit with a hammer. Why had Shannon revealed that dirty secret to Jake? And *now*? Couldn't she have picked a more appropriate time?

And when would that be?

"Now's not the time for this conversation," Jake informed them, mirroring her thoughts.

"We'll probably get killed soon anyway, Jake. So what's it matter when we have this talk?"

Mary could have gone without hearing that. If they were to just be killed after working so hard at survival, then all they'd done was a total waste.

"Okay," said Jake. "I give. What's on your mind?"

"Mary and I fooled around a long time ago, and…"

"Hardly fooled around," said Mary. "It was nothing."

Shannon looked as if she'd been stabbed.

"I didn't it mean it like that…"

Shannon was crying again.

Good job, bitch. Way to kick her when she's down.

"I know what you two did," said Jake. "I've always known."

Shannon opened her mouth to speak but couldn't. She only stared, her mouth gaping.

A trickle of heat rushed up Mary's back and into her neck. So, Jake hadn't been oblivious after all?

"I've known how you've lusted after Mary for a long time."

Mary was about to ask him how he knew this, but he answered before she could.

"You talk in your sleep, Shannon. And the dreams you have are usually about her. I mean, it bothers me some, but not as much as it should, I'm sure. I've tried for a long time to make things right between us, to be a good boyfriend. After a while, I just got tired of trying. I became less of a boyfriend and more of a big brother, just trying to keep you out of trouble."

Shannon sniffled. "I wish you didn't feel that way."

"I'm sorry. It's just the way it worked out."

"I can't believe you knew about Mary and didn't say anything."

"What *could* I say?"

Mary chimed in, "I'm sorry Jake. We didn't know what we were doing."

Or did we? It didn't really feel like girls messing around, anymore. Somehow, it felt different. After it had happened, she'd managed to ignore it, to suppress those feelings deep down inside her, but she couldn't fight the truth. It was *more* than just two girls experimenting.

"You don't have to say anything," he said. "I understand."

No, he doesn't. He thinks he does, but really, he doesn't understand at all.

"I'm sorry I never told you," said Shannon. "I was just too scared. I had this plan. More of an idea, really."

"What kind of plan?"

Yes, Shannon, what kind of plan?

"I don't know," she said, looking down at the ground. She plucked out a strand of grass and began fidgeting with it. "I guess I sort of hoped that maybe we could all… I don't know." She sighed.

"What?" asked Jake.

"I guess I'm trying to say that I had hoped we could all somehow share the relationship."

"A threesome?"

By the sneer on his face, she could tell he didn't get what Shannon was trying to tell him. But Mary got it. It wasn't that Shannon just wanted them all to share a bed, taking turns on each other, allowing Jake to be the rod they straddled and jaunted until getting their fix. Her meaning was much deeper than just that.

Why hadn't Shannon said something sooner?

"It sounds dirty when you say it like that." Jake held up a hand in apology, but before he could say anything, Shannon was talking again. "The three of us, yes, but sort of, I don't know how to say it."

Mary finished for her. "The three of us sharing the same love for each other?"

Shannon looked at her, a smile forming on her quivering lips. Her eyes seemed to glow. "Exactly. And of course, other aspects of the relationship as well."

On that part, Jake had been right. A threesome. Not just sex, but the emotional attachment as well. Mary wondered if, somewhere in a shallow pit of her mind, that was the reason she could never fully commit herself to Steve. What if maybe, just maybe, she had real feelings for Shannon? With Jake involved, it wasn't so scary anymore. It felt good.

It felt right.

I wonder if Steve ever worried about this?

Steve. God, she felt guilty about Steve. Surprisingly, it wasn't because he was missing. She felt the guilt of not feeling guilty about his absence. She hated herself for that.

"Sorry, Jake, I guess I'm just too fucked up to love." Shannon lowered her head.

"You *are* fucked up. But that's *why* I love you. What can I say? I'm addicted to drama." He smiled.

Shannon could only keep the bogus scowl on her face a moment before she laughed. "You're an asshole."

"Yep."

She shook her head. "You never let me quit, even when that's all I want to do."

"You wouldn't have anything to bitch about if I did."

Laughing, Shannon used her thumb to wipe the tears out of her eyes. She sniffled, wiped her nose with a forearm, and slowly exhaled. She quivered all over as her lungs released the trembling breath. "I'm sorry, Mary."

"It's okay," she said.

"I mean I'm sorry for all the hell I've put you through the last couple of months."

"It's okay, really. It doesn't feel like hell, not anymore."

Now, Mary was really confused, but this time it was her own thoughts causing it.

Shannon shrugged. "I think we all need to have a *long* talk if we get out of here."

"*When* we get out of here," said Jake.

The swift rustling of impending footsteps startled them. In a dash, Jake was standing, his knifed wielded, and ready to defend them.

Wendy reappeared and laughed at his seriousness. "Don't flatter yourself, stoner boy."

"What'd you do? Give up?" asked Shannon.

"No. While you sat here crying all over yourself, I went and found a house."

"You found it?" asked Jake, his voice rising with excitement.

"Yes, but don't shit your shorts. It looks just as I thought it would."

"And that is?"

"Old and abandoned."

"It is?" The disappointment was loud in Shannon's voice.

"I didn't exactly stay long enough to snoop around, but it looks that way."

Jake held up a hand to intervene. "If it's got a roof it doesn't matter. Maybe there's some water nearby. That's all we need to make it through the night."

Mary realized how parched and brittle her mouth and lips felt. Her scratchy throat made it difficult to swallow. The pores on her skin felt dry and achy for rehydration.

And a shower would be wonderful.

"I need to try and find a way to change the bandages on Mary's hand and shoulder too," Jake added.

"Shoulders," she corrected, turning so he could see the fresh wound. "In the lake when we were escaping, an arrow bounced off me. I must be a magnet for those damn things."

"Or an easy target," offered Wendy.

"At least you're all right," said Jake.

For now, she thought.

Jake offered both of his hands to Shannon. She took them. He tugged her up and held her close. She collapsed into his arms, snuggling herself tightly into his comfortable squeeze.

Mary had never seen Shannon hug Jake like that. Her chest burned with jealousy watching them.

She wanted to hug Jake like that.

PIPER

It was hard, but Piper managed to divert his attention away from Amy and focus on trying to escape. When he heard someone approaching, he froze and waited. Someone knee-high to Piper stepped around the front of his coop. It was a man, sort of. He wore a shirt made of burlap with a matching set of rough-stitched trousers. Each piece had been bleached to gray. He clutched a spear in his hand, the dowel pressed into the ground with the bladed end up.

He stepped up to the door and peered inside.

Piper was much bigger, faster, and definitely stronger, but the look in his visitor's eye crippled him with fright. All he could do was stare back and try not to scream.

The little thing cocked his head toward the sky and sniffed. When he brought his gaze back down to Piper, he was smiling a broken grille of brown and black teeth. "I smell terror."

Piper's breaths came in quick spurts.

"You are scared."

Piper wasn't sure if he was supposed to answer or just let the guy talk. He'd never seen anything so small, other than a baby. Its cranium was wrought like a piece of flesh-colored squash with fuzzy gray hair stuffed up under a stocking cap on top, and half of its face was covered with a matching bushy beard. He looked like one of Amy's goddamn lawn gnomes, but way uglier. *Must be one of the guards.* That this thing was up, walking around and speaking comprehensively was nothing short of a miracle. What had he stumbled upon out here?

"You are a big man," he told Piper. "Lots of meat on you. And your fear makes you smell delicious, but once we add some onion and chopped potatoes to your boiling blood..." Drool seeped from the corners of his narrow mouth, making it impossible for him to finish.

Piper was thankful to be spared the remaining words of the sentence. "You're going to eat us?"

He spoke softly, meant mostly for his own ears, but the little guy cackled high and shrill.

"You. We're going to eat *you*." He turned toward Amy who was watching him intently. "There are other plans for her."

Piper began to cower, his body shaking all over. He suddenly had the need to piss. He was afraid he might do it in his pants.

And when the guard cleared his throat, he did.

Piper didn't care. He was spooked by the little guy's every move, and by the way his guard smiled, he knew it. Holding the wooden shaft of the spear, he angled the tip toward Piper, stuck it through an opening, and nudged Piper's side.

"Let me have just a little taste," he cooed.

Piper writhed as the spear's tip pricked his skin. It did not hurt very badly, but it was really pissing him off. Piper wanted to grab the midget by its throat and squeeze until something cracked.

The gnome laughed, poking him under the armpit.

Piper cried out.

He heard Amy gasp from behind him.

Amy.

Bitch probably thought he was being hurt and that he was weak. He was not weak, but that last one did sort of hurt. He was still warm where the spear had pierced him.

The gnome came in again, but Piper was ready. He grabbed the spear just under the head and pulled inward. The shaft felt like a pencil in his hand. It was the little guy's turn to cry out as he was hoisted off the ground. Not releasing his grip on the spear, the gnome crashed against Piper's cage so hard it cracked the cornstalk bars.

Piper punched the stalk. It wasn't a good, solid punch, but it was forceful enough to snap the bars back. Then he reached through, snatching the thing by its neck and slowly applied pressure.

Amy squealed. "What are you doing? You'll kill him!"

"That's the plan, sweetheart."

"If you kill him..." She stopped.

The little guy's face was swelling. His shade had turned from pink to purple and his eyes bulged as his stumpy tongue lashed between his lips, trying to find air. Piper wanted to keep compressing until he crushed its throat, but Amy's unfinished statement was completing itself in his mind. *If you kill them, they'll really fuck you up.* He didn't know what they'd do exactly, but he could only imagine, and what he came up with wasn't pleasant.

What can be worse than eating me?

There was plenty.

"How can I get out of here?" he asked the dollop. "Tell me and I'll let you go." He couldn't answer Piper's question even if he wanted to, but that didn't stop Piper from shaking the little thing. "Which way should I take to get back to the lake?"

Before Piper's interrogation could be acknowledged, the gnome's neck splintered and caved in Piper's grip. The dollop's head slacked unnaturally to the side. The hands that had been slapping at Piper dropped, swaying limply.

The little fucker was dead.

Piper's skin went tight and crawly. He was suddenly freezing. The sweat on his skin felt like liquid ice. He dropped the little guy. There was a *thunk* when his body struck the ground. *You've really screwed up now.* His whole body began to shake, trembling as what he'd done began to sink in. Where he'd pissed his pants felt like ice water against his inner thighs.

"Did you kill it?"

"What do you think?"

"Why? When they come to check on us and see what you've done, they're going to torture us!"

"You don't think I know that? It was an accident."

"Do you really think that matters to them?"

Piper had never panicked before, hadn't even come close to it. But now he was a mess and nearly to the point of tears. He'd never done something so sloppy.

What are you talking about? You could have let Amy go, move out on her own, and find someone else to tolerate your bullshit, but instead you came all this way just kill her and her lover boy Gary. She wouldn't have told anyone about the other stupid shit you've done. She just wanted to leave, but your ego just wouldn't let that happen. See? You do stupid, sloppy shit all the time!

Now wasn't the time for his conscience to start adding its viewpoint to the situation.

"What should I do? What should I do?" He stuttered.

"You just killed us!" said Amy. "This is all *your* fault. All of it!"

He ignored her as he looked around. There didn't appear to be more of them coming. Not yet. But he figured they'd come looking for their friend sooner rather than later.

"What the fuck have I done?"

"You've killed us! That's what you've done!"

With no other plans coming to mind, he slammed his head against the stalks where the dead dwarf had cracked it. His vision went black for a moment, then slowly splotched back in. He checked the bars. They'd broken some more but were still a problem. This time, he took a moment to mentally prepare himself for the impact. He screwed his eyes shut, biting down on his bottom lip.

Then he brought his head forward.

The stalk broke under the force, allowing him to go through. He smashed into the ground, his breath blasting out of his lungs, and lay there coughing for longer than he'd have liked. He finally managed to find his breath and stood, slapping the dust off his clothes.

Amy watched him from her coop, eyes wide as spheres.

Oh, how he wanted to kick that look off her face. He wanted to do it so badly that he began to shake, but instead of caving into the temptation, he took a moment for some calming breaths.

"What are you going to do?" Amy asked. "You don't think you can just get away, do you? They'll find you. They're everywhere."

"I can handle myself."

An exaggerated huff of doubt came from Amy, and it was one that Piper completely agreed with. He seriously doubted that he would make it far before they caught up to him, but he was willing to risk it anyway.

As he was about to depart, he stopped, waiting for Amy to start begging him to free her, but to his surprise and disappointment she never spoke up. He looked back over his shoulder. She sat just as she had been. Instead of wide-brimmed shock on her face, there was only a scowl. He waited another second for her to ask for help. He looked forward to turning his back on her and walking away while she pleaded with him.

"What are you staring at?" she asked.

"Don't you want me to get you out of there?"

"Fuck you."

He hadn't expected that. He started to retort but stuttered. "Is that what you really want? Me to leave you in there?"

"I'd rather be trapped in here by those things than be out there with you."

"Fine. Then that's how it'll be."

He turned around.

"Piper?"

There it was. He knew she'd come around. Smirking, he turned around. "Change your mind?"

"If I get a chance to catch up to you later, I'm going to castrate you while you watch."

A cold hand gripped his spine. For a reason that he couldn't understand he totally believed her. And not only that, her vow spooked him. He'd never heard such words from her mouth before.

He scoffed, turned around, and marched into the cornfield.

Once he knew Amy could no longer see him, he ran quicker than he thought his legs could ever move him.

AMY

Amy was at the beach.

Sprawled out on a blanket, the sun had baked her skin to a golden brown. She couldn't move. The comforting heat of the sun had rendered her body useless, draining all desire to roll over and tan her back.

It felt good. Hot as all hell, but good.

Gary sat in a beach chair nearby. A three-foot-tall umbrella attached to the top of the chair was opened and shielding him from the sun. Legal pad in his lap, he jotted on its yellow pages with a pencil. He was deep in thought, and totally oblivious to the luscious landscape around them.

Probably busy at work on another bestseller. Some kids ran by, kicking at the sand and laughing during an intense game of tag. They turned toward the splashing water. *I'm glad we had kids, but two just isn't enough. Should have one more so we can call them the Three Musketeers.*

Then she remembered they didn't have any kids.

Poof!

They were gone. Vanished from the water. Their final swashes dropped back into the current and washed away.

She looked back at Gary. He hadn't noticed. His attention was still locked in the legal pad. The tip of his tongue poked through the narrow line of his tightened lips.

He's really going at it. He didn't even notice his two sons disappearing like that.

Why would he? He's dead.

"*Nooo,*" Amy screamed, reaching for Gary. She was too late. He vanished at the snap of an invisible finger. The legal pad hovered in the air a moment before dropping into the sand.

Amy screamed at the sky above. She demanded that her children and husband be returned to her at once. She pushed herself to her knees. Her skin felt tight and hot as she buried her face in her sand-sprinkled hands. As grit went into her mouth and on her tongue, she reached for the bottle of water that hadn't been there until now. She didn't question its arrival. She was just thankful that it had. She needed something to wash away the brittle bits of sand in her mouth.

Amy spun off the cap, raised the bottle to her lips, and guzzled.

What she ingested didn't taste like water.

She spit out the unknown fluid and raised the bottle to her face so she could examine it better. Red. The water was red. Then she remembered it wasn't water. It was blood. Little chunks of Gary's flesh floated around the bottom like the worm in a bottle of tequila.

She shrieked.

She was about to chuck the bottle into the ocean, but it was no longer in her hand. She decided to search the shore for it and noticed it had also vanished. The splashing waves no longer brushed the sand. The sand had turned into concrete. The bottoms of her feet burned. She stepped over to another spot, but it was hotter than the last. In fact, the concrete seemed to be getting hotter by the moment. She could smell something like cooked meat and realized it was her own skin. She pranced aimlessly back and forth until spotting Gary's legal pad.

Amy ran for it.

She slapped her feet on the paper. It was much cooler, but her feet were pounding and sore. She looked down. There was something scribbled on the paper, hints of lettering showed through the crack between her two feet. She spread her toes apart far enough to see the letters.

Two words, but they took up the whole page.

WAKE UP!

Amy almost squealed when she awoke, her head bonking the top of her cage. The memory of where she was and how she'd gotten there quickly returned. They'd put her in here, the little ones. Then they'd left her alone except to check on her every once in a while.

When she'd realized Piper was out there, she could hardly contain her laughter. Finally, the asshole was getting what he deserved. She didn't feel the least bit sorry for him. In fact, she still figured he was getting off too easily.

She watched him struggle, watched him panic, and she enjoyed every second of it, but then he killed one of them and managed to break through the cage. Bastard had the luck of the devil, and she knew it. She'd hoped this time would have been different, that he would actually be punished for the harm he'd done in his life.

Nope. He was free and had escaped into the corn. Maybe the things would find him, capture him again and slowly torture him as punishment. She hoped she would at least get to fulfill her promise of castrating him, yet as much as she would like to convince herself it could still happen, she seriously doubted it would.

Somehow, she just knew he'd never be recaptured.
Son of a bitch.

Indistinct chatter stopped her cold. A flurry of chills ran up her spine. They were coming back. What would they do when they discovered Piper had not only escaped, but killed one of their own? Would they take it out on her? *Why would they? I had nothing to do with it.* No, it had not been her fault, but she was the one that was here. They couldn't chastise Piper for it now, could they? No ma'am. She was all they had.

As the three more little ones approached, she asked God why he hadn't killed her too. Why had he left her alive and taken Gary? When they noticed Piper's cage and the dead one lying next to it, the small pact began to squeal a sound that pierced Amy's ears like needles. She cupped her hands over them and hummed, trying to drown out their badgering wails.

It didn't work.

So, she opted to scream instead.

Then they turned in unison.

Her scream died in her chest.

Their rage-fuming eyes were focused on her.

MARY

Wendy hadn't exaggerated. The house wasn't just old, it was decrepit, and riddled with age, molded flakes of paint clung to its three-story frame. The shingles that hadn't torn away had rotted to black clumps and the tar had dried up, forming little mountains of soot across the roof.

The barn was even worse.

Its door lay on the ground, weeds sprouting around it. The overall structure had shifted from long periods of abuse by heavy winds and crummy weather. Boards had separated from their bases and the spaces between seemed to be smiling a crooked, gap-toothed grin. Mary shuddered. The barn gave her the creeps. No matter what Jake said, they would not bunk in that thing for shelter if they couldn't get inside the house. She'd much rather take her chances in the corn.

They climbed the rickety steps onto the shaded porch of the farmhouse. It seemed much darker and cooler under the veranda. From where she stood, Mary could see just how forlorn the property actually was. It appeared as if it had been lost among the chasm of cornfields and they were the first explorers to rediscover it.

Two wicker rocking chairs, covered with spiderwebs and specks of dried leaves, rocked forward and back as if occupied by unseen sitters. Mary noticed a third rocking chair on the opposite side of the two.

She gasped.

It was small, just the right size for one of those munchkin things. Her skin tingled as gooseflesh scurried all over her. Her arms went rigid, and her breasts went prickly. Her scalp felt as if it were slithering.

Stop it, she told herself. *Could have been for a kid.*

She wasn't convinced.

"See what I mean?" said Wendy. "Abandoned."

"I've got a bad feeling about this place," said Shannon.

Mary, taut with fright, agreed, but decided to stay quiet for now and wait until she heard what Jake had to say about it. He'd been great so far on how to deal with this situation. She leaned against the stoop, watching Jake as he glanced from one side of the porch to the other. *Come on Jake,* she thought, *say something.*

"It's got a roof," Wendy added. "We can smash this window and climb through." The window she was referring to was a large, double-panel bay window to the door's right.

Shannon stepped closer, studying the window. "Oh my God…"

"What is it?" Mary asked.

"The window's boarded up."

Wendy threw her arms up. "Who cares? We'll kick them in."

"No. I mean it's boarded from the in-*fucking*-side."

Mary felt a shudder in her stomach.

"And these right here…" She pointed to another set of windows farther down.

They huddled around them. On first glance, it appeared only to be dark inside, but when they investigated more closely, they discovered that was not the case. The blackness was actually a tarp or some other kind of thick sheet that blocked any view of what was inside.

Shannon continued, ". . . they're blacked out."

"It doesn't mean someone lives here," said Wendy.

"It's obvious someone doesn't want anyone seeing what's inside."

Wendy laughed. "Look around you. There's nowhere else we *can* go. It's here, and so are we. Might as well use it to our advantage."

Folding her arms across her chest, Mary shook her head. She couldn't believe how stupid and desperate

Wendy was behaving. This wasn't just *her* life she was screwing with, it was all of theirs.

Shannon looked at Jake. "What do you think?"

All eyes focused on Jake, awaiting his input. He not only looked nervous, but terrified. It was clear he had no idea as to who was right and who was wrong. Mary realized for the first time he was just as clueless as the rest of them.

"Should we split?" Shannon said as she gnawed at her bottom lip, her arms straight and stiff by her sides.

Jake's opinion would be the final say in whether they were staying or going. They'd all go with what he said, no matter what his answer might be. Sighing, he stepped toward Shannon. "Maybe we should smash the window, and just peak a head through to see if anyone's in there." With Wendy to the left, and Mary to the right, Jake and Shannon were centered in front of the blacked window facing each other.

"And what if they are?" Shannon demanded. "Do we just apologize and be on our way?"

The wind began to blow harder now. The temperature was rapidly dropping with the setting sun. A light mist of fog slithered over the tops of the cornstalks, rolling and spiraling in a path for the house. It was growing darker and colder, and they were not dressed for the looming weather.

A decision needed to be made.

"Oh, for Christ's sake," Wendy said, as if Shannon were being ridiculous.

"Or what if it's trap?" Shannon brought a rigid finger to her mouth.

Wendy looked as if she wanted to slap Shannon.

Mary hadn't thought about that, but it could very easily be a setup. Piled up on the porch, grouped together like this, they'd be cornered with no chance of escape. Fleeing through the corn was out; those creatures were hidden out there too. They were probably there now, watching. Mary could practically feel their beady eyes on them, contemplating their next move.

What if they wanted us to come here?

Wendy raised her voice. "Don't you think if it was a trap they would have done something by now?"

"Maybe they're waiting," said Shannon.

"For what?"

There was a metal click from inside the house. The sound was familiar. It was something Mary had often heard when growing up. She remembered being nine years old the day her father had brought home a new rifle from a gun show in Minnesota. She'd been too young to care about the specs, and too distracted by its gigantic size. The barrel had shined so brightly it seemed to be glowing, diverting her attention from her father's instructions about safety and how to properly handle such a firearm.

It was pretty. And loud. And it made a very big hole in whatever it was aimed at.

Oh, shit.

Mary tried to warn them. She tried to raise her arms and shout. But she felt as if she was weighted down with sand and as if glass had filled her mouth. She couldn't move, or project a sound, and could only watch it happen as if she were sitting on her couch, viewing a violent, gory movie on TV.

Everything seemed to slow down.

Shannon opened her mouth to respond to Wendy, but her words were drowned by a sudden explosion. Glass shattered behind her. A cloud of red erupted from under her breasts. Then another swash of red splashed Jake's stomach, and spun him around so he faced Mary, gaping at her dumbly, before toppling over the railing and falling into the bushes below.

Shannon staggered but didn't fall. She seemed confused, glancing from Wendy to Mary. It was as if she was silently asking them what had just happened. She looked down at the billiard ball-sized hole in her chest, reached up, and dabbed it with a finger. She brought it up to her face. Blood dribbled from her fingertip.

Finally, it all seemed to make sense.

She'd been shot.

Shannon opened her mouth and looked like she was about to unleash a scream when the second blast resounded. Her head exploded as the bullet plowed through her skull, leaving only the lower jaw and some teeth attached to a wobbly neck. The tongue was slurping and lashing like a burrowing worm emerging from an apple and her arms reached about as if they were searching for something. Then she collapsed, her limp body bouncing down the shaky steps and coming to a blundering halt on the shoddy ground. Gooey chunks of brain and skull sluggishly oozed from the cavity that had once been her head.

Everything flashed, reverting back to normal speed.

Wendy and Mary gawked at each other. Wendy's mouth moved frantically, screaming with all her might, but Mary could barely hear it through the heavy buzz in her ears.

Then the front door swung open.

A hairy man charged out. His pale skin was the color of cream in the dwindling light.

Mary stood stupefied, monitoring it all like a peeping tom spying through a window into hell. She saw Wendy trying to run, evidently with hopes of fleeing, but she was struck in the head by the stock-end of the rifle the man clutched in his calloused, skeletal hands.

He shot Shannon and Jake.
He killed them.

What hope Mary had managed to cling onto through the day's insanity bowed to a heavy lump in her bowels. She didn't realize that she was crying until she was inside the house. How she'd gotten in there, she couldn't recall. Everything had happened in a hustle that if she had blinked, she would have missed it. She tried to move her hands, but they were stuck. When she looked down, she found her wrists had been bound by rope that burned and itched her skin. Something hard pushed against her back, prohibiting her from slouching or bending. *A chair.* More rope encircled her chest, pinching her breasts together as if trying to mound them into one giant bulge.

She'd been captured.

Captured? Seriously? How?

Had she tried to fight or to run? Probably not. She assumed she'd just remained frozen like a statue, unmoving and submissive, as he dragged her into the house and tied her up. She began to scream orders at herself as if she were sitting in the audience of a horror movie and yelling up at the screen: *Get free, girl! Don't stay there! You gotta get loose!* She agreed, but there was no way she could physically do any of those things.

When the man came back in the room dragging Wendy's flaccid body by the ankles, her arms stretched above her head limply like a doll, she understood this was no work of fiction.

It was horror.

True horror.

Gary Butler's stories were like kid's fiction compared to these last several minutes.

Gary's dead. Shannon's dead. Jake's dead. Probably Steve and Amy too. They're all dead.

They were dropping like flies that killed themselves by hurling their tiny bodies against the glass while trying to escape through a window. They were the flies, and this man, plus the little creatures, were the fucked-up window that they couldn't get through.

The door banged shut, encasing them in darkness except for the setting sun's orange light that funneled through the bullet holes in the window in linear lines.

It was real, every grisly detail was her scary, fucked-up life.

Wanting to cry, Mary could only laugh a hysterical cackle.

MARY

The man screamed at Mary through broken, jagged teeth. "Who are you people!"

His breath reeked like garbage that had been left baking in the sun during the hottest days of summer. His beard was dirty white, long and shabby, and drooped down to his gut. He wore a straw hat on his head, the kind with a large, round bill to keep the sun out of his eyes and off his neck. His long hair draped wildly over his shoulders with its milky, straw-like strands. His clothing was a matching set of tan slacks and buttoned-up shirt over a frail body. The shirt was long sleeved and tarnished with stains of all colors. He wore grubby work boots, probably once a light brown, but now mud-caked and crusty.

Mary pinched her eyes shut and looked away. His pruned face was so close to hers that she could feel his piquant, rank breath wafting against her cheek.

"I'm not asking you again, who are you?"

Wendy had yet to fully awaken. She'd been stirring about, but it seemed her neck wasn't strong enough to support the weight of her head.

Mary finally managed an answer. "M-Mary."

The old man stood up straight. "Those kids out there, the ones I killed, who were they?"

Killed.

"Oh God…" She began to sob. "They're dead…*dead.*" She tried controlling it, tried to stop, but she couldn't contain her reaction.

The old man put his hands on his hips. "What the hell were you doing snooping around my house?"

Mary wondered if she should even bother trying to convince him of what was going on out there. As crazy as he looked, she doubted he'd believe there was some kind of miniature monsters out in the fields, but she had to try. It was the truth, regardless of how he took it.

"We were being chased…"

"Chased?"

"Y-yeah."

"By what?"

"I don't know." She choked on the words, sniveling even harder.

He shook his head. "Stop that mess. You ain't got no business bringing those tears in this house. It's your own damn fault. It's your own damn fault you done brought the wrath of the Haunchies down on your asses!"

Her crying ceased at the name. *Haunchies.* What the hell was he talking about?

"What do you mean? We didn't do anything wrong." She forced back the tears, and started, "We were at the lake…"

"Whisper Lake?"

Mary nodded. She sucked in her bottom lip, hoping that chewing on it would help stop it from trembling, but her chattering teeth only pierced her lip, making it bleed instead.

He removed his hat. Thinning hair topped his dome and liver spots dotted his scalp. "They watch that area, all the way from Doverton to Plainfield." He ran a shaking hand over his balding head. "They picked you. You caught their attention!" The man began pacing, only stopping to speak. "They don't just pick anybody, don't just attack every random person who happens to come by."

He scratched his beard. When he pulled his hand away, white flakes hovered in the air a moment before floating away. "They attacked you? The Haunchies?"

She was confused. They were attacked, but she didn't know what they were. "I guess. They were these little fuckers, hiding in the trees and in the ground. They just kept coming…"

"In the woods near the lake is a ridge. That's where they bury their devil young. Babies, dead at birth, the others dying from disease, deformities and sicknesses that would hardly bother most folks. Kill them like they was nuthin'."

The ridge by the stream?

They'd been there just a few hours ago, but it felt like weeks, and they had been trampling over an unmarked graveyard. She remembered how they'd found Amy hunched over, drinking water from the brook like some sort of crazed animal. Maybe at that moment, she was. What she'd witnessed with Gary could have brought her to that. Mary could relate. After seeing Shannon and Jake slaughtered, she doubted she'd ever recover from it if she was alive later to try.

"The whole area's infested with them Haunchy bastards. Has been for decades." He stopped walking, staring up at the ceiling as if his memories were being projected up there.

Finally, Wendy managed to keep her head upright. How much she'd heard, Mary wasn't sure, but she was attentive now with her eyes glued to the old man, head resting against a shoulder, a welt swelling on her head the size of a baseball. She probably had a concussion and needed a doctor.

"You shot innocent people and act like it was nothing!" Mary screamed a guttural, ferocious sound that she used to save for her now-defunct band. She couldn't believe it had come from her, but the raw, pinched feeling in her throat let her know she'd been the one to do it.

"They were trespassers! They got what they deserved!" He leaned down, putting his face inches from hers. Thick, foamy drool snaked from the corners of his mouth like rabid spit.

Mary didn't break away from his stare, but she also didn't speak. They weren't trespassers. They were victims who just needed a safe place to go and had chosen his place. She wished they'd slept in the field.

The old man exhaled a harsh, irritated breath.

"It doesn't matter what I did to your friends. They weren't the first, and they most certainly won't be the last. Doesn't mean I like it, but it's what I'm supposed to do. It's my part of the agreement…" He stopped talking as if he'd almost disclosed vital and secretive information.

Mary wondered what he meant by that.

My part of the agreement…

She was even more confused and frightened. There wasn't much—if anything—about this old man that made sense, but she recognized enough to understand she was in serious trouble.

She and Wendy needed to get out of here right away, but they were both strapped down. Unless she could wiggle out of the ropes. Maybe if she contorted her hands just enough, she could slide them through the loops. She gave it a try but couldn't move her wrists at all.

If only she could cut the rope, but she didn't have a knife.

An image of a stainless-steel blade with a worn handle flashed in her mind as if it was right in front of her: Jake's knife.

He still has it, right? She tried to remember the last time she'd seen him use it. The memory was almost there, but not quite, as if it was trying to bleed through static. She was almost positive he hadn't lost it. *He must still have it on him somewhere.* How could she get it?

Mary imagined herself charging at him with her head hung low like a bull, still tied to the chair. It would catch him off guard, sure, maybe even knock him down. But would it work?

No way in hell…

One shot later, she'd be dead. Brains splattered like Shannon's.

Might be better than being trapped with this madman while hordes of knee-high monsters roam outside.

When he spoke again, his voice made her flinch.

"I've been doing this for so long, I can't even remember what year it is anymore." Laughing, he plopped his hat back on his head and looked at her with eyes sinking behind hills of wrinkles and crow's feet.

"I was forced into this a long time ago." He scratched the back of his neck with jagged fingernails. It sounded like spikes on sandpaper. "Of all the God-forsaken land in Wisconsin, those damn Haunchy bastards chose mine to settle on." He faced her, deadpan. "One night, they stormed my house. Broke through that window right there." He pointed at the boarded up double bay windows.

He continued, "They came during a terrible thunderstorm, by horse and buggy, straight from a carnival, dressed like clowns, ring-leaders, and acrobats. It was the damned scariest thing I ever saw." He stopped a moment to catch his breath.

"I've studied up on these bastards for years. A couple hundred years ago, they were known as Hauterieus and later adopted the name Haunchies. I read they were a simple tribe, Neanderthal-like, that lived deep in the forests of England. When the early settlers came to America, those damn Haunchies stowed away on the ships like rats, hiding in barrels, crates and chests. Some of the more savage bastards hid in the bodies of the dead after feeding on them."

Mary pictured their little bodies burrowed in the corpses feeding on the rancid flesh and meat. She could almost smell the disgusting odor of rot.

The man kept talking as if Mary wasn't there at all. He spoke as one would who was reminding himself of what he had to do that day. "Coming to America, they weren't treated much differently than they had been in England. As the years went by, they realized that they could live among the carnies comfortably, surviving by the carny code. They were welcomed among the other freaks."

Makes sense. Being that small, there wasn't really anywhere else they would have been accepted.

"They were quite the attraction. Stayed that way for a long time. Until Josiah became the sovereign of the Haunchies. He saw things differently than his ancestors. He didn't like the fact that they were nothing more than an attraction to be mocked and ridiculed. It revolted him to no end. Breaking away from the carnivals, they began touring on their own. To spectators, they were just performers, cursed with a disease that had prohibited normal growth. What they were really doing during these tours from town-to-town was searching. Do you know what they were searching for?"

Mary shook her head, swallowing the knot in her throat. It bulged in her chest a moment before finally sinking down. She needed something to drink. Her throat felt as if she'd been gargling nails.

"A place to live and call their own."

"They chose here?" She managed to ask.

The old man nodded.

"How? I don't understand how they could be here, doing what they've been doing, without anyone catching on."

He shook his head as if she were a dumb animal trying to roll over on its back. "They chose here because the animals in the woods would give them plenty of meat to eat, the soil was pure for crops, and the people—simple minded folk—would allow it. There wasn't much I could do to stop them."

"Bullshit." Mary started at the sound of Wendy's voice. "You could have called the police. Could have called the mayor, the governor, the national fucking guard!"

"That's where you're wrong. I couldn't do anything, and I still can't. Oh, I tried fighting back at first. It just didn't work."

"Why not?"

"They took my daughter. Brainwashed her."

A fire boiled under Mary's skin. She wanted to strangle this geezer. Why he was saying any of this made no sense to her, but she was more concerned with what he planned on doing with them.

He spat a phlegm wad on the floor.

"They took refuge in my fields. I allowed them to, although I really didn't have much of a choice. We made a deal that they could hunt on my land and plant their own crops, and they wouldn't come out of the fields. Hell, the whole town knew about them. Being a predominately Amish town, the Haunchies were welcomed to stay as long as they kept to their own and didn't interfere with Doverton life."

He scoffed, shook his head.

"When I wasn't looking—which I have to admit was often—my daughter Leanne would sneak off to visit them and give them food. She actually started to *fall in love* with one of them. I came home one night to find them little shits all over my house, an infestation of Haunchy bastards. They were coming to tell me things were changing, and Leanne was coming to *live* with them. You see, they had plans of expanding, of turning against the Amish, taking over Doverton and turning it into Haunchyville."

"You had other plans." Wendy wasn't asking. It was a statement.

Nodding, the man backhanded the tears that had misted in his eyes. "We *all* had other plans. Me and three other families took our rifles into the fields…"

The same rifle he'd used earlier, Mary assumed.

His eyes were locked on Mary, but he stared through her. "We followed their paths through the corn and into the woods. We found their little village spread through the trees, on top of the ground and under it. We torched every bit of it. The ones that managed to escape…we waited for them, picking them off one-by-one as they fled." He snickered, although he didn't seem to be amused.

"I must have killed forty or so of them myself, and they got four of our small group. We eventually put out the fire and stormed what was left of their little village—which was mostly charred sticks—and killed the ones we could find.

"I looked high and low for Leanne, but didn't find her, so I came back to the house and waited for her to come home." He sighed.

"Did she?" Although she despised its telling, Mary couldn't help but to be intrigued by the man's story.

He shook his head. "The Haunchies came and showed me what I had done to her. She died trying to help them escape. I burnt my own daughter alive because I couldn't accept that she loved them. *I* killed her."

Silence filled the room like a heavy thing. When the man spoke again, his voice was a shaky, uncouth tone. "When we'd failed at slaughtering the Haunchies, the Amish cleared out of Doverton. A new deal was drawn up between them and me…"

He took a deep breath as if admitting a great guilt. "And ever since then, I've been afflicted with the duty of being their watcher. Their protector. Guarding them like a common dog."

Mary's spine crawled.

"Because of Leanne, I promised to keep them safe either until they all die off from starvation or disease, or until God grants my prayer of letting me die. I've been tempted a time or two to take my own life, to end this torment, but I don't, for Leanne. She would have wanted it this way. They're frail, weak, and need medicines and immunizations, so I get what I can for them. Someone needs to protect them until they finish what they started all those years ago…"

He pointed to the door, beyond it. "Claiming Doverton as their own."

Mary squirmed against the ropes trying to free herself. This was going to turn bad, even worse than what it already had been. This man was just as dangerous, if not more so, than the Haunchies.

"I've spent half a lifetime trying to keep trespassers *out* of Haunchyville, but every now and again some would get in. I'd tell them what I have to tell you now. Once you get in, you can never leave. That's the rule. You enter Doverton and you never get out of Doverton."

Mary screamed, unleashing a shriek that could have shattered windows had they not been boarded up already. She struggled, throwing her weight from right to left, rocking the chair in an attempt to topple it. She hoped it would break apart when she hit the floor.

Everything stopped with the sudden impact of the wooden rifle stock bashing against her temple.

Everything went black.

AMY

Amy was stripped and then led to a corral by a chain attached to a metal collar around her throat. The corral was lined with barbed wire, rows of it close together with even more contrived spikes for added security. She was barefoot and the craggy, uneven ground caused the soles of her feet to ache and throb. Her skin, rough with dried mud, felt dingy.

And the lacerations across her back stung like knife stabs with each step she took.

When they'd discovered that Piper had murdered one of theirs and escaped, she'd been questioned. She had answered them honestly and accurately. She told them all they wanted to know, but it hadn't been enough, so she was punished. Severely. Three of them whipped her with an instrument constructed of bamboo and briar vines.

Two of them, both male, guided her with the chain while two other males ran to the rough-and-ready gate and opened it. All of them were crudely dressed in burlap that had been stitched up the sides to create one-piece uniforms. Symbols that Amy didn't recognize bedecked the material. She assumed they were soldiers of some kind, and the symbols represented their rank.

"Get inside," the high-pitched voice demanded.

She didn't dare refuse. She entered the pen.

Once inside, she scanned it over. It was like the back of a farm where pigs were kept. There were separate sections, divided by more barbwire, but all the same size. She counted four, but there could have been more.

"Get on your knees," one holding her chain said.

She obliged. The mud was soft and cool under her knees. He released the hinges of her collar, letting it drop to the ground with a wet slap.

It was a relief to not have the extra weight tugging against her. Her shoulders and upper back tingled, but faintly underneath her muscles were constricting. It felt as if she was about to get a horrible cramp.

The other three circled behind her and, as a team, put their tiny hands against her buttocks and shoved. She fell forward, her breasts sinking in the deep mud. It didn't hurt and maybe it wasn't supposed to, maybe it was meant to be demeaning. If so, it had been.

Amy felt smaller than those who'd shoved her. She knew if she really wanted to, she could overpower them and make a run for it. But where would she go?

Where *could* she go? She was just as dead out there as she was as their prisoner, plus she was just too fucking tired to run. It felt as if she'd been completely drained of all her strength.

She also understood she was being submissive again, just as she was when Piper subjugated her. It wasn't something she was proud of, but she was unable to stop it from happening. She'd grown too comfortable with submitting and didn't know how to respond in any other way.

The four gathered together whispering and only casually glancing over at her. Something about their hushed tones and devious looks made her very nervous. She didn't like it. They were planning something.

When they faced her, each holding a piece of the chain like a belt for whipping, she knew what their plan was.

More punishment.

She prayed they killed her this time.

PIPER

Piper's lungs burned.

He hadn't stopped running since his escape and he wasn't planning to reduce his speed anytime soon. He wasn't running away, though. Not anymore. He had decided to return, so he circled back in the corn, making his way back to their camp.

He stopped by the nearest tree and scanned it up and down. He found a limb thick enough to hold him and climbed up to observe them from a safe spot in the tree. He could practically see everything.

It looked like a small and clandestine village. There were huts throughout the area that had been crassly manufactured from corn, mud and branches. Smoke billowed out from openings in the tops that Piper assumed were their chimneys. He could smell a faint smell of spices and something that reminded him of pork loin, but not quite. His stomach growled. He hadn't realized how hungry he was until he caught that smell.

Can't think about that now, he told himself. *Need to stay focused.*

The fuckers had taken his knife and gun, and he planned on getting them back.

He just didn't know where to look.

Another thought struck him. He could find one of the natives, capture *him*, and then interrogate him to find out where they'd stashed his stuff. Once he got his weapons back, he was going to go after them—not just the tiny people, but also Amy and the others she'd brought with her. That bitch from the hotel, the one who'd teased him? She was going to get it really bad if they hadn't beaten him to it.

Through all this hell, there was a pinch of heaven. He could harm Amy and her friends, and the best part of all, this little tribe of tiny shits would take the blame for it. He was a sheriff, after all, and he was pretty confident no one would question him.

Climbing down the tree, he had to strain to keep from laughing.

AMY

Amy snapped her eyes shut and waited for the blunt strike.

"Stop this," a voice ordered.

Amy peeked with one eye and, through her blurred vision, spotted someone approaching. Although he was also small, he stood at least a foot taller than the others. She opened the other eye and saw that he was a genuine dwarf, or at least looked to be. He had a helmet of wavy, brown hair and was arrayed in garments that seemed to have been hand-sewn from ancient cloth. His pants were blue, the shirt was white, and the matching blue jacket was buttoned at the stomach.

"What were you about to do to this delicate creature?"

The four shared a look of fear as they slowly lowered the chain. It appeared none of them wanted to fess up to what they had been planning.

"Were you going to harm her?"

He got no response.

"Were you?"

No response, still.

He looked over to Amy with repentant eyes the size of golf balls, and on a head not much larger than a small melon.

"My dear, what were they about to do to you when I arrived?"

Amy felt the corner of her mouth curve upward. She was glad he'd asked.

"They were going to beat me."

His woeful appearance shifted. His mouth twitched and his eyes narrowed. "Oh, *were* they now?"

"Yes. Again."

His eyes widened. "Again?"

She turned around, showing him the wounds on her back. She heard him hissing through clenched teeth behind her.

"I see."

She quickly turned around to see his rejoinder. He had already taken his gaze from her and had it aimed upon his men.

"You dared to harm her? *This* one?"

"S-sorry..." One of them managed to mutter before being slapped across the cheek by the larger one.

"You do not address me until I have permitted you to speak! How dare you harm this one? You know my plans for her. She was to be held until I came to speak to her myself."

"But sir, the other one killed Orion and escaped. She saw it happen."

"Did she assist in the slaying or the escape?"

No one answered.

"Why was *she* punished? Why was *she* stricken? Orion's death is most unfortunate, and it will be avenged, but to chastise *her* for it? That's appalling and uncalled for."

Amy had to admit she enjoyed witnessing him scolding the smaller ones. It couldn't make up for what they'd done to her, but it was a damn good start.

"Get over there and help her up."

They obliged, rushing over to her and allowing her to brace her hand on their shoulders and heads. She made sure to push down on them extra hard as she stood up. Once she was on her feet, she was a tad woozy.

"Allow me to introduce myself. I am Warder, the king of these..." he looked at the others, frowning, "...savages. And you are the one they call Amy?"

"How do you know my name?"

"There are guards all over. Their eyes see all, their ears *hear* all, and then they report it to me."

He looked up at her like a child wanting a cookie. "I know all of your names. Wendy, Steve, Jake, Shannon, Mary and the one you weep for was called Gary."

The mention of his name brought on a fresh batch of tears.

Warder raised his hand and wrapped his chubby fingers around hers. She jumped when he touched her. "Now, now my sweet. You will forget him soon enough. There are imperative plans for you here with us. You will be my bride."

A breath of fright tickled the back of her throat. She choked on a disgusted scream.

"You have been chosen to bear my children. We need more like me that have been born of a normal such as you. My mother was a normal and my father was one of them." He nodded to the pending four who were awaiting his next behest.

"I have been fortunate enough to survive these harshest of winters and the most sweltering of summers. I rarely become sick. The ones like them, they'll be lucky if they last another year. In order for my species to survive, we must crossbreed. Someone needs to carry on once I'm dead and gone."

The scream that had been ingrained in her throat dislodged itself and burst forth from her throat. Dropping to her knees, she continued screeching, doing severe damage to her throat.

"Silence her." Warden spoke as if he were ashamed for having them do so.

Something solid slogged her head.

Then everything went dark.

MARY

The truck bounced over a gulley, throwing Mary into Wendy.

Mary opened her eyes. Stars moved slowly above her. She could hear the rumbling of an engine and smell the dirty exhaust coming from pipes underneath her. She realized the stars weren't moving at all, she was. She was in the bed of a truck moving at a leisurely pace to somewhere she could only guess. Wherever it was, she doubted it was a nice place.

It felt like winter outside. Her body shivered and her teeth clattered.

Wendy bumped Mary off of her. "I was wondering if you were going to wake up. I was beginning to think you might be dead."

Mary felt as if she should be. Her head throbbed in the front, shooting jagged tendrils of pain through her skull. It felt as if there was something heavy slowly squishing her brain.

She could remember screaming, the old man grabbing his gun and then nothing. The way her head was pounding, she assumed he'd bashed her.

Hard.

Mary lay on her back at Wendy's feet. "W-where are we?"

"I don't know. We're tied up in the back of his truck. I think he's taking us to them."

"Are you sure?"

"No, goddammit, I'm not sure, but if I had to lay a wager on it, I'd say yes."

Though it was hard to do, Mary sat up with a grunt. Her arms were knotted behind her back and her ankles were bound together. She pushed her feet against the other side of the truck to hold herself in place, though from the bouncing and rocking of the truck, it would be hard to stay that way for long.

Now that she was upright, she could see the wasteland of dying corn as it passed by. In the moonlight, the stalks no longer looked brown, but a soiled gray.

Her head had begun to throb more severely as the pain swelled, thundering so badly that her skull felt as if it were splitting open. Then her stomach cramped, her ears clamored, and splotches danced in front of her eyes. Unable to lean her head over the side of the truck, she turned away and vomited in the bed.

"Oh my God!" Wendy cried, scooting away from the puddle coagulating near the tailgate. It began to seep out from under the latch, leaving a sticky trail on the dirt road behind them. "That's so gross, Mary!"

Mary dry heaved a couple more times. Strings of thick wet goo hung from her lips. She wiped her mouth on her shoulder. The moon glimmered in the globs of mucus on the strap of her tank top, and it stunk. "S-sorry. I didn't think I had anything inside to throw up."

"Looks like you had enough in there for the both of us. Fucking disgusting."

"How long have we been driving?"

"Hard to tell. I'm willing to guess fifteen minutes, maybe more. But we haven't gotten very far. He's been moving slower than shit, but still managed to hit every bump along the way, which doesn't help my bladder any."

Mary realized how bad she needed to empty her own bladder. It felt full and saggy like a water-filled balloon. She ignored it and asked, "Is this road going through the fields?"

"I think so. We're in pretty deep. I can't believe how big these fields are. Has to be over a hundred acres we've driven through so far."

With all this corn to hide in, and the surrounding forests, it would be next to impossible to find the Haunchies unless you knew where to go, and even then, they could still retreat to their hidden tunnels.

She wondered if The Watcher even knew how many tunnels ran underneath Doverton.

Probably not.

Mary looked at the cab. She couldn't see the man distinctly, save a pale shape of a head and a pair of shoulders. The truck bounced over another hole. Without being able to use her arms to stop herself, she rolled backward, bumping against something firm. Her legs whipped to the side, bringing her upper torso around and on top of Jake's corpse.

His jaw was yawning and stiff, as if frozen in a silent scream. There was nothing in his eyes that remained of Jake, only a terribly shocked expression marking the vacated casing of his body. She looked to her right and saw what remained of Shannon nuzzled against him. Luckily, her head was blocked by his shoulder, sparing Mary from having to see its mangled remnants.

She couldn't bring out a scream or any kind of reaction other than horrified surprise.

"I didn't want to tell you they were back here. I hoped you wouldn't notice them."

Mary barely heard Wendy. What had absorbed her focus was the recollection of a plan she'd thought up back at the house before everything went dark. *Jake's knife.*

"Holy shit!"

Wendy started. "Jesus Mary, you can't just scream like that. You scared the shit out of me!"

Mary got up on her knees. "You have to help me, Wendy. You have to help me." She checked up front. The old man hadn't noticed anything, not yet, but surely, he would soon.

"Help you do what?"

"Jake's knife. He still has it doesn't he?"

Wendy's eyebrows rose, and she seemed to understand without Mary having to explain. Mary was thankful for that. She was unsure of how much time they had before they reached their destination.

Vigorously nodding her head, Wendy said, "I think so. He kept it in a holder on his belt, behind his back."

Mary briefly wondered how Wendy knew all that but pushed the thought away for now.

Jake was on his back and partially wrapped in some kind of tarp. "How can we get to it?"

Scooting on her rump, Wendy joined her. "We have to roll him over and get it out."

"How?"

Neither of them could use their hands since they'd been girded behind their backs.

Sucking in her bottom lip, Wendy reached out with her leg, nudging him with her heel. She was barefoot and only kept grazing his hip. Mary understood that Wendy was trying to use her foot to turn him. Wendy adjusted her position so she could use both her feet. It didn't work, either. Finally, she just pushed him up on his side with the bottoms of her feet and held him there. Through clenched teeth she said, "Hurry, he's heavy."

"I can't. My hands are behind my back!"

"Use your teeth!"

"My...teeth?"

"Hurry!" She grunted.

Groaning loudly enough to be heard over the clap of the truck, Mary got on her knees and leaned over. Her face was near enough to his ass that she could kiss it. This close, she saw that he was not wrapped in a tarp, but an old, filthy blanket that smelled like piss and shit.

The truck dropped again. Wendy fell back, dropping Jake. Mary's knees slipped out from under her. She crashed forward, getting a mouthful of fusty blanket.

Cursing, Wendy sat up, a grimace of pain shrouding her face.

Mary couldn't breathe pressed up against the blanket like this. The stale odors clogged her nose and made her eyes water. She tried to suck in a breath, but there was nothing there but fabric and a foul taste. She tried calling out to Wendy, but the sounds were muffled against the blanket. She pulled in a deep breath, expecting to feel relief when the air pushed its way into her lungs, but instead she coughed. A few tries later, she was able to breathe again.

"Jesus." Wendy frowned. "What happened to you?"

"N-nothing, let's get this over with." She stole another peek up front. All seemed fine.

"Okay," said Wendy. She stretched onto her back. "I'm not going to fall again." She slammed both feet against Jake, shooting him up on his side again.

Without giving it another thought, Mary dove in, clamping the blanket between her teeth. Twisting her head this way and that, she wrenched the blanket up. It gave some, but there still wasn't much slack. So, she tried again, tugging harder. The blanket started to rise. Screaming behind it, shooting foam-like spit from her mouth, she worked until it tore free. She dropped on her side, unmoving and panting.

Mary watched as Wendy shoved with both legs. Now with the blanket out of the way, it shouldn't be hard to get him turned over. Wendy growled until Jake finally rolled, lodging with Shannon's corpse.

Wendy slithered over Mary, using her teeth to remove the knife from its sheath. She looked back at Mary, smiling behind the knife, her eyes wide and perky. It was the most life she'd seen in her since meeting her yesterday. It felt like months ago when they'd first met back at the store. She cursed Steve for having to pee. If he could have held it for a few more miles, people would still be alive. She hated herself for thinking that way, but it was the truth.

"How are we going to use it?" Mary asked before she smacked her lips, trying to get that awful taste out of her mouth.

Wendy looked back over her shoulder, probably checking on the man, then sat on her rump, bringing her feet around in front of her. She wiggled her toes. "He didn't tie *my* feet." She put the handle between her ankles, the blade pointed at Mary. "Turn around, I'll get the rope off your hands, then you can do me."

Mary was quick to sit up. She had to check on the man herself. He must not have had much hearing left, because he was still oblivious to their actions, or maybe the truck sounded louder up there where he sat. Whatever the reason was, she was grateful for it. She shimmied back until Wendy told her to stop. She could feel the coldness of Jake's blade against her skin, and some dry, scabby scuffs that Mary assumed was blood.

"Just don't cut me."

"I can't make any promises."

Actually, she couldn't care less if Wendy sliced off a finger as long as she got loose. That was what really mattered. She could handle having four fingers if it meant she was no longer tied up. The tightness gave some. She could jiggle her hands. It felt wonderful just to be able to move them again. Finally, the rope dropped, releasing her hands completely. She pulled them around and examined them. Even in the dark, she could see the bruising around her wrists like a bracelet. She took turns rubbing each one, helping the blood flow back through them. They tingled as if they were pumping rice instead of blood.

"My turn," said Wendy.

"Hold on," Mary answered, spinning around. She took the knife from Wendy and began working on the rope at her ankles. "Give me just a second, I've gotta get my feet loose."

Wendy began humming the song "Footloose" as Mary sawed the rope. She swore if she didn't stop soon, she'd use the knife on her. Finally, the blade sliced through the rope and hit the metal of the truck floor. It made orange sparks when the knife struck it.

"Okay, *now* it's my turn." Wendy held her hands up to Mary and she went to work. She knew they didn't have much time left. She could smell the faint smell of a fire, and also what might have been a pork barbeque. Her stomach seemed to scream, demanding it be fed immediately.

But she ignored it with the dread of knowing they were almost to their destination.

PIPER

Piper had snuck back into the village where he now crouched behind a small hut. He was both surprised and annoyed that not one creature had come within reach so he could nab them. They'd been scurrying about, moving as if they were preparing for something. Something important. Whatever they were up to, he didn't like it. They moved in rapid fashion, only speaking in passing.

He'd heard rumblings of a celebration...and a bride.

There was no one near where he was hiding, so he decided to move in closer. Hunched over, he trotted around the right side of the hut, moving across a path and stopping behind another hut. He peeked through the hole that he supposed was meant to be a window. It was vacant inside. Sighing, he rushed around the back, keeping as low as possible at the speed he was moving. He tried two other huts—with the same result—which brought him farther into the village. He was getting dangerously close to them, but if he wanted to get one, this was how he was going to have to do it.

The next structure he approached was flat, rectangular and long. He cautiously looked through a small gap in the stalks. His mouth dropped open as a gasp caught in his chest. It looked like a butcher's shop inside. Slabs of meat hung like clothes in a closet. Different sizes, different cuts, but all appeared fresh. Blocks of ice had been stacked around the meat to preserve them. Then he spotted the butcher's block and what sat dissected on top.

Gary.

He'd been stripped and flayed. His cock was a bloody, jagged stump that looked like a broken cigar dipped in ketchup. His chest was opened, and the white bones of his ribs yawned. Piper didn't want to see any more and quickly moved on. He should feel some kind of victorious gloat at seeing Gary mutilated, but instead, all he felt was sadness. He didn't understand why it depressed him so much but seeing Gary like that was like a hard slap of reality.

That would be his own fate if he failed.

Piper could *not* fail, no matter what.

He crouched behind another hovel and took a break to catch his breath. It was brighter this far into the village; torches lit the area like streetlamps. Salty streams of sweat ran down his face. The image of Gary still haunted him.

Finally, as rested as he was going to get, he decided to continue onward.

Piper stood up.

Then he heard a cough. It was soft like a toddler's. With his back against the hut, he eased his way to the window and peered in. What he saw wasn't a toddler, but one of the creatures. It was no bigger than a two-year-old child with breasts like acorns poking her dress made from rags. A female. Her cheeks were puffy on top of jaws formed like a half moon. Her small eyes were like the porcelain eyes of a stuffed animal. Her hair was pulled into a styled bun on her head, and it appeared as if she had pointed ears on each side of her head.

She sat in a chair fashioned out of dehydrated corn stalks. The cushion looked like a sack of rice. In her lap was a quilt that she was sewing. She began to hum as she worked. The melody was quite pretty, and with her sweet little voice, Piper kind of enjoyed it. He listened another minute before continuing.

Instead of going to the back, he went around to the front. There was a door that looked more like a hatch. He'd have to crawl to go inside. He looked closer and realized not only would he have to crawl, he'd have to go in on his side. He'd probably get stuck halfway in, giving her plenty of time to get away and find reinforcements.

He needed to think of something.

He returned to the window, glancing inside once more. She hadn't moved. Hadn't even noticed him creeping around out there. *Good. Just keep humming.* He turned around, stepped back and kicked.

The wall caved in.

The little woman-thing gasped and was on the verge of screaming when Piper barged in, snatched her out of the chair and cupped his hand over her mouth. She was light and her body felt frail. If he squeezed much harder, he'd break her.

"Don't scream," he demanded. She didn't try, nor did she struggle. He could feel her frantic breaths coming from her nose, tickling his fingers. "I need something. And you're going to help me find it. Nod if you understand."

She nodded.

AMY

Amy had been washed and cleaned. She was now being escorted to an old storage shed located on a property adjoining the cornfields. She had seen a house on her way in, but it had looked vacant. There, she'd been scrubbed by a pack of females dressed like little dolls who sang songs as they worked, like the Munchkins from *The Wizard of Oz*. Using rags and buckets of soapy water, they'd washed her roughly, though they moved delicately around her wounds and private parts.

Then they'd left, leaving her unaccompanied.

She lay nude on her back, bound by her wrists and ankles on a cot that was maybe just a foot off the ground. The ropes on her hands had been hiked up to the ceiling, over the railing, and looped through metal hooks embedded into the floor. They came down, knotting around each foot, displaying her legs as if in stirrups and about to give birth. She couldn't lay them flat no matter how hard she tried.

There was a small, crank window at the back of the shed. It was open to allow in some fresh air. A small paper lantern hung from a hook, casting a dim orange blush in the tight space.

Her nude skin gleamed.

The thin aluminum door slid open, throwing a yellow-orange bloom inside. By the way the light danced across the walls, she realized that the glow came from a fire somewhere outside. Slowly, the aroma of burning wood drifted in, making her ache to feel its warmth. She needed it, and not just for her body, but for her mind.

A petite form stood in the doorway lit from behind, encasing its features in murky shadow. Judging by the height, she guessed it was the one who'd introduced himself as Warder. *My soon-to-be husband.* Her chest felt heavy, as if someone had put their foot between her breasts and was gradually pressing down.

"Hello, my dear," he said, entering the shed. He stopped at the foot of the cot. It was too dark to see his face, but she could practically feel his eyes roaming her body.

It made her uneasy. Sure, she was a hostage to a community of pint-sized people and about to be forced into a marriage to secure the existence of their race but knowing that he was gawking at her naked body made her feel absolutely terrible. She hated how vulnerable she was. Tied up like this, there was nothing she could do but let him study her.

"You're not very talkative at the moment, but that's fine. I wanted to see you." He came around the side of the bed and was now the taller one. It allowed him to see her. *All* of her. As he stepped into the light, she saw him running his tongue across his lips and the way they wetly smacked sickened her. He put a hand on her calf, and she flinched at the touch of his calloused skin. As he moved, he slid his hand slowly along her leg as if savoring the feel of her skin.

He released a stuttering wheeze.

Her nipples, standing rigid, were hard as nails when he pinched them.

Gasping, Amy squirmed.

She could tell he liked that.

Warder rubbed down her stomach, fingering her navel before moving to the closely cropped stripe of hair between her legs. He tickled her, gliding his fingers across the spiky texture.

Her skin crawled.

"The moment I saw you, I knew you were the one."

He pinched a small clump of flesh beside the patch of hair. Her body jerked from the sudden bee sting sensation. His lips twisted. He apparently enjoyed her fidgets.

Amy pulled away from him when one of his chubby fingers tried to enter her mouth. He raised his hand, balled it into a fist, and slammed it down like a hammer against her belly. She wanted to pull her legs up but couldn't because of the bondage. She choked on her huffs, feeling as if she were being strangled. A speckled fire burned in her stomach.

"I didn't want to hurt you. You asked for that." His voice was stern, but not angry. "You may not understand or be willing to accept what I'm going to give you, but soon you will come to relish it. You will learn to honor me, and obey me, through sickness and in health."

"Oh God…"

"It might not be easy, but I will break you." He smiled. "I welcome the challenge."

She had no doubt that he could. Hell, she'd allowed Piper to control her for so long, it probably wouldn't be as hard as Warder figured it would be.

Slowly, he extended his index finger and smiled.

He stepped away and moved back down to her feet, then stepped between her opened legs. All she could see of his movement was the top of his wavy hair bouncing as he came closer. His face reappeared between her thighs, beaming a grin.

Amy was tempted to shrink back, or to try throwing her knees at him. But she knew it would only bring her more punishment. As repulsive as it was, she would have to let him do what he wanted.

He raised his finger, whirling it like a wiggling worm. She didn't want him touching her, but braced herself for it. She could feel hot water streaming down her face. Her tears. Knowing this made it even harder to hold them back.

His smile faded at the sounds of her sobs.

"You shouldn't be sad, my dear. I will take care of you. Do as I wish, and you will never have to worry about anything again." He returned to her side, coming closer.

"You should feel honored that out of all the women who have come and gone, you are the one that I chose to be my bride."

She didn't feel honored. That was the furthest from what she felt.

He lowered his mouth to her breast. "They are so beautiful. So soft."

Rubbing his nose across her skin, he gently kissed her breast. Then he girdled his thin lips to her stilted nipple and licked it, flipping his tongue back and forth before he sucked it into his mouth. She'd always been busty, but compared to him, they were enormous. He gripped it with both hands and began kneading it like a kitten. He sucked, fondled, squeezed, and cooed like an infant.

She snapped her eyes shut, trying to keep her mind off what was happening to her. She wanted to think of happier times, but nothing came to mind. She tried imagining Gary, but that only led her to the memory of his death, and right back to where she was presently. Amy thought about Warder's idea of consummating the marriage. It felt dirty to even consider it, like sex with a child. Her stomach crinkled up like a paper ball.

With Warder nursing on her like a calf on a teat, she pictured him naked. If he was proportioned down there in accordance with the size of his body, his penis shouldn't be very big.

That's a plus, she thought. *At least it won't hurt too much.*

Then she cried.

He bit her nipple, causing her to yell, and then made raspberries against her breasts. She realized he was trying to laugh but couldn't.

His mouth was full.

PIPER

Piper stood before a wall of guns with his penis hardening in his pants. He was holding the female, who he'd learned was named Beth, in front of him by the top of her head, his fingers interlaced with the thin locks of her hair. He needed to lean forward slightly to do so. Rifles, shotguns, and pistols adorned the wall, glistening in the gloomy cot as if they'd just been polished.

"H-how did you guys come up with all these guns?"

"We kept them."

"But you can't use them. Why would you keep them?"

"Some came from trespassers and the others from people in town. We keep the weapons of the ones we abolish. Sometimes we use them to trade for food."

Trophies. Piper admired that.

He pushed her, steering her in the direction he wanted to take. They arrived at the handguns. There were some mounted on the wall like tools on a pegboard and others were in a wooden barrel. His pistol wasn't on the wall, so he checked the barrel.

There it sat, right on top. He gasped when he saw it. His hand shot out, quickly snatching it from inside the barrel. He held it up to examine it. The clip was still inside. It looked as if they hadn't tampered with it in any way. He stuck it behind his back, clamping it in the waistband of his pants.

"Where would they have put my knife?"

"Over there. All the blades go over there." She pointed toward more barrels, but these had handles of various utensils protruding from the top like umbrellas in a stand.

He pushed her toward them. There looked to be a lot more blades than guns, and he had no clue where to begin. "I'm going to need your help."

He let go of her. She winced as he tugged his hand out of her hair. There was a steady ache in his lower back now from having to lean for so long. Hopefully, it wouldn't lock up on him.

"Help me find my knife. It's about this long." He showed her the length by the space between his two index fingers when he held them up. "Wooden handle. Can you read?"

She nodded.

"It says 'Here comes the pain' on the blade, just above the handle."

She looked confused and frightened.

He put on his best smile. "Hey. I can't do it without your help. This'll all be over soon."

She nodded and took a couple steps back as if she was afraid to turn her back on him., Piper couldn't blame her for not trusting him now that he had both hands free and all these weapons around. He wouldn't if the roles were reversed. Finally, she dared enough to turn around. Her arms were rigid by her sides, her fingers nervously plucking at her dress.

He watched her a moment before getting to work himself, making sure she didn't try to run or do anything else that would be stupid. He saw a lot of cool blades of all different lengths and girths. Some were jagged and others were smooth. There was even a sai and some other types of swords. *Had they butchered the Ninja Turtles?* He scanned several more, but still didn't find his knife.

When he was about to give up and just choose one, Beth asked, "Is this it?"

Piper looked at her. She stood a few feet away holding a knife with both hands. He stepped closer, squinting his eyes as he examined the blade. At the nestle of the handle, there it was: *Here comes the pain.* He smiled, genuinely happy for the first time in days.

"Yes, it is. You found it." He pranced over to her and took it. He held the knife out, slowly scanning its beauty. God, he loved this knife with its hook at the end, the way it felt it in his hand, the sound it made when it clenched raw meat as he was hollowing out a carcass. This knife was meant to be his. He knew it the day he first spotted the blade in a display case at a flea market outside of Landon. The salesman knew it too. They'd discussed the knife a great deal, even after Piper had already paid. He could feel himself wanting to cry over the reunion.

"I helped you. Will you let me go like you said?"

He shook his head, pulling himself away from his thoughts. "What'd you say?"

"Can I go? I did what you wanted. Please? Can I?"

He smiled again. "Of course you can." He twisted his wrist, aiming the blade outward. Beth's little eyes widened. "You can go right now."

He punched the knife into her scrawny throat and yanked it back. A shower of blood spurted from the massive gap. She staggered back, pawing at her throat. Blood continued to pump through the cracks of her fingers. Her mouth moved, mewling out wet gargling sounds, and then she fell back on the floor, her arms splayed away from her body. She twitched a few times before finally going still. The expression on her face was haunted surprise. Her pale skin was already turning blue as her life drained from her in a dark red puddle.

Piper studied what he'd done. He'd almost decapitated her with his knife. All that was keeping her head attached to her shoulders was a belt of skin and some sinewy matter.

He went back to the room, exploring the selection like one would while grocery shopping. He was looking for a rifle, maybe two, that could assist him in carrying out his plan.

MARY

"We're going to Haunchyville," said Wendy. "I'm actually pretty excited since I've never been there before. It should be a lot of fun. I wonder if they have a gift shop. I collect shot glasses. Wouldn't an 'I heart Haunchyville' shot glass be a wonderful addition to my collection?"

Wendy's sarcasm was either her way of dealing with everything, or she'd completely lost her mind. Mary settled for a little of both.

"Are you going to make a move?" Wendy asked, leaning over the side of the truck, and gawking at what lay ahead.

Just beyond the woods was a glow. They'd already passed through a small forest of charred, skeletal trees and spiky grass, presumably from the raid all those years ago that the old man had told them about. The village had to be what was up ahead.

Mary wanted to act. She was trembling with anticipation. She clutched the knife behind her back, gripping it so tightly that her palms were sweating. But it wasn't the right moment. Not yet. "Just be patient."

"Oh, yeah, sure. I'll just hang out until you get both of us *killed*."

Mary had no intention of getting either one of them killed, but if Wendy didn't shut up, she was going to plant the knife in her mouth and slice out her tongue.

They'd discussed the possibility of leaping from the back of the truck and trying to find their way out of here through the woods, but by doing that they would only be putting themselves right back to where they had been, which was lost and running in the woods. Mary and Wendy agreed they were tired of running and wanted some wheels. So the plan to kill the Watcher and take his truck had been hatched. They played rock-paper-scissors to determine who'd be the one to slay the old man.

Mary had lost.

The truck slowed to a halt, the last bits of gravel crunching from under the truck. The brakes squealed, reverberating through the stalks in the contiguous fields. The corn continued into the black of night on each side of them until it met the woods, but the road they'd been traveling was blocked ahead by an aluminum gate, like the kind that was used to lock up a pasture, and it was fastened with a thick chain.

A road waited on the other side of the locked gate, and a sign on two wooden shafts informed her of its name. Mystic Lane.

The name gave Mary the creeps. Something was just wrong about such a forsaken, barren place having a beautiful, peaceful name. She brought the knife around to her lap. Wendy saw it and nodded. She started to scoot toward the cab where there was a small sliding window in the back windshield.

"Wait," said Wendy.

Mary stopped. "What is it?"

"Someone's coming."

Mary quickly returned the knife behind her and slid back, hanging her head over the side. She could see two flames floating in their direction. As they neared, she began to make out dim shapes. She realized the fire wasn't actually floating, it was two Haunchies carrying torches.

"Be calm."

Wendy nodded and gulped.

The two of them went through the motions of being tied, keeping their hands behind them. Mary prayed their captors were dumb enough to believe it.

Two dwarfed figures simultaneously appeared at the gate. There was a faint rattling of keys, then the chain. One of them tugged at the chain until it only dangled from the post and the other one pushed the gate open. Together, they walked to the truck. Both were armed with teensy spears and dressed in rags.

Ropes were being used as belts and severed rabbit's feet hung from the bands of their trousers.

The bald one, whose head looked like a scoop of vanilla ice cream in the moonlight, had a knife sheathed to his scrawny thigh. He stayed back a foot or so, watching the girls as the other walked around to the driver's side.

"State your business, Watcher."

"Bringing you some intruders, Troll. Two dead, two alive."

The one he called Troll nodded at his partner. The bald one nodded back. Stepping into the glow of the headlights, Mary saw his face was horribly wrinkled with scars. Pockmarks dotted the top of his bald head. He continued around the side of the truck, stopping at the rear tire. He smiled up at the girls. "These should do just fine."

"How do they look, Lashus?"

"They sure are pretty." He climbed up on the tire to get a better look. Mary could smell the stench of decay all over him. She remembered how her dog used to smell after rolling all over a dead animal. For a reason Mary couldn't fathom, whenever her dog stumbled upon something dead, he needed to get the smell fixed in his hair.

I wonder if Lashus here enjoys it too.

"See one you like?" asked Troll.

"Oh, yeah." His eyes were fixed on Wendy.

The pinch of a scream began to rise in her throat.

Lashus laughed. "Uh-oh, she's a squealer. I like it when they make noises like that."

Wendy looked at Mary as if wanting her to do something. She could probably stick Lashus with the knife, but doubted she'd make it much farther than that. Waiting was the only option at this point.

They were trapped like rats.

Wendy managed to find her voice. "Stay away from me."

Mary wished she would keep quiet.

"She's a feisty one too," said Troll. "Probably has a smart mouth on her."

"Nothing a few lashings wouldn't help."

They both laughed and it had been enough to shut Wendy up.

Troll patted the side of the truck. "Go on through, Watcher. Warder will be pleased."

"I'm sure he will." The gears grinded and the truck shifted. Then it slowly began to drive forward.

Mary could still hear the two Haunchy guards laughing as they rolled by.

The truck passed through the gate, enveloping them in the darkness of the woods. The trees hung over the dirt path like a canopy, blocking out the moon and stars. It was much darker in here.

The truck traveled along at a molasses pace.

"Now, Mary." Wendy crawled to her. "Do it now or I'll do it myself."

"It's so dark. I can hardly see."

"Then give it to me."

"No. I'll do it." It wasn't that Mary craved killing someone, she just didn't trust Wendy with the knife. Out of the two of them, Mary figured it was best if she kept hold of the knife. If the others were still alive, they'd surely agree.

She adjusted her stance to a squat.

"There you go," said Wendy.

Mary took a few deep breaths, willing up the courage. Finally, she waddled up to the cab, not coming out of her crouch. The back window was open only a crack, but it was enough that she could put her fingers through. If she could open it without him hearing, then she could just slide her arm through and slit his throat. Then they'd have to brace themselves until the truck stopped. Once it did, the plan was to pull the old man out of the truck, steal it, and go for help.

Not a perfect plan, but it was all that they had for now.

Mary tucked her left leg under her for balance and eased her left hand through the gap. The metal was cold and rigid against her palm. She wondered if she'd be able to move it.

Wendy joined her, keeping just to her rear.

Mary pushed against the frame. It didn't budge. She'd hoped to just slide it over, but apparently, she would have to put some weight into it. He would surely hear it if the metal happened to scrape.

She looked through the glass.

It was dark in there without interior lights. This was going to be a lot harder than she'd first considered. *Not really*, she told herself, *just stab until you hit something.*

Mary felt a nudge on her shoulder. She glanced back and could see Wendy giving orders through clenched teeth and a narrow line that was her lips. She couldn't understand her but had a pretty good idea what she was saying.

Stab the fucker!

Evidently tired of waiting on Mary, Wendy moved past her, gripped the window with both hands and pulled. It moved, but not much. However, it should be plenty of space for Mary to do what she'd planned to do.

Holding her breath, she eased her arm through the opening. It was warm inside the truck. The air was thick. She angled her wrist, positioning the tip of the blade near his head. She canted her body away from the window so she could put more force behind the thrust. The realization that she was about to kill a man was not lost, but she wouldn't allow herself the time to feel any grief. She'd take months, maybe years after they were far from this place, to wallow in the guilt.

He was actually leading them to their demise. This was self-defense.

Sort of.

Stop stalling and do it.

Mary snagged her bottom lip between her teeth and glanced at Wendy again before she reared her arm back and brought it forward with a grunt.

Something caught her by the wrist and began squeezing it, trying to make her drop the knife. She could feel her wrist cracking under the constricting pressure, but she wasn't going to let go of her weapon.

"Nice try girlie!" he yelled above the roar of the archaic engine.

She cried out. It was the old man! He had her hand clutched in his.

"What's wrong?" Wendy shouted.

Mary tugged back, trying to dislodge her hand. It wasn't working. She struggled to use the knife but couldn't do much at all other than shake her hand.

Then he pulled.

Mary shot forward. Her head struck the top of the cab. Everything flashed bright for a moment, throwing off her balance. She wanted to fall, but the old man's painful grip on her wrist kept her up. Then she felt helpful hands slide under her arms, not only to help keep her braced, but to try and pull her back.

Wendy.

"Let go of her!" Wendy's cries sounded as if they were in a bubble.

Mary wondered if she still had the knife. She flexed her fingers and could feel the hardness of the handle under them. Surprisingly, she hadn't dropped it. With her bearings returning, she sprang to life, pushing against him. His arm bent back towards him, but only a tad before he drove it back. He racked her elbow against the paneling causing it to shoot sharp tingles up to her shoulder.

This wasn't working.

If it stayed like this, she'd drop the knife for sure, and if that happened, she'd just jump out of the truck and take her chances in the woods and fields. *No. We need the truck.* She'd grown tired of this battle and was ready to bring it to an end. They were taking the truck, and this old man who'd slaughtered two of her friends was *not* going to prevent it from happening.

Mary shoved Wendy out of the way then plunged, the force of her hips knocking the paneling aside enough that her body collided with the old man. She heard the splintery crack of his breaking arm. Her satisfaction was overwhelming when he began to scream through his phlegm-filled throat.

Mary hung outside from the waist down, but from there up was inside the cab. She couldn't wiggle her way all the through, but she didn't need to. The old man pulled his arm back. It dangled from his elbow limply. She used his distraction to her advantage, gripping his frizzy beard in her hand and jerking his head down while concurrently bringing the knife up.

The blade pierced his eye. She didn't stop driving it in until the hilt met his forehead. Blood sluiced down her hand as warm, thick, and gloppy as soup. Its copper scent filled the musty interior. His tongue lashed outside his mouth as if trying to find the knife and pull it out.

Then his body shifted left, bumping the steering wheel and turning the truck...

...toward a drop-off.

During his spasmodic fit, the old man must have planted the pedal to the floor, because the truck was gaining speed as it neared the perimeter. Mary saw the drop-off illuminated in the headlights as the truck careened over the edge. She tried to pull herself through the window, but she was held tight.

I'm not going to survive this...

The front wheels spun in the air for what felt like minutes. When they found ground again the truck bounced. Mary's legs shot up, the small of her back cracking against the top of the cab. There was a sharp pain there, but it quickly vanished, then she couldn't feel her legs anymore, but she definitely could hear them breaking and chinking like giant celery as the truck tumbled down the hillside. It didn't hurt though, and she was thankful for that, because it sure sounded painful.

Mary saw the giant oak tree a second before the truck hit it.

Her hips shot free from the window.

She saw the windshield even quicker.

Then she saw nothing.

WENDY

The front of the truck was crumpled around the tree bark in an embracing heap of rusted metal. The driver door hung open. The old man lay partly in and out with the knife jutting up from his face like a flagpole. Smoke bellowed out from under the hood, a steaming miasma that smelled of antifreeze and oil.

Wendy had been bounced from the truck when it teetered over the hill, but now she leaned against its bed for support. She wasn't sure how bad the wound on her head was, but it felt swollen and was definitely bleeding, so that meant it was bad enough. The vision in her left eye was blurred and she figured some ribs were broken, because it felt as if someone was stabbing her lungs with arctic nails every time she took a breath.

She didn't know how long she had been unconscious, but it didn't seem like it had been that long, although she was pretty certain someone must have heard the crash and would be coming to investigate before long.

She came back to the truck to find either the old man's rifle or Jake's knife. She preferred the gun, but if she couldn't find it, she planned to pull the knife from the old man's skull.

It was hard to move around swiftly from the soreness and pain riddling her, but she managed. She checked the ground around the old man for his rifle but found nothing. The bed of the truck was also empty. What was left of Mary was folded against the tree and piled on the hood in a bundle of pale flesh, black clothes and blood. Ropes of moonlight cut through the trees overhead, showing Wendy more than she'd wanted to see of Mary. She'd actually grown to like the kid and didn't want the memories of her to be clouded with that image.

Too late for that.

Then she spotted the gun.

Pinned against the dashboard was a rifle that looked as big as her. Wendy didn't know much about guns, but it was obvious to her that this one was old. The barrel had specks of rust dotting it, and the wood had gone from a rich tan to a dark, tarnished brown. Holding her breath, she leaned over the old man's folded body, grasped the gun and hefted, straining with her back to lug it out.

Now that she was armed, she thought about searching for ammunition or possibly even extricating the knife from his eye as backup, but she didn't want to touch his filthy dead body.

Suddenly, she began to identify the distant chatter and howls of looming Haunchies coming to see what the commotion was about.

She hurried, jogging through the pain. She thought of Gary, remembering how he would rub her shoulders and massage her feet after a long day at work. Something warm and salty ran down her face as a smile formed. It wasn't thick enough to be blood.

It was tears.

She was finally starting to cry as the realization that Gary was dead pounded down on her, causing her to stumble. The dark ground came up to meet her, and when the unyielding soil connected with her chest, it felt as if her breasts had been slammed through her back. She couldn't breathe.

When she tried to rise, she felt a heavy weight on her back. Then she understood that it wasn't only the apprehension of Gary's demise weighing on her, it was a *Haunchy!* It chattered in her ear, hysterically laughing and hooting as its miniscule hands pawed and slapped at her face. The coarse, haggard texture of burlap rubbed the nape of her neck, making it itch. As Wendy clawed at the ground, she also bucked with her hips while trying to fling the critter off her back.

He didn't seem to be going anywhere though.

She still had a grip on the rifle, but there was no way she could safely use it, not with the Haunchy behind her.

She flipped over to her back, burying the Haunchy under her. He spat a cough when she landed on top of him. She hoped he didn't have a knife. Any second now she expected to feel the piercing of a cold blade in her lower back.

He began to squirm beneath her, writhing and twisting as he tried to get out. She lifted a few inches and dropped back down on him again. He groaned. His movements became less spastic.

She slammed back on him again and again. Finally, she stood up, using the rifle to help her get to her feet. She looked down to find that the Haunchy was only dazed. She wanted to blow the bastard's head off but didn't want to the noise of the shot to attract some of his friends. Instead, she raised the gun above her head by the barrel and brought the stock down onto his head. It caved under the handle into a ball of jagged skull and mud-like matter.

Then he was still.

Wendy lingered just long enough to ensure it was dead before retreating farther into the woods. There was a pale outline up ahead which she slowed down to examine. The light of the moon was filtered by thick limbs, but she could see enough to recognize that the shape was at least the height of her waist, and it had thin rods coming to sharp points at the top.

An iron fence.

She stopped before it, looking beyond the fence and onto the surface of land past it. Silhouetted in the dark blue veneer of night were rocks spaced evenly apart and they continued on for an acre or so. As she gave her eyes time to adjust, she started to realize they actually weren't rocks at all.

They're tombstones.

Penetrating up from the earth like little fangs, they were hardly large enough to notice. Seeing the diminutive graves sent a flutter of shivers up her back. Her head prickled.

Wendy decided to go around. It would take longer and was probably more dangerous, but this area was almost too much for her to bear. She skulked past the graveyard, keeping her eyes averted. It was dark ahead, nothing but blackness with plenty of shadows for things to hide in. Maybe she should sneak back to the dirt road. It would be risky, even with the rifle, but it was better than going to Haunchyville. There was no way she could fight *all* of them. She didn't even know how many bullets were left in the gun. There might not be *any* bullets left in the gun.

She stopped walking for a moment, looking around as she concocted a plan. If she kept going the direction she currently was taking, she'd end up in Haunchyville, but if she turned around, she'd backtrack to the bunch that was probably now inspecting the wreckage or had moved on to hunt for her. If she went right, that would probably only lead her *deeper* into the woods.

Left.

That was the only logical direction to go.

And that was where she went.

Wendy looked up as she walked, carefully scanning the trees above her. She didn't see anything ready to pounce on her. Her night vision was well-adjusted, so if she hadn't spotted any lurkers up there, then that probably meant there weren't any.

Then she heard voices up ahead. Crouching over, she scurried to a nearby tree like she was prancing across hot ashes and then ducked behind it. Out of all the others around, this specific tree stood out. Leafless and bare, the bark looked to be rotting. Its withered branches hung stiffly like dead, gaunt arms.

She hunkered down. There were more cornfields nearby. Not only could she see the dried stalks, but she could smell their crispy scent like old leaves and sugar.

A small group of Haunchies had gathered and were talking anxiously. She hoped they wouldn't decide to walk toward her. She would be easy to spot and if they found her now, she'd have nowhere to run. One of them pointed right at her. Her heart lurched, her muscles stiffened. Did they see her? He averted his gaze away from her and then pointed in another direction. She exhaled slowly through her pinched lips, slightly hissing as the air simmered out.

He hadn't seen her.

Wendy turned around, leaning against the tree. The bark was soft against her back. Very soft. She nudged her elbow against it. The tree sunk under the pressure. *It's not a real tree. It's fake. Why would a fake tree be out here?* Wendy turned toward the tree and shoved it with her palms flat out in front of her. The tree caved almost all the way in but did not break or tear. It reminded her of rubber novelties from a Halloween store. The tree had been sculpted, molded, and made. She felt around the formation. At the bottom, her hand brushed something hard. She had a good idea of what it was.

She stood up, raised a leg, and kicked it.

It was a door. Just like the trapdoor at the shack that she and Jake had used to save their lives earlier. This was another opening to their tunnels. She nearly cried out with excitement. They would never think to check for her in their own tunnels. This kind of route had saved her life once already. It was too good of a plan to fail.

She peeked around the tree one last time and saw that the group was still oblivious to her. As she scurried into the tunnel, she'd never felt prouder of herself in all her life.

WENDY

On her stomach with the rifle strapped over her back, Wendy maneuvered her way through the tunnel by her elbows. It was hard trying to move with the gun, but she wasn't going to leave it behind. She towed herself forward. This tunnel was tighter than the one she and Jake had used earlier. They'd been able to crawl on their hands and knees in that one. It had been strenuous but was much more doable. This one hardly seemed possible. The dirt was enclosed tightly all around her, making it almost too hard to breathe.

It was also dark, so dark she had to blink her eyes to make sure they were even open. Snaking along like this was going to take a long time, but she was just fine with that if it meant her freedom and survival.

Dirt rained down in flakes up ahead. She stopped. There was a muffled gasp above where the dirt had sprinkled down. Wendy held her breath and listened. She could hear indistinct murmurs. Groaning? *Growling.* It was growling. Then she heard the gasp again, this time followed by a cry.

Female.

Amy.

She recognized the tone even muted through the dirt. She wiggled onward, stopping directly beneath the sounds. Above her in the dirt was a circle of wood. *Another trapdoor.* Wendy struggled onto her side, put her hand on the door, and delicately pushed it open. She poked her head through the opening. The sounds were louder and clearer now. She gave the location a quick glance and realized she was looking into a tool-shed of some kind. It was dim in there, the only light being what was coming from a lantern hanging in the corner. It hardly cast enough luminosity to see anything, but it was glowing just the right amount for her distinguish enough of what was happening in here.

Centered in the room was some kind of a table or bed, low to the ground, and designed in a way that it looked sadomasochistic. At the foot of the slab stood a tiny, naked body layered in a coating of sweat, its hips were thrusting, the minute buttocks flexed and then relaxed as it pulled out.

Repetitive slapping sounds resonated throughout.

Although it was somewhat bigger than the others, she was certain it was a Haunchy. He leaned back his head, eyes pinched shut and teeth grinding as he grunted toward the ceiling.

On the table, Amy stared off to nowhere in particular with hollow eyes, her bottom lip clamped between her teeth. Her face was wet, presumably with tears. Her body bounced with each pitch of the Haunchy man's hips, her full breasts swishing this way and that.

Wendy climbed out of the hole.

The little man's body began to quake. He nearly shrieked as his body was ravaged with shakes. Wendy recognized the male climax even in something as unfamiliar as a Haunchy. He was almost crying by the time he finished.

As he panted, Wendy jacked a bullet into the rifle's chamber. There was one bullet in there at least. The little man froze when he heard the *ca-clack*.

"Who's there?" he asked, out of breath.

"One of the group that you didn't catch."

Amy gasped. Her head jerked up. "Wendy? Is that you?"

"Yep. It's me."

The little man turned around, his pinky-sized erection was glazed and softening. He did not look amused. When he noticed the rifle, there was a quick shimmer of fear across his face, but it was quickly replaced by a sneer.

"You have got a lot of nerve coming in here."

He looked at the opened door in the floor, then returned his eyes back to her. "Found my tunnels, did you?"

"Oh, yeah. They've worked out for me quite well. And we killed that watcher of yours. He tried to bring us to you, but we got him first."

"You lie."

"How do you think I got his gun?"

He looked at the rifle and a brief look of defeat fluttered through his eyes. His hands clenched and unclenched repeatedly. His penis had shriveled to the size of a raisin.

Wendy clucked her tongue. "Now, what do we do here?"

"You shoot me, and everyone will hear it. They will come for you."

"Oh, I'll be long gone by then." She flicked her head toward the hole in the ground. "Got my own path."

"Wendy. Untie me. Please."

"We'll see."

Amy's eyes widened.

"You can't imagine how satisfying it is to see you like that, and also knowing what just happened to you." She exhaled a heavy breath like someone smelling the freshest air. "Makes me almost giddy."

"Please, Wendy…"

"You think I'm just going to let you go after what you did to Gary? After what you did to *me*? To *us*?" She realized her voice was rising in pitch and bordering on hysterical, so she took a moment to calm it.

"Where you're at is where you belong."

The little man used this momentary distraction as an opportunity to attack. Arms outstretched, he lunged for her. His mouth was opened wide and growling.

Wendy caught the flicker of movement in the corner of her eye. She whipped around, the rifle pointing forward, and fired. The bullet entered his yawning mouth, and exploded through the back of his skull in a splintery swash of red. He twirled three full circles before crashing to the floor in a limp contour.

Then she turned to Amy.

"Wendy, don't do this. I understand how you feel. I love Gary. I do. Please. I didn't intentionally set out to hurt you."

"You think that'll help you in any way? I don't care if you did it on purpose or not, the fact is that you still *did* it!" She circled around the bed to Amy's side.

"We were doing just fine until you came calling for help again yesterday. And like always, you made things awkward and terrible. Now Gary is dead!" Her eyes were misting. "Because of you, Gary is dead!"

Explosions echoed outside. There were screams and shouts as more explosions came. It sounded as if a battle was ensuing out there.

Wendy ignored it, keeping her eyes on Amy as she moved across the room.

Amy was crying now. "I hate that he's dead too, Wendy. I'll never forgive myself for it, ever." The words seemed forced through her sobs. "But I'm sorry that I hurt you. If I could trade places with him, I would, but even if I did…" Amy took a deep breath, "…he still would rather be with me than you."

Amy began to laugh as Wendy thrashed about the room in a rage. Wendy screamed, kicked the slab Amy lay on and smashed the walls with the gun stock. Then Wendy spotted the lantern dangling in the corner and hurried to it. She snatched it from the hook.

"You bitch," Wendy growled.

She pitched the lantern as if it were a ball. It hit the bed, exploding into a blanket of fire.

Amy's breathing exhilarated Wendy as the fire began licking up her sides. Her huffs turned to shrieks as the scorching flames spread across her, enveloping the bed in a field of fire.

Wendy looked on in bliss.

PIPER

When the shot thundered Piper quickly ducked behind some old oil drums and pumped the lever on the stolen rifle. He looked around. The dwarfed residents immediately halted whatever they were doing and, in a herd, rushed toward one shanty. He had no idea who'd fired the shot, but obviously the little clan wasn't expecting it.

He hurried onto a path and opened fire, dropping them one at time. The ones that fell tripped the ones behind them, bringing even more down. This was fine for now, he realized, but it wouldn't last. He needed to do something bigger that could incarcerate them. He studied his surroundings, and when he saw what he was looking for, he smiled. *The torches.* He darted to the nearest one and snatched it in passing. Then, running to an opening of a hut, he heaved it.

It struck the roof, igniting it.

He grabbed another torch and ran along a path as a group of the little things began to take chase. He neared the cornfield and chucked the torch ahead of him. It landed somewhere in the corn. It might as well had been a bomb the way the stalks went up. As dry as they were, it took no time for them to catch fire.

Then, he took cover in another shanty, loading bullets into the rifle. As the bitter aroma of smoke filled the air, he began to laugh, listening to the desperate cries of shock and alarm from the inhabitants.

WENDY

Wendy had to leave the rifle behind. Without it, she was able to move through the tunnels much more quickly. As she ventured forward, she thought back to that moment in the shack with Jake. She'd allowed herself to become wide open, showing him her feelings and he'd used them against her. Her lips curved higher. She admired that. It was something she probably would have done. At that moment, she hadn't noticed what he was doing. She'd just taken the bait and fell literally into his inviting arms.

His muscular arms, his broad chest.

There was a tingle between her legs.

Damn it. Why?

Her turgid nipples were probably leaving lines in the dirt as she shuffled along. She hated it, but it also felt good the way the ground massaged her breasts and rubbed the soft walls neighboring the inner cave between her legs. It felt almost too good to handle and she had no clue as to why.

Survival. That was why.

She was alive and happy about it, so her body was reacting accordingly. She heard a moan and giggled when she realized it was her own voice. *I'm being ridiculous.* But she couldn't help it. She'd made it. That was enough leverage for getting at least a *little* giddy as the ground molded around her, touching her in just the right places. It wasn't as good as her last time with Gary in the hotel, but it was all she had, and she would take it.

She wondered if she'd orgasm.

She laughed again, but it quickly turned to screams when her hands raked across emptiness. The ground disappeared out from under her. She flung her arms forward, swatting nothing but open space.

Then she plunged.

It seemed as if she fell forever. A light appeared below her, rippling and twisting in shapes. She could hear water dripping before splashing face first into a thick pool of liquid. The obscure water filled her ears and nose, flooded into her mouth. She swallowed some. It tasted like what she imagined raw sewage would.

Submerged in the rancid water, she sucked it in only to regurgitate it right back out. It was a disgusting cycle. She kicked and grappled, finally managing to paddle her way to the top. Her head lashed out from the water, and she gasped and gagged. Her mouth was filled with a rotten aftertaste.

Where was she? What was she in? She looked around. Another tunnel was above her. It slanted like a slide. The moon shone through the hole up top, casting a soft disc of light onto the soppy murk she was treading in. Something hard bumped against her. She cried out, but quickly caught herself. The solid object floated behind her, bopping against her as if trying to get her attention.

It had.

She turned, wanting to know what the hell it was. The light didn't quite reach it. She had to pull it into the small circle of brightness.

When she grabbed it, she noticed how it felt slimy and cold like raw turkey. She pulled it to where she could see it clearly and then screamed again, snatching her hand back as if it had been burned. It was not a cold turkey, but a cold female corpse. Its purple-pruned skin had wrinkled gullies across her face. She looked like rotted fruit. Her long hair had matted into thick clumps and was plastered around her shoulders. She wore a muck-covered silk robe that felt like old panty hose stored in a damp basement for many years. The corpse's breasts were deflated bladders, hollow orifices that left her chest flat. Filled to the brim in the canyons of her chest was rice.

Wendy could not create a reason as to why they would have packed rice in there. Had she been used as a buffet table, or was this some kind of religious burial practice that she'd never heard of? She felt herself gagging and heaving. Then she disgorged another wad of vomit across the cadaver. The rice began to move as the warm liquid seeped in.

It wasn't rice at all.

It was maggots.

She scanned the gloppy pit through her teargorged eyes. All around her, on the hilly inclinations blockading the small cavern and even in the water itself, was movement. Twisting and turning as it slithered this way and that. The whole area was covered with the flesh eaters.

Shrieking, she swatted the corpse away from her and paddled to her right. The slanted tunnel was just above her. As she examined it more closely, it dawned on her that it actually wasn't a tunnel at all.

It was a shaft.

Her hand struck something compact and firm which brought out another scream. She was afraid of what this could be. It was flat and muddy.

The edge!

She'd made it to the other side. She could get out of this carcass pool.

With her hands planted on the side, she lifted herself out of the water.

Wendy didn't allow herself time to rest. She ran straight for the tube and her getaway. It was encrusted with dried blood so thick it that looked like paste. She briefly considered going back the way she'd come until she felt the ground contracting under her feet like sand being pulled into the sea.

She wanted nothing more of this place. She wanted *out!*

Her arms went into the tube first to grip the sides. It was slippery and she lost her grip, dropping back down on the rock. There were wet squishes under her toes as she flattened maggots when she landed.

Her grip held on the second try.

Using only the strength of her arms, she hiked herself up, her feet kicking open air until she had shimmied into the shaft. Freedom was now a short distance away. She crawled to the opening in no time.

Her hands flogged out first, pawing at the sky. The air was much colder above ground. Wendy's arms pimpled with goose flesh as she made her way out of the hole like a Wendy reborn. It seemed to fit. She *had* been reborn.

She'd been forced to become a new person.

The air was thick with the smell of burning brush. To her, it was the most wonderful fragrance in the world. If she could bottle it up and sell it, she would. The smoldering scent meant only one thing: Haunchyville was burning.

Wendy was thankful to have this moment, this time to relish. She had won. She'd been victorious. Everyone else had fallen, but she had made it out. Alive. She hated that Gary wouldn't get to celebrate this new life with her, but she would always make sure he was the focal point of her past-life's pleasant memories. She owed him that much.

She tilted her head back, allowing the ravishing scents of destruction to enter her nostrils. It tingled her skin just thinking about all the new possibilities her new life had to offer.

Cha-chook.

The sound came from behind her. She felt the coldness of a gun barrel press against the back of her head. Her heightened spirits collapsed into a mass of dread.

"Wendy." The male voice sounded pleased.

Who is he? How does he know my name?

She nodded without turning around.

"It's nice to see you, again."

Her skin not only crawled, it ran.

"You may not remember me, darling, but I sure as *hell* remember you. The name's Piper Conwell. You're gonna come with me, and we're gonna have *a lot* of fun together."

ABOUT THE AUTHOR

Kristopher Rufty lives in North Carolina with his three children and pets. He's written numerous books, including *All Will Die, The Devoured and the Dead, Desolation, Pillowface*, and more. When he's not writing, he's obsessing over gardening and growing food.

For more about Kristopher Rufty, please visit his website: www.kristopherrufty.com

He can be found on Facebook, Instagram, and Twitter as well.

Printed in Great Britain
by Amazon